PRAISE FOR *AFTL*

"Kim Taylor Blakemore hits her stride in this well-plotted page-turner of a novel. The prose shines with her unique lyrical voice. Cannot recommend highly enough!"

—Terry Lynn Thomas, *USA Today* bestselling author of *The Silent Woman, The Family Secret,* and *House of Lies*

"*After Alice Fell* is an enthralling, haunting, and harrowing gothic mystery that sweeps the reader into a post–Civil War New England that consists of broken families and even more broken minds. Easily one of my favorite books of the year, this story stayed with me long after I'd read the last page. I absolutely loved it!"

—Emily Carpenter, bestselling author of *Burying the Honeysuckle Girls* and *Reviving the Hawthorn Sisters*

"Blakemore pulls you deep into the mind of a woman haunted by a harrowing past and the fallen ghost of her sister. Family secrets, terrible regrets, and hints of murder lurk around every dark corner of this well-drawn, Civil War–torn world. As the mystery of Alice's death slowly unravels, you simply cannot look away!"

—D. M. Pulley, author of *The Dead Key* and *No One's Home*

"Superbly crafted, Kim Taylor Blakemore's *After Alice Fell* is an enthralling story of absolving guilt and seeking the truth. It's a captivating historical thriller that kept me turning the pages way into the night."

—Alan Hlad, internationally bestselling author of *The Long Flight Home*

"Taut, tense, and terrifying, *After Alice Fell* is a harrowing novel that will make skin crawl and hearts break. Blakemore's latest is a sophisticated, meticulously woven historical suspense of loyalty, loss, and deception. With a nod to Shirley Jackson's claustrophobic settings and intricately drawn characters, Blakemore has created a haunting thriller that will pierce the security of her readers."

—Amber Cowie, author of *Loss Lake*

PRAISE FOR *THE COMPANION*

"A captivating tale of psychological suspense."

—*Publishers Weekly*

"A slow psychological burn."

—Criminal Element

"Blakemore's descriptions are rich and vivid . . . Secrets, eavesdropping, sinister happenings, and a forbidden relationship all make for a riveting historical thriller reminiscent of Sarah Waters, *Burial Rites* by Hannah Kent, or *The Confessions of Frannie Langton* by Sara Collins."

—Historical Novel Society

"A vivid and sensuous domestic drama, *The Companion* is also an atmospheric crime story."

—Emma Donoghue, bestselling author of *Room*

"Sarah Waters fans, welcome to your next obsession. *The Companion* is an elegantly written tale of beautiful lies and ugly secrets, a reminder that love's transforming power makes not just angels, but monsters. Telling one from the other will keep you guessing until the end."

—Greer Macallister, bestselling author of *The Magician's Lie* and *Woman 99*

"*The Companion* is a brilliant study of all that makes us human—our terrors, regrets, and passions, and the lies that shape our worlds. Kim Taylor Blakemore's novel is both astonishing and captivating, and it will leave readers spellbound."

—Lydia Kang, bestselling author of *A Beautiful Poison* and
The Impossible Girl

"As her date with the gallows approaches, Lucy Blunt is struggling to understand why she is at odds with society. In a literary tradition stretching from *Jane Eyre* to *Alias Grace*, her intoxicating account took me to another time and place. A confession with the illicit excitement of a thriller, *The Companion* offers everything I like about modern historical fiction: a resonant voice that brings women's lives out of the shadows."

—Jo Furniss, bestselling author of *All the Little Children* and
The Trailing Spouse

"A vividly rendered and chilling tale of murder, desire, and obsession."
—Sophia Tobin, bestselling author of *The Vanishing*

"With exquisitely vivid and lyrical writing and a subtly layered narrative, *The Companion* is a fascinating and beautiful novel. If you enjoy Sarah Waters, you'll love Kim Taylor Blakemore's latest."
—Lily Hammond, author of *The Way Home*, *Alice & Jean*, and *Violet*

"*The Companion* is a totally absorbing read—beautifully written, atmospheric, and intriguing. Kim Taylor Blakemore's characterization is both convincing and compelling as she evokes the gritty reality of nineteenth-century life to great effect. I loved this book."
—Lindsay Jayne Ashford, bestselling author of
The Woman on the Orient Express

"Lucy Blunt's account of her journey to the gallows is a study in female wildness, perhaps constrained but definitely untamed, in this compelling novel. The writing is honed, fresh, and intensely physical, pulling the reader headlong into the heroine's tough, sharp-eyed world. Lucy's wit, courage, and resourcefulness render her sympathetic; at the same time, her watchfulness, her almost obsessive reading of others in order to gain advantage, is masterfully conveyed. Blakemore's understated psychology—in particular her grasp of the petty yet crucial maneuverings that take place between rivals—held me entranced until the end."

—Maria McCann, author of *Ace, King, Knave*; *The Wilding*; and *As Meat Loves Salt*

"Moody and atmospheric, *The Companion* is a compulsively readable treat. Blakemore's meticulously researched world captured me from the very first page, and her intriguing, unpredictable characters kept me guessing until the end. An utter delight for lovers of classic gothic literature!"

—Elizabeth Blackwell, bestselling author of *In the Shadow of Lakecrest* and *On a Cold Dark Sea*

After
Alice
Fell

OTHER BOOKS BY
KIM TAYLOR BLAKEMORE

The Companion
Bowery Girl
Cissy Funk

After
Alice
Fell

A Novel

KIM TAYLOR
BLAKEMORE

LAKE UNION
PUBLISHING

Text copyright © 2021 by Kim Taylor Blakemore
All rights reserved.

Published by Lake Union Publishing, Seattle

www.apub.com

Amazon, the Amazon logo, and Lake Union Publishing are trademarks of Amazon.com, Inc., or its affiliates.

ISBN-13: 9781542022705
ISBN-10: 1542022703

Cover design by Faceout Studio, Jeff Miller

Printed in the United States of America

For Alida Thacher and Thea Constantine
&
Dana, always

Chapter One

Brawders House
Harrowboro, New Hampshire
August 1865

"Is it her?" The ward attendant holds up the oiled tarp. He chews on his dark mustache. Blinks and clears his throat. "I am sorry, Mrs. Abbott. I must ask."

I clasp and unclasp my reticule, the metal warm between my thumb and forefinger, the click comforting, steadying in this room with white tile walls and black grout. There's a single circular grate in the corner; yellowed paint chips from the ceiling clog its pipe. The cold pushes through the floor, needles of ice that poke my thin-soled boots. Ill chosen, meant for summer, not this chill room. But I hadn't thought; I put on the first pair I found and last night's stockings, too, hung from the bedpost because I was too weary to put them away.

A note delivered, too blunt:

Alice Snow deceased. Please collect.

The driver who delivered the note had waited, slumped against his hansom and fanning his face with a folded-up newspaper. His horse, roan and swaybacked, drooled and ground his teeth. The air shimmered and blurred the edges of the fence and abandoned barn across the road. It was too early and already too hot.

I had missed an eyelet when buttoning my boots earlier, and now the leather cuts into my ankle. I rub the heel of my other shoe against it until the chafed skin burns. Paint chips drift into a crevice of the tarp's fabric, stick like snow to the crown of this dead woman's head. Neat, straight part and white-gray skin. Strands of ginger hair blood stippled, a tangle loose and dangling. A mottled stretch of bruising across her forehead. I lower my gaze to the floor. There are divots there, hollows and gouges. Her body is cooled by a leather-strapped block of ice. The body who is Alice. Alice so still, Alice under the tarp.

Alice, my sister.

She is not meant to be here, her mouth agape as if she were about to share a thought, like she used to when she was very young, her finger to her lip, a shake of that ginger-red hair, then "Marion, I wonder . . ." Or "Marion, it's an odd thing . . ." Her voice trailing away as she swallowed the words or clamped her jaw because I interrupted, finishing out whatever it was she wondered about or found odd. "Everything in and of itself, Alice, is so very odd that one must just consider it normal. Otherwise, you'll drive yourself mad."

The attendant stares at me.

"It's her."

He lowers the tarp, pulling it up to her forehead. It is too short. Her left foot pops free: a dark welt across the bridge, crisscrosses of cuts, thin long toes. Maybe she'll wriggle them now, as she used to. "Look, Marion. I'm royalty. Look at my middle toe, look at its length."

"You'll need to sign the certificate."

There, on the small desk by the square window that looks out on nothing, on a wall of brick and pipe, is the document. Smaller than I would expect. Simple and harsh.

Record No.: *4573*
Name: *Alice Snow*
Sex: *F*
Date of Birth: *February 3, eighteen hundred and forty-one*
Age: *24*
Date of Death: *August 3, eighteen hundred and sixty-five*
Cause of Death: *Accident. Acute mania.*
Signed: *Lemuel Mayhew* MD

I've seen too many of these, pinned too many to uniform lapels. I've seen so many dead: Antietam, Poplar Springs, Spotsylvania. Men stacked on carts, tarps too short to hide the high arches and missing limbs and nails roughly cut. I've signed so many letters, whispers from the soon dead to their loves. *Forgive me. Help me. I am almost at heaven, Mother.*

One signature and Alice will be released. One signature to absolve this place of any responsibility for her slipping from the roof, absolve the staff from finding her body splayed on the pebbled drive, half tangled in the sharp thorns of pink hedging roses. I dip the pen and hold it above the signature line. Ink beads at the nib and splatters.

"What time was she found?" I keep my eyes on the ink, watch it soak and spread along the short edge.

His foot scrapes the stone floor. "You'd need to ask Dr. Mayhew."

"But Dr. Mayhew isn't here. He's upstairs with my brother. You are here. Mr. . . . ?"

"Stoakes. Russell Stoakes."

"Mr. Stoakes."

The ink is a river now, rippling around the paper, a black frame around my sister's name, her death, the date. When I hand it over, he'll place it in the brown folder with her name printed neatly on the edge.

He waits for me to sign. He is as cold as I am, has his arms crossed over his barrel chest and fists curled round his elbows. His eyes are a muddy hazel and flick with resentment. It's not his fault he's been assigned this duty. He taps his finger on the corner of the iced table. "She didn't suffer."

"Yes, she did."

I turn from the desk, holding out the official certificate officially identifying the now official death of my sister, Alice Louise Snow, and watch as the attendant shoots a glance at it before setting it atop the folder.

"She's afraid of the dark." I take my gloves from my pocket and fumble them on. "I must find my brother."

The door sticks as I open it and step into the hall. Low voices slip and mumble from both directions, from under other doors and away down the tunneled walk. Away from the white-tile room with black grout and my Alice too silent under the tarp.

Metal wheels squeal and chitter behind me, loud and then silent. I stumble forward, my chest tight, hand grasping for the solid wall. The brick is chipped and scratched from too much use.

Mr. Stoakes's footsteps are heavy on the stone behind me, following with enough distance to keep out of my thoughts. The light is dull, just a slit of sun through high casement windows, heating the narrow glass and sheeting the interior with layers of dust.

"Don't follow me." I grab at my skirts and gather them.

He reaches for my elbow. "Best I help."

I twist and claw away from his grip. "Don't follow me."

My sister lies on a bed of ice. Our brother, Lionel, waits in the garden. He's met with Dr. Mayhew but refuses this task. They've left me to attend Alice, and now I am lost in a jigsaw of halls and occasional gaslit lamps bolted to the wall. Steam pipes run the length, banging and knocking.

"Mrs. Abbott?" The attendant's voice slips around corners and then is gone.

I follow the pipes through a door to a tunnel of red brick and a low, heavy arch, lamps spaced twenty paces apart, and then another door to a hall with squared walls and rippled paint and metal-latticed windows. A dance of signs, black iron, white letters, arrows every which way. Utility. Store C. Store D. Room A13. Utility B. Morgue.

I turn my back to that one, though I know if I follow that arrow, I'll be on familiar ground. I'll be back with Alice and can start again, trace my steps to the stairwell and up to the side door in the cheerful visitors' lobby. It's just a matter of steps, then, to the double doors and wide porch. Certainly, Lionel will be waiting. He'll hand me up to the hansom cab; I'll take out my handkerchief and wipe my forehead. "It's so very hot," I'll say and watch the jonquils lining the long drive doze and dance in the sun.

But I don't want to go back to Alice. I can't. I can't see her body on ice.

Utility. Store C. Store D.

My chest tightens. I press against the wall, hand to stomach, breath pulled through the nose. I scrape my fingers to the brick. I am lost here with Alice.

She is meant to be alive. How can I tell her now how sorry I am?

My knees give way. A door bangs, and there's Mr. Stoakes, lumbering over. He passes the doors. Store C. Store D. Room A13.

With a squat and hmph, he's on his haunches. He blinks, rapid fire, and tightens his lips into a smile. "We can't have this, Mrs. Abbott."

"Yes, I'm sorry." I flatten my free hand to the wall. Let out a bark of a laugh. My heart slows. "I'm not like this, really. It's the shock. It shouldn't bother me; I was a nurse—"

"I'll help you up now." As he stands, he keeps a hold on my elbow, light like a comfort. "There we are. Let's find your brother."

"There you are." Lionel looks up from his watch, thumbing the case shut and sliding it into his vest pocket. He leans against the white railing in the one streak of sunlight, his hair bright copper, much like mine, darker than Alice's. The sun reflects in his glasses as he turns to me. His coat is as blue as the sky behind him, as if he had been set by a painter upon this porch, the coat and bright-sheened vest provided from a costume closet. *A Languorous Day*, the painting might be called. No one the wiser for the setting. No matter the confection of porticos and porches, vine-weaved lattice and wide sunny lawns, nothing masks the purpose. It is an asylum, and until last night, my sister was an inmate within its walls.

Lionel nods to Stoakes, then crosses to me and lays his hands on my shoulders before pulling me to him in a strong grip.

My ear presses against the pouch of tobacco in his coat pocket. He rubs the back of my neck, lays his cheek on my head, and his breath warms my scalp for only a moment before he steps away.

I smell like death. It's why he moved away. The decomposing skin, the rot of liver and belly, the stench of gases, the sweet mildew and musk of it threads my black widow's weeds and hair. Alice wraps around me like a shroud.

"My God," I say. "What have we done?"

"Not now." He glances behind, to Stoakes, his eyes apologizing. Then he strides down the stairs to the pebble walkway, just one glance over his shoulder to make certain I'm following him. "Come along, Marion. The cab is waiting."

He leans forward to talk to the driver. The horses are edgy; the cab rolls back, then forward.

I take his hand and clamber to my seat, folding my skirts round my thighs and settling into the cracked leather. The driver in his faded coat turns his head halfway to hear us. His hat is dark rimmed with sweat and matted with horsehair.

"Move on." Lionel rests his hands atop each other, snaking his gloves between his palms.

The carriage sways and starts forward.

"We're all that's left now."

Lionel stares at a rip in the fabric, right near his shoulder. It's been poorly mended. "Don't be silly. There's Cathy. Toby."

"Your family," I say. "Not mine."

We slow for the gatekeeper. He chucks his crutch under his arm and uses the gate for balance, his left trouser leg loose below the knee, swinging with the motion. *Where?* I want to ask. Antietam, Fredericksburg, a nameless creek in Virginia muddled with late-spring runoff: I might have held his hand. Or lied and said there would be ether when there was none.

The driver turns the horses to the road. The light flicks through silver maples, planted to maintain privacy.

"She wasn't well. If you'd been here, you'd have known." His voice drips with accusation. "Not at the end. My God, she nearly—"

"I don't want this argument now."

"You made a lot of excuses for her."

I shake my head and look down at my lap, at the tangled mess I've made of the thumb of my glove. I've picked it apart, cotton and silk now torn and in knots.

Lionel stares, too, then pulls the glass open. Just outside his window, orange dahlias and red heleniums line the drive, riotous and bloated with too much color. Just outside mine is the brown brick building that holds Alice in its bowels. Two workmen sit astraddle the far peak of roof. One fans his face with a wide-brimmed hat, staving off the heat and mosquitos. The other slaps at his arm, then turns up his palm to stare at whatever's left of the bug before wiping it off on his trouser leg.

"I was going to visit," I say. "When I'd settled. This week or next."

"She'd have refused to see you."

"Why?"

"Do you need to ask that?" He points out my window to a narrow road that meets with ours. A mule with heavy head pulls the buckboard. A simple pine casket rests in the bed. "There's the wagon."

The driver sits wide kneed, round backed, his chin jutted forward. He pulls the traces, slowing the mule, ceding the roadway to us. With a quick nod, he doffs his soft cap and holds it aloft as we pass by.

My chest burns with each breath. I force myself to watch our driver. I count the stitches along the back of his brown coat. The fabric is faded nearly yellow at the shoulders. He's mended a rip in the hem.

Lionel's wife, Cathy, will be waiting at the house. She'll have cleared the dining room and gathered muslins. I don't think I can take her condolences any more than I could take them when Benjamin died.

The horse whip bends and swings in its stand near the driver's thigh, and he looks averse to using it. Other drivers flick and play the leathers on their horse's backs, but he leaves it be, churrs and hums instead.

"Toby shouldn't see Alice like this," I say, my eyes following the swing of the leather. "He's too young."

"I'll look out for him." Lionel stretches his neck, first one way, and then the other, before staring out his window glass.

There's a quick movement along the stone fence. A shard of sun reflects off a white cap and pale wrists and forearms. A girl, wraith thin, scrambles over the fence, hands waving, black hair frizzled at the forehead. She jogs next to us, reaching out to catch the doorframe. Her eyes are the palest of green, nearly incandescent against the scarlet birthmark marring her cheek and jaw.

"Mrs. Abbott. Oh please, Mrs. Abbott." A wide scar rides along her chin and curves up as she speaks. "I need to talk to you."

Lionel leans over me. "Get away from the carriage."

"No, I need to talk to Mrs. Abbott. Please . . . stop the horses."

The driver flicks his long whip so it snaps the air by the girl's leg. "Get back to work, Kitty Swain."

"Oh, stop. Charlie, stop." She calls and waves, stumbles in a divot as she sprints to keep pace.

The horses are urged to a trot. The girl gives up, lifting and dropping her arms to her skirts. She stares at me, her mouth moving and something akin to pleading in her visage. But the words are lost in the horse's clops and the squeals of the carriage axles.

A spit of sweat, icy and sharp, stings my neck. I remove my kerchief from my sleeve and dab. But I turn my head, compelled to take one last look at this pompous brick building with the inviting porch and grated windows and a cupola ringed with lightning rods. A single-paned glass window in the middle dormer catches the sun and holds it. Each wing's roof is steep pitched—easy enough to slip.

Three stories. Four along the left wing where the ground slopes away. An accidental, unfortunate fall. Sunken eyes, gaping mouth, criss-crossed slices and scratches from the thorns. Bruising on her forehead. Blood-stiff hair.

Three stories. Four at the apex.

How did you get on the roof, Alice?

Chapter Two

Maple and elm branches arch over the road, cling tight to the edges. The trees are heavy with cicadas, the air vibrating with their chatter. Teeth on metal. The branches tap and scrape the top of the brougham. One of the insects drops past my window to the dirt.

Lionel and I pass an hour in silence. The dirt road curls to the right, a thin track between the trees. Midway down we pass the husk of a once-grand house. Now it is nothing but long windows of shattered glass and weeds crawling up the brick. The old Burton manse. Silent and empty these past ten years, ever since the murders of the poor wife and her companion.

We turn to the Post Road, follow the wind of the river until we are amidst the tumble of Harrowboro proper. The town is full with mourning, though it has been months since the war ended, since Lincoln lost his life; no one looks askance at our cortege. I stop counting the women in weeds black as mine—flicking a broom on a porch, bending to a basket to coo at a babe, balancing wash on a shoulder, exiting the dry goods, the druggist's. Dull cottons, heavy laces, jet bead brooches, lapel pins that hold an image or braid of hair in their cases. I turn my head from the legless beggar, the newsboy lifting the afternoon paper with one arm and the sleeve of the other pinned tight. By the livery, the women thin out, their figures just ghosts of skirts flitting between the shops. Three new photography studios have opened between Adams and School Street. At least now the tintypes will be of the living.

At Manufacturers Row, we slow and plod and lurch forward, accommodating carts piled high with woolens and mules pulling great carts of lumber. The brass dome of Snow & Son gleams. I turn my eyes from the reflection, but Lionel stares at it straight on. The windows are shuttered; a note with a black border is pinned to the door.

The buildings give way to farms set back behind low stone fences and fields and weeping trees. Then, another hour, and there is the house. Plain white wood, black-paned windows, the whole of it rambling every which way over the contours of the land. Lionel has removed the grand elm we used to swing from, leaving the house exposed and sharp edged like a broken tooth.

"Ahey, ahoy!" There's a flash out my window: Lionel's son, Toby, runs alongside us, his knees pinked and dimpled, his short breeches tight around his stout legs. Old Saoirse chases after him, white braid against her back, calico skirts flicking up fine dirt, her fingers just missing him as he jumps away.

He's pale, his eyes the same faded blue as his mother's, like gingham too much worn. It still hurts to look at him. How much he resembles Lydia, as if she shimmers under his skin instead of under the earth with a simple granite marker. His nose has the same quick upturn, and mouth the same curve to the lips; all of it so pleasing on his mother— *Lovely Lydia*, we called her—but somehow giving pause when observing the child. As if all of Lydia's features have been copied by an apprentice.

We come to a stop in front of the house. The windows are festooned in black. A long ribbon hangs from the front door. Cathy has been industrious during our absence.

Toby jumps the two granite steps and peers at the wagon behind us. He opens his mouth to say something, but Saoirse has caught up and stands in his way.

Lionel reaches across me and clamps his hand to the window frame. "Why is the boy outside? Get in the house."

I lay a hand on Lionel's forearm. He shakes it off, clambers over me, fumbling with the handle before shoving the door hard enough it clangs against the brougham's body. He curls his hands to the frame and takes a breath. His cheeks have turned a mottled red.

"Lionel . . ."

"See to our sister." He jumps out and strides to Toby, lifting him into his arms and over his shoulder. Toby's hands flap on his father's back. Saoirse turns to me, lifting her palms in surrender before following them.

The old roan blows out a breath and jangles the traces. I fiddle open the clips to the glass between us. "Do I owe you money?"

"The asylum paid."

"Will you help with the coffin?"

The driver—Charlie—purses his lips and scratches a dark patch of stubble on his chin. His eyes mark each window of the two-story house and land on the open door. "You'll need to bury her soon."

"I'm aware."

He twists farther to look at me directly. Something shifts in his features. "I'll do such."

"Oh, Marion." Cathy floats down the front steps, crosses to the cab, her dove-gray skirts clutched high to avoid the dirt. The crinoline swings and settles when she lets go to reach up for me. "Oh, Marion. This is too much death." Her eyes are button black and restive, and her dark brows come together as she looks to the wagon behind us. She puts her hand to her mouth, stumbling back on a foot and catching herself. "We'll need more towels."

I step from the cab, my stomach roiling and legs still feeling the sway of the carriage. The two drivers take the coffin between them, each to a handle. The melting ice drips a dark line into the drive, a thin stream of water and mud.

"I have the dining room ready," Cathy says.

"Thank you."

She scuttles in front of me. "I'll have Saoirse bring more towels."

The chairs have been pushed against the wall, ready for vigil. The summer curtains, pulled closed, leave the room a dingy beige. There is no air; the windows have been closed against the heat. Cathy's added another leaf to the table, laid the muslin on the waxed wood. I turn to the serving cabinet. My eyes follow the new wallpaper's tangling green vines and florid palm leaves. Underneath there is still the pale peach that Lydia had sent from Boston. But Cathy is fond of this. The rug has been rolled back. The men's feet echo, and if the mirror were not layered in black cloth, I would see their reflection as they set Alice's body to the table.

Cathy's left a bouquet of summer blooms on the cabinet top. I run my hand across them and then crush bits of lavender sprig she's laid to the side of a large bowl of water. A basket is set to the floor with colored rags rolled and stacked. I need to thank her, but the thought of another debt sits heavy.

There's a scrape and bump above my head, from Toby's room. Lionel is playing with the boy, distracting him; perhaps they're playing hoops and sticks inside, which Cathy forbids.

Leather is pulled from brass; the ice has been unbuckled, or what's left of it.

"We'll crack it outside," one of the men says. They'll crack it so we can slip the shards around the body, hide it away under the muslin.

"It's not necessary," Cathy says. "There's no one to call on her."

"I would like to sit vigil tonight." The lavender is brittle; I press a thumb to it, raise it to my nose.

Cathy nods. "The ice, then."

The pine box rests on the floor. The men make quick work of the lid. I keep my eyes to the wallpaper. Every third vine on the wall changes pattern, turns another way, hides a bright-orange floret. Why did Cathy replace the original? There was nothing wrong with it; it was not out of style. It was an extravagant thing to do, and in the middle of the war.

"Hup," one of them says. One at Alice's head, the other at her feet, and they've laid her to the table with only a rustle of muslin and a light bump to the wood.

"The ice is under the yew, when you're needing it." I glance to the door, at Charlie with his cap stuffed in his belt, watch him step to pick up the leathers and roll them tight. He takes the hammer from the cabbie and sticks the handle in his belt next to his cap.

Cathy, at the head of the table, rubs and rubs her hand over her bodice. Then she lifts the watch pinned to her waistband. "Is that all?"

"That's all, ma'am."

"You'll find lemonade and cake in the kitchen. Before you go."

She moves from behind the table to close the double doors. Her hand is on the knob as she turns back to the room, and she twists it back and forth. Her eyes travel the long boards of the floor.

We must look. We must look.

The coffin's top leans between two windows. The nails show, ready to return to their place. The long box stands alongside. I turn, catch the tip of a nose and curve of forehead, force myself to look. It's not Alice here. It's a body. Alice left when she fell off the roof. This is just a body.

Cathy's lips tremble. She lets go the doorknob and takes a hesitant step.

"Will you read from the Bible, Cathy?"

Her face relaxes, eyes alit with relief. "Yes, of course I will."

"Then I shall wash her."

4573. This is the number stitched above Alice's left pocket. Neat and small, in a blue thread. The cotton gown is shapeless, the buttons obscenely large. One has been ripped from the collar, and the one below is sewn with red thread. I fold back the fabric: Alice is barely there. The poke of ribs, breasts small and shriveled though she is but twenty-four. Her stomach is concave, slung between the jut of her hipbones, marbling now in greens.

I shift Alice to undress one arm and then another. Cathy murmurs from her perch on a chair, peering up every so often from the Bible she holds flat to her lap. She murmurs, and outside the glass the cicadas buzz.

Alice is light as air; I expected the weight I'd grown used to when preparing the men at the field hospital. Like the dead men, she is silent and does not complain about the indignity of her naked body exposed to all and sundry.

I fold the garment and set it on a chair, though my only plan is to burn it. The water in the blue filigreed bowl is tepid. I circle the washcloth, squeeze it, and listen to the drops.

Her skin has begun to slough from muscle and bone. I hold her hand, press the cloth between the fingers. Her nails are short from biting them; a bad habit she never broke. We have the same curve to our ring fingers. I rub at her wrist, but the mud-brown ring remains stubborn. I turn her hand, palm up. The underside of her wrist is white, the veins a blue black.

I round the table. Touch my thumbs to a bruise that runs from temple to temple, then run my gaze to the faint stippling of color across her chest, across both upper arms. Another band of yellowing at the wrists. Again, across her thighs and ankles. Across the tops of her feet. Each band of discoloration uniform in width. Like leather belts buckled one hole too tight.

With a quick turn, I yank open a curtain for more light. Cathy straightens in her chair and stops reading.

"What is this?"

She won't look. Her eyelids flit, and she gives a minute shake of her head.

"What did they do to her?"

The Bible slips from Cathy's lap, hitting the floor with a thud as she stands. Her eyes slide across Alice's body, and she lets out a sharp gasp. "Oh, no. Oh, Alice."

I slap the cloth to the table and stride to the door, out to the hall, lunging up the stairs past the walls of bilious peonies, turning at the landing to Toby's room. The door is ajar. Toby shrieks a laugh. I push into the room, find Lionel crouched on the floor in the center of a cast-iron train set. Toby shrinks into the corner by the hobby horse.

"Have you seen her? In all this time, have you ever seen her?"

Lionel stands and steps from the circle of flatbeds and caboose. He grips my arm tight near the elbow and half pushes, half pulls me from the room. "Not here."

"Did you visit her?"

"She didn't want to see me."

My shoulder catches a picture frame, tilting Mother's image and pushing the far corner against the curio.

"You're hurting Auntie." Toby cowers against the door, a stuffed toy rabbit crushed between his hands.

Lionel turns to him, loosening his grip. "Get back in your room."

Toby darts past us, bouncing from Lionel's leg to the railing before tearing down the stairs.

"Don't let him—Lionel, don't let him."

The boy is too fast. He slips past Cathy, aiming for the dining room, stopping in his tracks at the door.

No one moves. We all stare at Toby staring at Alice on the table. He turns his head: to me, to Lionel, to Cathy.

Cathy circles round him to pull the door tight. "Come here, my boy." She drops to her knees and draws him to her, enveloping him in the billows of her skirt. He arches back, quivering and tense as a bow, and lets out a scream. He bats her hands from him, clawing at her cheek, kicking to be let go. She fingers a scratch on her jaw, then slaps him.

"Cathy!" Lionel presses past me.

The boy totters back from her, chest welling, face purple with shock and rage.

"When will she leave us alone?" Cathy's hands fist her skirt. "When will she ever leave us be?" She clamps her jaw and stands, wiping at the scratch now beaded with blood. "I want her buried."

Behind the house, skirting the pebbles and rush that line Turee Pond, Lionel and I lug the coffin. There are piles of burnt wood where the glass house once sat. The path we follow is muddled with chokeberry and Queen Anne's lace. The icehouse crouches between maples and oaks that tint the light pale green and hold in the clammy air. The coffin bumps my thigh.

"Nearly there." Lionel steps over a twist of root.

Up a small hill, to the family plot, to a burst of sunlight and shimmering air and a deep hole to the right of Father's, Mother's, and Lydia's. The grass of Lydia's grave is scattered with twigs and feathers. I turn my eyes to the dark rectangle mouth that will soon swallow Alice whole.

We set the box on the lip of the grave. The yardman, Elias Morton, stands nearby. Lionel sent for him. Paid double to make certain the job was done quickly. His white hair curls from under his stovepipe hat, settling on the fray of his collar. His milky eyes follow Lionel and ignore me.

No words. The men take a handle each, crouch low, and drop the case into the ground.

I let out a breath, rake up a fistful of earth, then open my fingers so it sifts and scatters on the pine box.

"I'm sorry, missus." Elias stares at his boots. "So sorry."

Lionel stands with his hands on his hips. "She'll be better now." He looks at me across the pit. "She never forgave you for leaving her with us."

I choke down a sob and turn away. I cannot watch the rest, when I know how the dark terrifies her, and now she will be encased in it. When I know my brother is right. I do not deserve forgiveness.

Chapter Three

Perhaps I should get up from the bed, open another window, the one facing the kitchen garden. I've been lying here since we buried Alice, watching the shadows slip across the room and the sun darken to a thick burnt orange. But Cathy's down in the garden, her voice a burble and sometimes a coo and sometimes "Toby, stay out of the tomatoes," and "Toby, Toby, where are you?"

Toby laughs and shrieks as only little boys can do when hiding from stepmothers amidst plants and hedges and the knife-edged shadows of a sinking sun.

Lionel and Cathy have given me this room at the back of the house. Alice's old room. The windows face both the kitchen garden and Turee Pond. The bed sits next to the glass with a wide sill to hold my morning tea; the writing table has three drawers and a squat shelf. My childhood wardrobe has been dragged from the barn and repainted in robin's-egg blue. Pink roses snake down the wallpaper. Cathy's set a clock and a vase of posies on the fireplace mantel.

A fine little room trying so desperately to be cheerful.

"You'll be more comfortable down here," Lionel said. "And Cathy's bought all new linens for you."

What he meant was they would be more comfortable with *me*—the widow with no means—not underfoot. I haven't determined yet how many *thank you*s and *sorry*s will be enough.

It comes then, a rip and tear to my heart, that this is not a temporary situation: this is what happens when one's husband is killed with half his regiment on Monett's Bluff.

I can still see the casualty sheet, posted atop the others until the watered silk walls of a room once elegant bulged with names of the missing and dead.

The ward attendant tapped the sheet and bellowed, "Forty-seventh Pennsylvania. Twenty-ninth Wisconsin. Eighth New Hampshire."

A soldier in nothing but frayed gray trousers lurched up from the floor and yanked my apron for attention. "That's my brother's regiment." He scratched under the bandage on his face. "That's Franklin's men! He'll have got 'em good. Is he on the list? Can you look? Can you tell me if my brother's on the list?"

"Stop scratching. It won't heal." I kneeled to him. Put my hand atop his to still it.

"Will you look for me? Look for my brother, Franklin Branch."

The room felt wadded with cotton, all the sounds muted but the constant thump of my heart and the soldier's voice. *Will you look? Will you, Nurse?*

"Eighth New Hampshire?" I stepped over and past the wounded, holding my skirts tight against me in the narrow hall. Jostled between cots and surgeons and soldiers who stood or swayed—too well for a bed, too injured to be returned to their troops. Crying and moans and the uproar of more carts and more men echoing from the street to the vestibule. I stood on tiptoe to see over the men who'd gathered in front of the lists. Started at the *A's*.

There. *Benjamin Abb*—. One name amongst scores, the last three letters cut off in a crimp of glue.

It was late before I returned to my billet. All day I'd sent missives for the wounded and dying, my fingers stained with ink. Now I sent my own.

City Point May 4, 1864

Dear Lionel,
Benjamin is dead. Tell Alice. She will not lament his
passing. For me, I tell you plainly I cannot mourn a man
I did not love. He quashed that sentiment too soon and
required it again too late.

I am enclosing a rebel two dollar bill for Toby. His
birthday is next Friday if I have my days straight.

Thank Cathy for her letter of last week, it brought
cheer. The lemon drops were a marvelous surprise.

As ever yours
—M

Lionel's return letter was placating and kind. Alice's was honest.

Here. May 25.
I didn't do anything wrong. Come home.
—Alice
AND—I'm not sorry. About Benj.

The columns of roses on the bedroom wall dissolve and reform into
the white of Alice's skin, the brown-purple bruises, the blood-tangled
hair that took so long to plait.
She didn't suffer.
She did. Of course she did. All her life.
I gasp for air and bolt up. Hold in a moan and rock forward,
elbows jabbed to my thighs. I want to crawl out of my own skin,
away from the sear of guilt. I left her here, when I should have come
home.

There's a soft knock on the door and a turn of the knob. A small shoe slides in the opening. I grab my wrap from the end of the bed and pull it round me. Toby slips just inside the door.

"You should wait for an answer first."

He twists the seam of his breeches pocket, then lets it go and wipes his finger along the edge of his nose.

"Did you hear me?"

"Yes, ma'am. I should wait for an answer, then you will let me in." His gaze circles the small room, stopping on the round clock atop the mantel. He points at it and contemplates the black scrollwork hands, the bulge of the face, the gold gilt numbers.

"It's eight and six," he says.

"Yes. Eight thirty." So, I've slept. The sky is tinged butternut and gray.

"You missed dinner."

"I did."

"We had raisin pudding." He scratches under his chin. His nails are mooned black with dirt.

"What do you need, Toby?"

He shakes his head then turns around, picking something up from the hall floor, and backs into the room. He grimaces, gripping a tray by its corners so as not to upset the bowl balanced at its center. The spoon slides to the lip.

"Let me." I rise from the bed, take the tray, and set it on the desk. The broth is tepid, no steam; a dab of grease floats on the surface and then clings to the interior of the bowl.

"Do you like beef tea?" I ask.

He pulls his chin into his neck and shakes his head.

"We have something in common, then."

"Mama said it's fortificious."

He calls Cathy "Mama"—I suppose it's expected. Still, it has only been three years. He was five when Lydia drowned. Old enough to remember her, I think. Is there a prescribed passage of time that must pass before the mantle of *mother* moves from one woman to the next? Perhaps the word comes prior to the affection, for I see little of it between the two now.

My nose curls at the smell of the broth. I unlatch the window. I'll tip it to the ground once everyone's abed. "You can give your . . . Cathy . . . my thanks."

Toby sets one foot on top of the other. He frowns then, and blinks. His lashes are so long. "Where's Alice?"

"She's gone away."

"But she just came back."

"Oh, Toby." I kneel and touch his shoulder. "Alice is . . . She isn't coming back. She's with God now."

"But I saw her." He swallows gulps of air. His eyes widen, the pupils slipping to black dots. "Who'll keep away the Bad Ones?"

Alice in the corner, twelve years old, balanced like a stork on one foot, finger scraping the paint and plaster, not turning around. *"They're out there," she said. "Right outside the window."*

"There's nothing there. Please Alice, come downstairs. Come down, don't wake Mother—"

"There are no Bad Ones, Toby."

"Yes, there are." He points to the glass, now flat and black but for the flicker of gaslight reflected from the hall. "Out there. It's why she slept in the glass house. To keep guard."

Alice believed night creatures lived in the pond—fiends that came from the Narrows, where the pond pinched and bent out of sight. She drew the creatures in the corners of her notebooks. Wire wings stitched in mismatched feathers—white tufts from an owl, black plumes of the long-tailed duck, the emerald offering of a mallard—six red beetle legs with single talons, a dragonfly body with horse's tail, eight eyes split into honeycomb patterns.

We weren't allowed to go there as children. It is deep, the slip from the edge a surprise, the stone too smooth for scrambling feet and hands.

Alice drew the Bad Ones sanding the surfaces every night, lingering on lily pads near the deepest crevice, waiting for a poor soul to slip.

Elgin Miller's son—1812, 10 years old
Marjorie & Hester Bickford—1834, 8 & 10
Israel Foley—1737(?) 72 and perhaps drunk
Mayhew Greenleaf—1788—wheelwright

More names, written in neat ink on the back wall of her wardrobe, so small she used a magnifier to add each to her roll of the dead. The wardrobe now in Toby's room. All the names she'd created or recorded from the stones in the town cemetery now covered with paper and glue.

Stephen Lang—1854—24 yrs old, to wed Timothy
Lamprey's daughter
Mildred Larkin—1855
Theresa Messer—1855

The summer Mother died, wasted and anguished with pain. The summer Alice turned fourteen and suddenly refused to speak.

Lydia Snow—1862

I did not make the funeral. *We are too much entangled in war,* I wrote. *Alice will be of good use for the boy, as I am of good use for the Union.*

Alice's return letter was a drawing of me splayed on the lily pads, the creatures crouched on my abdomen and poking the sockets of my eyes with the tip of a gnarled walking stick.

Smoketown Hospital, MD Nov 1862

Dear Alice,
Your letter (drawing) was much disturbing and I am
distressed enough as it be. If this is my punishment for not
attending Lydia's funeral, if this is so—to have this hor-
rible drawing seared in my mind—then it is too much.
If this is to tell me you are angry, it is too much. I am full
here with terrible enough scenes, and men in pieces and
many ill with dysentery and some will not make it home.

Sister, you must look to the sunlight. You do remem-
ber that, to look away from the dark. You must be a good
aunt now for that little child.

I must go. It is far late. I am sending two dollars and
this bead bracelet as a token of my everlasting love to you.
It is simple, yes, but it sparkles in the light.

As ever yours
—M

There is no air tonight. I've left the windows thrown open on the off chance of a whisper of breeze. I twist on the bedsheets, searching for a spot less hot than the space I just occupied.

The clock ticks, though I cannot see the time. Late, I know. I sent Toby from the room, listened to the squeaks and groans of the floorboards as Cathy took him to bed, took herself to her room. Lionel calling a goodnight from the landing and knocking the balustrade with his knuckles, just as Father did for us. Then later, his footfall on the stairs. The latch of the kitchen door as Saoirse locks up, then treks across the gravel drive to the road and the cottage at the crossing she shares with Elias.

I squeeze my eyes shut, clench my fists to my stomach, wish for sleep. Listen to the tick of the clock. But images sift and turn: strange Kitty scuttling along the stone fence, the pipes of the asylum basement, the lavender I crushed to powder, the marbled green of Alice's stomach as if she were transforming to stone.

I breathe through my nose, in and out, my limbs so heavy against the bed. Bones without muscle.

Tink tink tink.

The noise comes from the hall. I pull my robe from the bed iron, shrug it on, then lift the candle and turn the doorknob.

The light slips across the parquet on the floor, creeping up the walls and through the pattern of irises and mourning doves. I can see us all, hear us—Lionel and Alice and I, tumbling down the stairs to the landing. A snow day. Father waiting out front with the sleds. Mother leaning off the top railing.

"You make sure Alice has her mittens," she calls down, her voice still strong, her cheeks ruddy with life.

Lionel shoves his arms in his coat, then winds a wool scarf round and round his neck. He's taller than me, whisper thin, and knobby at the knees and elbows. When did he grow so?

I lift Alice's coat from a hook. "Come on. Father will turn into a penguin."

"Where'd you hide all the mittens?" Lionel leans over the storage bench, digging through and then lifting out the pairs. He twists round, kneeling to Alice. "Hold out your hands, little bluebird."

I button my jacket to the neck and grab my wool cap. "Don't forget her hat, Lionel."

"I won't forget the hat."

"I don't want a hat," Alice says, and shakes her curls.

"You'll take your hat," I say.

"I'll be ten on Friday and you won't be able to tell me what to do anymore."

"That's right." Lionel stands with his palms on his hips. "You'll rule the house and all the world. And Marion will have to listen to you instead of us having to listen to her."

I watch the ghosts of us that linger still, that rush out the door and let in the blistering cold. Trudging to Wagon Hill in our snowshoes and Alice bobbing along on Father's shoulders. Lionel and I dragging the sled and blowing air that freezes to spirals.

A scrape of a chair in Lionel's study pulls me back from the memory. A swirl of tobacco smoke floats through the half-drawn door just across from the stairs. Then he is there, leaning his shoulder against the doorframe. He's in robe and slippers, his hair mussed on one side. "Am I making too much noise? Or are you looking for a drink too?"

"Do you remember taking the sleds to Wagon Hill?"

He blinks and squints at the wall, his eyes flicking back and forth, as if he's flipping the pages of a book. "Huh. I haven't thought . . ." He swallows and gestures for me to enter. The room is as small as mine, stuffed with an overlarge desk, two low leather chairs, and a round rosewood table upon which lie his pipe and an empty glass.

"Take a seat."

The chair is well worn, the arms cracked and darkened with oils. Lionel's had more than one drink; his movements are too thought out. He leans close to the cabinet. "I know you're not a sherry drinker. Whiskey or rum?"

"Whiskey."

With a half smile, he pulls the bottle from a shelf and holds it to the light. Makes a show of pouring the liquor for us. "It's a little rough. You'll need sugar."

I take the glass from him. He holds up a finger, then removes a sugar tin and tiny spoon from behind a row of books, flicking open the top. "Now you're an accomplice to my sugar thievery."

"I haven't had sugar since I don't know when."

"Now you shall." He stirs the sugar, then taps the spoon to the glass. *Tink tink tink.*

I let out a short laugh.

"What's funny?"

"Nothing. It's been a long day."

"I'll drink to that."

"Let's drink to Alice."

He flops back in the chair. His whiskey spills on his hand, and he turns his wrist to lick it off. "Sorry. To Alice, then."

The sugar doesn't help; the whiskey burns my mouth and sears my throat.

"How's your room?"

"I've been billeted in cow sheds and attics. The room will do. Your generosity . . ."

He stops me with a wave of his hand, then closes one eye and stares at his glass.

"It's all been such a muddle," he says. "Since Lydia drowned. She was very good to Alice. Patient. She was always so patient."

"Yes."

He glances at a bookshelf. A tintype lurks behind a manual on brass bolting. Lydia in a gingham dress, white-blond hair, a spray of flowers held in her lap, a peacock brooch on her breast. She is about to smile; the edge of her lip is blurred. She will have held it until she was told to relax and then laugh. She laughed at so much.

"All a goddamn muddle."

"You have Cathy now. I'm glad for that."

He cocks his head, watching me, first one eye shut, and then the other. "Yes. Cathy."

"I am sorry about her brother."

"First battle and Paul gets a bullet in the eye. How's that for luck?" He drops the glass to the table with a clatter. "Bull Run was supposed to have been it. Remember? People took picnic baskets and sat on the hill. Had beer and sausage while the fifers played."

I lean forward, press my hand to his arm. "You were good friends."

"Until he called me a coward. And other things." He pulls his arm away. Clears his throat and leans his head against the chairback. "Wagon Hill wasn't steep enough to sled."

"It wasn't?"

"No. Too close to the brook. Too short a slide. You're thinking Tilton Hill. Remember? There was that one birch Bremmer wouldn't cut down. Right in the middle of the path. If you went too fast— remember when Alice went too fast? God, she went flying off that sled. Straight in the air and thumped to the drift. Just one shoe showing."

"That couldn't have been her."

"Why not?"

"She wasn't allowed to ride alone. She rode with me."

"Then I must have taken her myself. Let her go wild once." He lets loose a laugh, his eyes following the arc of her flight, the candlelight gleaming on his glasses. "That was the last winter Mother . . . I didn't get supper. Father locked up the sleds. Remember?"

"Where are her things?" I ask.

"What?"

"Alice's things. Her clothes. Those wooden birds she loved. Her locket. All those journals and sketches. Her things, Lionel?" I set my glass on the table between us. "There's nothing here of hers."

"Don't blame me for her."

"I don't blame—"

"You're the one who left me with her. You and your Union."

"I wanted more than mending socks and sewing uniforms."

"And look what it got you." He slugs his drink. "Now she's dead. Maybe it's better. I think it's better. For everyone."

I flatten my hand to my thigh and stand. "You're drunk. I'm going to bed."

30

His attention slips, then he shakes his head. "You agreed to the committal."

"I shouldn't have."

"The last time Cathy found her, she was holding Toby out the upstairs window by his wrists."

"There must have been—"

"Stop making excuses for her." He lurches up, cradling his drink to his chest with one hand and pulling on his lower lip with the other. "I won't be made guilty for this."

"She was covered in bruises, she—"

"I don't care."

"Lionel." I shake my head. "You don't mean that."

He drops back to the chair, his head bowed, the glass pinched between his thumb and fingers. "I told her she was going to visit you. To pack her trunk. Bring a coat because it's cold in Maryland." His voice rasps and chokes on itself. "I said I hired her a cab. She waited on the porch all that morning and—"

"I can't hear this."

I lurch back to my room. It is stifling hot. Stagnant and sour. "My fault." Three paces to the fireplace. There's Benjamin, under glass, in his uniform and sporting a grand swoop of beard. "My fault." A turn to the window. The moon has risen, a dust of gray on the tips of silver birch, on the roof of the boathouse, across the skin of water.

I touch my hand to the pane—the window's been latched tight. This one over the pond. That one over the garden. I don't remember closing them. I press the heels of my hands to my forehead, rub at the sweat.

Why would Alice hold the boy out the window? But there wasn't a why with Alice. The beautiful girl with the jangled brain answered only to herself.

I promised her I'd always be there. I promised.

"My fault."

Chapter Four

Cathy serves breakfast on the back porch. "To spare us all from the heat," she says.

To spare us from the dining room and the mirror still festooned in black crepe, I think. To spare us all from grief.

The porch is approached through the narrow ell of the kitchen and down a short flight of steps. It hugs the back of the house, the floorboards and ceilings a patina of blue milk paint and graying wood.

She doles out chicory coffee in measured pours, three quarters of a cup each, and then the milk server is held up. Her left eyebrow raises in question, as if today I will tell her I am fully tired of milk.

"Just a drop," I say.

"Surely more," she answers. But there's a look of relief when I refuse more.

Lionel flips through yesterday's *Statesman*, rolling a corner between his thumb and forefinger. Cathy waits, tilting slightly forward, the server tip clinking the rim of his cup.

He glances at it, eyes bloodshot and tired, then back to the paper. She pours the milk—a dram and a dab—before slipping to her own chair and setting the milk to the side.

"No milkman today?" he asks.

"We're just a little—" She gives a quick nod and reaches her hand to me, covering my own. Her palm is clammy and sticky with sweat. "I hope you slept well."

How could she ask that? My limbs ache from sleeplessness, from lugging the coffin, from the constant repeating image of washing Alice's cold hands. Only when the sun rose and tipped the trees did I rest at all, awakened by the sound of Saoirse clanking pans in the kitchen.

"I slept well as could be."

Toby flips his toast over, pressing it to the plate and smearing jam in concentric circles.

"Toby." Cathy grabs the plate and holds it up. "There are starving people."

"Give him the plate." Lionel doesn't look up. He pushes his own plate of half-eaten toast rimmed with dried egg yolk to the side.

"There are starving people, Lionel."

"Give him the plate."

Toby kicks his heel against the chair leg. He's lost interest in the plate. He's absorbed now with the pond. He points at it, then twists round so his elbows catch the top of the chair's back.

"Nothing moves," I say. The pond is dark and viscous, disconcerting in its blankness.

The birch leaves are already yellowing, the maples beginning to curl. Reeds and rushes strangle the curve of the east bank while the west rim is a jut of granite and exposed roots, permanently pooled in shadow and black lichen. At the far reach, the pond narrows to a pinched channel, and beyond the channel the waterway makes a sharp bend shaped like a broken finger. The Narrows.

"Toby. Sit." Cathy's sigh is long. "I think we should plan the fall garden, get a head start. The fresh air will do you good, Marion."

"The garden." I nod, then finish the chicory in a gulp and slide the cup away. Just yesterday, Alice was laid to rest. Now there's biscuits and blackberry jam. "We can discuss the merits of planting broccoli versus squash."

Toby lays his cheek on his palm and stares at me. Cathy keeps her head down and picks at the crumbs on her plate. She's flushed pink. Lionel fiddles with his spoon.

"I'm sorry," I say. "That wasn't kind." My throat tightens. I push the chair back to stand. I know I've hurt Cathy; I know Lionel disapproves. He taps his spoon to the tablecloth, tilts his head like Father did when one or the other of us had broken some rule, and purses his lips the same.

"Don't." I rise and catch the chairback with my hand, my vision sparking at the edges, the drone of the cicadas beating my ears.

Still he fiddles with the spoon. *Tap tap tap.*

"Will you join us in town today? For service?" Cathy asks.

"I prefer to stay here." My mouth fills with an acrid taste. "I've some correspondence and . . ."

Lionel leans back, his arms crossed and the spoon flicking in his fingers. A dab of milk beads and then darkens the crease at his elbow. "You should make an appearance. At the very least."

"Can I stay with Auntie?" Toby slides back to his seat and stares at his father.

"No, you may not."

"There is solace there." But Cathy's gaze darts away and back as she says it.

"Perhaps for you. Not for me."

"You should come to town with me one day. Welcome the new headmaster of St. Albans. And his wife."

"I don't know her."

"You know him. Thomas Hargreaves. That student who weaseled himself around your husband. He married last year. Or was it the previous?" Cathy looks at me as if I should know this. "She's Jenny Wright's cousin. From Goffstown. I'm sure you know her. Ada?"

"I don't know her."

"You've been too long away. It will all feel comfortable soon. Won't it, Lionel?"

"Meet them if you must. I won't." I do not add that I hate them; that I hate St. Albans Academy and its perfunctory eviction of Benjamin's books and my possessions from the dean's cottage, the solicitous letter that spared little apology. And Thomas Hargreaves—always at the table, uninvited, and always too late in the evening pontificating with Benjamin on Latin subjunctives and the nature of one teacher or another's morals. "I won't meet them."

Breakfast is cleared. After a fuss over Toby's jacket and Cathy not finding her kerchief, they depart for town. I stare at my bedroom door, waiting for the house to sigh and take a breath. But the building doesn't settle to silence. It groans and pops, wheezes and moans. Alice once said it was like wood fairies having a dance and a prowl for sweets.

No. That's not right. I told her that. She had crawled into her wardrobe, and nothing I said lured her out. Not even when I promised that I'd caught the Fairy Queen and locked her in the birdcage.

"It's just the house, Alice. You've heard it all your life."

"I can't hear it anymore. I can't."

She would scream. I knew it was coming and that Mother was just down the hall, napping, already too ill. I yanked open the wardrobe and crept in, blocking her arms as she flailed her fists in great circles.

"I won't let them in," I said. "I'll keep you safe."

Her lips tightened against her teeth. I clamped my hand over her mouth so she wouldn't bite.

"Let me sing you a song, Alice. Let me sing a lullaby and all will be right."

Now we lay us down to sleep
I pray dear Lord our souls to keep.

She stopped flailing, grew rigid as a board, the flats of her bare feet knocking against the other wall. I lay down beside her. Pulled her hair into ringlets round my finger. I wanted to pull it. She was too old for tantrums; thirteen, already curved like a woman and catching the cooper's eye.

She screamed anyway, her breath hot against my hand.

I twist to the window, the memory edging away and scuttling under the bed. My skin flushes hot, unbearable under the stays in this horrible black dress that keeps the day's heat gripped tight in its fist.

Outside is no cooler, but I can stretch my arms and take a full breath. Out back, a few loose chickens stab their beaks to the ground, clawed feet spreading and contracting with each step. Their red feathers are dulled with dust. No matter the flap of wings and the pecks between the quills, still the dust clings. They climb up and over the remains of the glass house, four posts still standing at the corners, up and over the charred boards and black soot and earth, disappearing in the cattails at the water's edge.

Why has it all not been cleared? Surely a hazard, a strange thing for Cathy to allow to remain. All shards and sharp edges and the glint of danger that called to little boys.

It is like two separate houses: the inside a fuss of brocades and competing wallpapers, glass figurines of goats and rosy-cheeked children, settees reupholstered in damasks, and side tables of tiger maple. The exterior austere and tipping to rot.

I spy a square of fabric, pink and gay, stretched taut between a cracked globe lamp and the curved runner of an overturned rocking chair. It is a piece of quilt. I grip the corner, tugging it loose. The cloth is crusted with soot. The pattern underneath is bright still, calico and plaids, circles and squares, bits of old dresses—Alice's, mine, a border of singed brown velvet from an old suit coat of Father's.

I press the fabric to my chest, as if by holding it to my heart I can conjure the days Alice and I pieced it together, when her fingers were losing their childish clumsiness and gaining a young woman's confidence. When Mother's hands were plump and quick with the needle, and the three of us worried away the winter hours with small talk of future husbands and what to make for dessert. When Alice still spoke at all.

I crumple the cloth in my fist, shooing off a hen, and turn back to the house. But I hesitate, not wanting to sit inside in the thick heat. Instead, I stride past the vegetable garden, out to the front yard, blinking against the sudden thrust of sunlight. No elm to mitigate the glare, just a broad stump and withered grass. There's the black crepe on the door, hanging still and limp.

It comes to me then, like a kick to the stomach. Alice is not coming back. She's in a box in the ground with no light to give her succor. I drop to my knees, push my hands in the dirt, and can't stop the keen that scrapes my throat.

I want my sister.

Surely there's a coach. Even on Sunday, there must be at least one. I stumble on a deep rut in the road, glance back toward the house and beyond it the road to Harrowboro. I've come far. The dirt shimmers, the heat lifting and swirling. I slow at a copse, aching for shade, for a moment away from the stares of the sheep and the saw of insects.

I have no bonnet, nothing to prevent the burn of sun on my scalp. I unbutton my collar, fan my handkerchief though it's damp with sweat.

There's a faint clink of metal, and the clop of hooves. The Runyons must be coming back from church; they are two farms farther up and won't deny me a ride.

I dab the kerchief to my neck and lips. Smooth my hair. Watch the chestnut nag and cart approach, Mr. Runyon's blond hair like webbing, the long-stemmed pipe chewed between his teeth. Mrs. Runyon seated behind, just the top of her blue bonnet bobbing.

Mr. Runyon slows the cart and peers down at me. "Where you to?"

Mrs. Runyon settles her new babe to her breast and tilts her head. The bonnet is the only thing soft about her. "Are you well?"

"I was waiting for the coach."

"Hmph." Mr. Runyon glances at his wife, then the road behind. He pushes the pipe stem from the one side of his mouth to the other. "There's no coach of a Sunday."

"I need the coach." I raise my hands, then let them fall. There's a sharp taste of salt on my lip. I'm crying. I'm standing on the Post Road in dust-stained clothes, the handkerchief I hold stinking of soot and charred at the edges.

"Come up back with Essa now. We'll see you to home, and tomorrow there will be a coach. You can rest assured on that."

Essa pats the edge of the cart. "Climb on up and meet the new one."

"I need the coach."

"Climb on in. Can't stay out here too long, lest you're courting sunstroke." Her voice sways and murmurs, like she's talking to her babe. "Climb on in."

She takes my hand as I clamber over the back, pulls me close so our shoulders bump when Mr. Runyon turns us around and the wheels thump and drop.

The babe has a thatch of black hair. Bubbles foam and pop along his pursed lips. He grabs her shawl and lets it go.

"What's his name?"

"Frederick Hiram." She gives the boy three pecks on the head and leaves her chin to rest there. "Your brother told us the news."

"Sorry thing, that." Mr. Runyon gives a hard clamp on his pipe. "She was a good girl."

"Better this way, though," Essa says. "Better for her."

Frederick Hiram gurgles and squeals.

"Shush, love."

I squeeze shut my eyes, but there's Alice, falling from the roof. I open them and stare out at the roll of fields dotted white with sheep. A dark shape slips in the grass. A fox.

I wave the quilt piece. "Leave them be!"

The fox startles and slinks under the bramble, but not without a callow glance at me, yellow eyes near translucent.

The nag huffs a breath and shakes her head, flinging saliva and sodden hay.

The boy's gurgles turn into a high wail. His skin turns a shade of purple, and Mrs. Runyon lifts him up and plops him down. "He's got a voice on him, he has."

"That he has," Mr. Runyon avers. "That he has."

Frederick Hiram stops all of a sudden, the sway of the cart lulling him to quiet. His lids droop heavy. Mrs. Runyon pats his back and cuts a quick glance to me, then squints at the dust from the road. Her face is wide and flat, too big under the flap of bonnet, and she bites a loose bit of dry skin on her lower lip, muddling whether to ask why I was wandering the road of a Sunday.

I swallow back a laugh. Maybe I should tell her. I'm off to Brawders House, I'd say. I'm off to the asylum. See if she'll just nod and pat Frederick Hiram's back. Maybe she'll give me a queer look, the one reserved in the past for Alice, now turned toward me.

Or perhaps the boy will choose to scream again, so I keep quiet and watch the pastures until we reach the drive and Mr. Runyon stops and sets the brake.

"Will you not come in?" I ask. "I'm sure Cathy—"

But the words catch in my mouth, like cracked stone. I grip the cart edge. Alice stands at the side of the road, barefoot and clad in a thin cotton chemise. Hands clasped in front of her, red hair parted in the middle, hanging straight to her hips. Rose lips, a spray of freckles, eyes the color of moss.

"Alice."

Mr. Runyon clambers down from his seat, blocking my view as he walks to the back of the conveyance and unlatches the gate. He reaches a rough-worn hand to help me down.

Still Alice stands there, the skirt of her dress stained black, half-moons of earth under her nails, a swipe of mud on her neck. She stares at her bare feet, then watches as I descend from the cart, my legs tangling in my skirts. My body shakes. I step toward her.

"Give our condolences," Mrs. Runyon says. She covers Frederick Hiram's head with her shawl to protect his scalp from the high sun.

Her husband returns to his seat.

Alice is no longer on the roadside.

A rush of breeze, hot and sharp, flattens the seared grass and scatters the few sheep, setting them to bleat and trot to the shadows of the old barn.

Then a thick quiet before the nag shakes her head and jangles the bit.

"Our condolences," Mrs. Runyon repeats. "Our condolences."

The drive waves and shifts as I walk to the house. Toby stares from the dining room window, his palms flat to the glass. He's talking, his mouth moving, brows pulled down in a concentrated focus. But he watches me. Keeps talking and watches me. Gives a little wave that I return before taking the steps.

The door is ajar, the hall cool. Toby stands in the frame of the dining room door. "Shh." He looks to the top of the stairs, then reaches for my hand, slipping his in mine. His fingers curl, plump and sticky. He leads me into the dining room and points at a seat.

"Here she is." He lets go my hand and struggles with the chair, pulling it out. Pointing for me to sit. Patting my shoulder when I do.

It faces the mirror. The crepe has been removed, folded, and set to the cabinet. I stare at the silvered glass. A little boy and a plain woman with a swatch of dirt on her cheek peer back.

His lips are moving, hot sweet breath, no sound, focused on the chair across.

"Toby."

He clicks his teeth, the only sound from his wordless mouth, and his fingers drum the fabric on my shoulder.

"Toby."

My stomach twists. No. I shrug his hand off, then turn to grapple for his arms. His thighs push against my knees, and he looks at me with colorless eyes, those lashes so long and curled, furling and unfurling.

I shake him. One hard shake. "Toby!"

He smiles and then turns to the doorway. Cathy rounds the corner. She fans a riot of flowers on the table: goldenrod, chrysanthemums, an armful of asters. "Aren't they . . . Are you all right?"

"It's hot."

"Go ask Saoirse for a vase, Toby." Cathy cups his cheek and gives him a peck. "And a glass of water for Auntie."

When it is the two of us, she turns to the flowers, lifting a stalk to strip the leaves. A ladybug drops from a stem, stretches its shelled wings. Cathy holds out a finger and waits for it to crawl onto her palm. "Look." She smiles at me, as if sharing a marvelous gift. "She's good luck. We'll keep her in the house." With a flick of her wrist, she tips the ladybug to the table. It lands on its back. Its legs flail and wings flap and close until it rights itself and crawls to the safety of a broad leaf.

"You should have asked them to stay."

"I . . ."

"Where were you going?"

"I wanted the coach."

"There's no coach on Sunday." A milky liquid seeps from the stem and beads along the stalk. She swipes it with her thumb, then looks around for some rag or towel to clean her hand. There's nothing but the black crepe.

"Why?"

"I want Alice's trunk."

"I'm sure they'll send it."

"I have questions for Dr. Mayhew. She shouldn't have had any access to that roof."

"You won't find comfort."

"I am looking for none." I grab the table edge and push myself up. "I just want to know."

But Cathy isn't listening; she's rearranging the flowers, a single frown line marring her forehead. "She was never at peace. Always . . . What good does it do to stir the dead? It changes nothing. Nothing at all."

Chapter Five

But the dead stir me. Three nights the same dream.

I stand in the upstairs bedroom of a house we've taken for a hospital. The walls are plum, the green curtains rusty from the blood of the hands that tie the fabric back. Dr. Rawlings wears a rubber apron. He crooks his finger to me.

"You will close their eyes." But there are hundreds of soldiers, too many, the line of cots a mile long.

"I can't."

"You must."

I bend to the first man. Place my hand to his forehead, then swipe my palm over his lids. "Fare thee well," I whisper.

The next to the next to the next. Blue eyes and green, empty sockets and clouded white.

"I can't."

Alice is here, kneeling before a limbless, lifeless body, drawing the eyes shut. The locket dangles from her neck.

"Why are you here?" I ask.

She looks up at me. A cicada pushes its way past her lips, its blunt red-brown head dipping as it crawls to her lower lip, transparent wings unfurling in a tissue-paper whisper.

I wake in a knot of sheets and nightclothes, the room close and musty. The wallpaper on the bed's edge buckles and bubbles. I press a finger to smooth it, but it won't stay put.

There's a tap at the door. I hear Toby breathing through his nose, trying to be quiet.

If this is his habit, it will need to stop. "I'm indisposed," I say. "If you need something, go ask Saoirse."

The knob twists left and right. Stops.

"Did you hear me?"

"Yes."

"Then you must say 'yes.' And 'sorry.'"

"Yes, Auntie. Sorry." But he doesn't leave. He still stands on the other side of the door, the toes of his shoes just visible in the gap.

"Toby?"

He slips a blue jay's feather under the door. Blue and black, tipped with white.

Alice came home with treasures, seeds and nettles, dandelion down and thistle silk stuck to her hair, in the weave of her skirts, clinging in tufts to the fine hair on her arms, like a tumult and chaos of clouds. Dirt beneath her nails, grit in the whorls and eddies of her palms. The trees that ringed the pond bore witness to her and she to them—an etch of initials, a trinket or bobbin or discarded laces were secreted away in slits she'd carved in the tree trunks. Sometimes I'd find buttons missing from a bodice or skirt. Other times a hairpin went missing. Not stolen, though. Replaced with an acorn. A twig with a red-tipped leaf. The bud of a spring iris. A blue jay's feather, tipped with white.

"Thank you," I say.

"You're welcome."

You're welcome, Alice said. And her voice was like bells.

Benjamin's picture has been moved. I've gone to the kitchen for coffee and come back to it moved. It was on the mantel; now it sits on the sill. Saoirse's been cleaning and not putting things back in place. My journal shifted from the bedside drawer to the desk. The wardrobe door ajar.

I close the door, replace the portrait, and move the silk bookmark to the next blank page of the journal.

"Saoirse."

I hear her milling in the front parlor, her hoarse hum in constant refrain.

"Saoirse."

The humming stops. She comes to the hall and peers across to the dining room, then down the hall to me. She chews her lower lip. "Did you call me?"

"I did. I—"

She pulls at a dust rag and then swipes it across the top of the curio cabinet.

She has grown old. Too old to keep doing this. Too old to scold her for something as ridiculous as a misplaced portrait. At least I have it.

"Are you ailing, missy?"

"No. No. I . . ." I pick at the doorframe with my thumb, then lift the edge of wallpaper running its length. A tiny line of penciled letters runs along the seam. The paperer's marks. "Thank you for taking care of my room. But I wish to do it myself."

She shifts her jaw left to right. "Are you settling with us for good?"

"I don't know." I spread my hands and shrug, wait for her to look away. "I don't know."

"Well, that's that, then." She turns to make her way back to the parlor.

"Saoirse."

"Aye?"

"What did Alice do?"

She stops. Flaps the rag against her thigh, then folds it and tucks it into her apron pocket.

"Saoirse."

"About killed the child, she did. If Missus hadn't found them, who knows what."

"But why?"

"Not my place to say."

"You knew her, Saoirse. She'd never . . ."

But she raises her hand to stop me and walks back into the parlor.

Later, I find Cathy and Toby in the field. They've set one archery bale against the old barn and another, closer, painted with rings of yellow and red and blue. A beginner's distance. The sheep, normally lounging by the barn's shadows, have wandered to the stone wall facing the road and house; some lie in the sun, others rest their heads on the crumbling wall and stare at nothing.

Cathy is dressed in an open vest, loose shirt tucked into her skirts. Sleeves rolled to the elbow. Hair loose and tied with a single ribbon. She settles the bow in Toby's hand, curling his fingers round the grip.

"Nose to the string, Toby." She bends down to sight along the bow with him, corrects the cock of his elbow. Then she steps back, hands to hips, watching the arrow release and arc and drop to the ground.

"Well. Not terrible," Cathy says. "Maybe we can convince your auntie to join us?"

"I'd like Saoirse to stay out of my room."

"If you wish. It's your room."

"They haven't delivered Alice's trunk. It's been four days. I want her things."

"Archery is much more fun to worry about."

"Cathy—"

"Wait. One more try, Toby."

A single arrow lies near Toby's feet. He bends to reach it, and the bow swivels and drops.

"It's too large. Is it Lydia's old one?"

Cathy shrugs. "Do you want your own bow and arrow, Toby?" She glances over her shoulder at me. "We can go to town."

Toby squints up at Cathy, then shoves his hands in his pockets and rolls on his toes. The empty quiver on his shoulder twists and bumps against his thigh.

Cathy picks up the bow and holds it out to the boy. "I forgot how much fun this all is. We haven't done this . . . well, since . . ." She shakes her head. "Your aunt is an excellent archer, Toby. Did you know she won Mrs. Brown's Academy tournament five years running?"

"That's not true."

"You did." She kicks out a back foot as she grabs an arrow, nocks it, and takes aim at the far bale. The arrow makes its mark with a thud, feathers quivering against the yellow bullseye. "Then I won."

Toby stares up at her and frowns. He reaches for her leg and grips it tight.

"Let go."

He shakes his head.

"Go get the arrows." She ruffles his hair, then grips his shoulders and jostles him. "Toby. Let go."

He steps back, then meanders from arrow to arrow, pulling one from the soil or off the ground and dropping them in the quiver. Midway to the barn he drops to his haunches, poking at something in the grass, then holding it aloft on the tip of an arrow—a cicada husk. He flicks it and moves to the barn.

"Lydia was the archer," I say. "She won those tournaments. Not me. I left midterm. My mother needed care. And I had Alice. You know that."

"But he doesn't remember Lydia. So, it's easier if I say it was you. Not so many questions." She unties the hair ribbon, combs her fingers through the locks, and then watches Toby as she ties the bow. "I loved Lydia. But if I tell him about that, he'll ask for more. And I'm not willing to tell more."

"He should know of her. He doesn't need to know she drowned, I understand not telling that, but—"

"No." She cocks her head and stares at me. In the sunlight, her eyes darken to jet glass. "I'm his mother now. If you had a child, you would understand."

"I don't want Saoirse in my room. Things have been moved."

"All right."

"And I don't need to have had a child to know Toby shouldn't be lied to. Lydia was his mother and she loved him. He should know that."

"Isn't it enough he's lost Alice? Isn't that enough for a little boy?" She runs a hand across the back of her neck and turns to watch him.

He waves, the arrows clutched in his hand.

"I can't have children." She picks at the leather wrapped on the bow's handle and shrugs. "You could and chose not to."

"My sister . . ."

"Your sister wasn't a child. She was many things, but she wasn't that."

"How did she get on the roof of that building?"

With a long exhale of breath, Cathy moves to collect the other bow. "How, indeed."

"I want to know."

"Do you know you've never once talked about your husband? Where in the world did he die? In a swamp? In a field? A bullet? A minié ball? Dysentery? Did some other woman give him a Christian burial? For God's sake, will you ever order his tombstone?"

"Be quiet."

"There's been too much loss, Marion. We need to let go of it and hold on to the living."

Benjamin and I were a marriage of practicality. He was Head of Latin—
"Soon to be head*master*"—and in need of a wife. My father was impatient for me to wed and to take Alice with me. His "happy accident" whom he coddled as a child became his embarrassment as she grew and her quirks became habit. How to explain a mute daughter? One who freezes midstep to smack her hand to her face not once but six times, always six, before carrying on? One who knocks her head to the wall in the morning and paints exquisite miniatures of flowers to give as gifts in the afternoon?

Our paths originally crossed in the aisles of St. Albans's library, which carried five times the books Mrs. Brown's did. Alice wanted an astronomy text. And I had none to give her nor instruction to guide the lesson I gave her. It had been years since I graduated from Mrs. Brown's, and music and literature moved me more than the stars. I stepped to the counter, for women were allowed no farther in the rooms, wrote my request on a slip of paper, and waited for the clerk to return. The door swung open behind me, bringing a rush of brittle leaves and slicing air. It was Benjamin, smelling of musty books and leather from the satchel slung across his chest.

"I have seen you before," he said. His beard was trimmed but not full gray, and he knew I would admire the angles of his jaw and cheekbones, making sure to pose like an actor in the one beam of sunlight.

I laughed, and pressed my fist to my lips to stop it.

"Why do you laugh?"

"I don't."

"You do."

He cleared his throat and peered past the counter to the stacks. "Mr. Eliot is never here when you need him here." Then his eyes turned to the paper I still held in my hand. "What are you looking for?"

"A book. For my sister. She's ill . . . I would like an astronomy book to bring her."

"Your sister is in luck. We have many to choose from." He tucked the books close to his chest and tipped his head. "Follow."

His back was broad, straining a coat that shined at the elbows. The clerk came around the corner, eyes blinking furiously at my presence amongst the stacks, but Benjamin waved him off. "This young woman—what is your name?"

"Marion. Marion Snow."

"Miss Marion Snow is in need of a book, Mr. Eliot. A text that ponders on the infinite measure of the universe. We shall get it for her." He strode on. "I have seen you at the lyceums on Wednesdays. Last week was particularly sodden, was it not? A treatise on corn. Corn! We are choking in the grip of our southern brethren's penchant for slavery and we are given a treatise on corn." He glanced back and winked. "Not that the subject is without merit, if you find it has merit."

"It is of importance to the hogs."

"Why, it certainly is, Miss Snow. It is quite that." He stopped so suddenly his bag swung and bumped against my chest. "Here." He pulled down a large tome from the top shelf. "This is complex. With mathematics. Is your sister good with mathematics?"

"Yes, she . . ."

"Because I am not. But I am excellent with Latin. So, she may avail herself of my tutoring."

He came to the house regular as clockwork, Tuesday mornings. I sat with him in the parlor, and Alice lurked at the top of the stairs. There was no denying I waited for each Tuesday, impatient at the slow tick of the clock. His voice, as he lectured and read, was rich. His eyes were richer. "Here is a very fine illustration of Neptune, Miss Snow." He twisted in his chair to call out to the hall. "I shall leave the book open to it."

"You spoil us," I said.

He turned back to face me. "I wish to marry you."

The room hummed. My cheeks burnt. Alice came down two steps and stopped at the creak of a board.

"Your father has agreed."

"Why me?"

"You do not simper. I have not once heard you complain. We are agreed on the slavery issue." He tamped a pipe—I remember the match did not take and he tossed it to the plate on the side table in the parlor. But it missed and dropped to the rug, leaving a small smear of black that never scrubbed clean. "And I wish to marry you, Miss Snow."

"I don't want to marry."

"All women want to marry."

"That isn't true." I slid forward on my chair, clasping my hands around my knees.

"What do you want, then?"

I looked out the window, at the dark hedge and the line of white where the road intersected. A dappled shadow from the great tree spread across the drive. "I want . . ." But all I could conjure was a field without end, and myself looking back at myself from the horizon's bowed edge. Yellow flowers, knee high. "I want myself."

"But you have Alice." He raised a finger. "And I have agreed to Alice. She will have a home with us."

So, Alice and I changed houses. The cottage was too small; we were all underfoot of each other. I refused his bed as often as I could. I did not wish for a child. I had been burdened enough ministering my mother and then Alice. I could not fathom the want of a child who would tug my skirts and hold me to its needs. By Christmas the first year, he ignored Alice. By the second, he ignored me. Visits to Turee grew less frequent. Lionel's wedding. Toby's christening. Father's funeral. A summer afternoon.

"You are a selfish woman," he said. "You shirk your duties to me. Not to her, of course. Never to Alice."

Chapter Six

Turee, Aug 10

Dr. Mayhew,
I wish a meeting to discuss irregularities in the procedures
of Brawders House that led directly to my sister's death.
I also request a full accounting of her treatments and the
efficacies of each. This will go far to alleviate my concerns,
and to stay me from filing a more formal complaint.
I will call on you directly, this Wednesday, 10 a.m.
Should this be an inconvenient time, please respond, oth-
erwise the meeting stands as requested.
Marion Snow Abbott

I set the pen to its holder, and then press and rock the ink blotter
to the paper.

Nothing in their explanation fits. It doesn't fit Alice's poor, wasted
body. Something bites and scratches at my thoughts. I look out the
window to the pond, following the course of a dragonfly as it hunts for
prey on the gloss of water. The afternoon sun cuts through the western
trees; the dragonfly is emerald and black in turns. It lifts and dives, hovers and waits. Patient and careful.

I fold the letter, open the single drawer, remove my wallet. A few bills, still, that are mine alone. Then I put the letter and the bills in my small knit purse and button it to my belt.

Cathy sits at her desk in the parlor now. She's changed from her archery garb, sits with a curved back over the house ledgers. Toby stares from the settee, one foot kicking the leg.

"I'm going to Turee," I tell her. "I have a letter to post."

"Can I come?" Toby asks.

"Why?"

"I'll buy you an ice." He pulls his lip down with a finger and taps his nail to his tooth. "I have money. And you're very sad. Ices help."

"Well, I . . ."

He gives a solemn nod.

Cathy drums a pencil against her chin, then turns to us. She points the pencil tip to the ledger, then drops it to the pile of receipts. "Come here," she says to Toby and reaches out, pulling him to her chest and covering his head with light kisses. "You are very sweet to think of your auntie."

He pushes against her thighs and squirms, then pecks her cheek. "That's enough."

She rests her hands on his shoulders. "Are you too big for kisses?"

"I'm buying Auntie an ice."

"That sounds like a grand idea." Her gaze catches mine. "We'll all go. I could use the walk."

"Are you sure? You look busy and—"

"It's just the household accounts. They can easily wait." She plops the ledger on top of the papers and pushes it all to the back. "An ice, and maybe a look at the new bonnets at Mrs. Emmet's is just the ticket." With a quick motion, she shuts and locks the desk tight.

Toby runs ahead of us, the flap of his brown poplin coat waving behind him. He has found a long stick and swings it above his head like a broadsword. Our parasols are more decoration than shade. Cathy's brought a fan and flicks it in a circle around her face. A deep flush darkens her cheeks and neck. She has overdressed for the heat, a plaid of gray and mustard. Our skirts swing and settle, lifting the dry soil in puffs.

"An ice in town. We could have shaved a bowl from the block in the icehouse, you know." Cathy squints and stares through the maple trees to the fallow fields of the Humphrey farm. The farmhouse windows are black. Widow Humphrey's two boys lost their lives early on in the struggles. Spotsylvania. The black bow remains on the door. She walks out of the barn toward the hen house and lifts a hand to us. We return the greeting. Cathy goes back to flicking her fan. "She should move to town. She'd have an easier time of it."

"Do you think she'd leave the land her boys were born on?"

"She has their pensions."

"It's not enough to give this all up. There's barely enough to cover food. You know that. I give you Benjamin's. You do the books."

"Don't be so sharp."

"Don't make foolish remarks." I dig at the collar of my dress. My nail catches, and I hear the small rip to the lace as I pull it free. "I'll stop in this week to see if she needs a hand."

Toby stabs the hard earth, poking and crushing the cicada shells that stick to the stone fence and the bark of the trees and litter the road.

Cathy loops her arm through mine and nudges my shoulder. As if we are close, as if she could jostle Lydia's memory out of the way, kick it into the grass. She looks at me and blinks, and she knows I think her an interloper. Perhaps I should judge less. Give her a nod for stepping in (so easily, so blithely) to rescue Lionel and Toby. *I will care for this little family*, she'd written not long after Lydia's funeral. *You keep to your cause.*

"I'm sorry," I say. "It's hot. You know that makes me tiresome."

"You're forgiven." She tips her parasol to the sun so the flowered pattern repeats on the road. She peers up through the lace and ribs. "I should have worn a hat."

"You can buy one at Mrs. Emmet's."

With a shrug, she lets her fan drop and swing from her wrist. "You could do with a new one. Although the straw suits you. Even if it is black."

The trees thin out, leaving the dirt road bare to the sun. A row of clapboard cottages line the edges, laundry hanging on ropes between the houses. Petticoats and undershirts and children's dresses. A wicker basket sits by a pole and awaits the folding. On the right, the mill pond is glassy green. Terrence Markam's house reflects like white stone in the water. The image is solid enough it seems one could step onto it and glide to the millworks on the other side. The water slips over the mill gates to the canal beyond, and the rush of it gives us a spray of cool mist as we walk by.

"Nothing's changed here."

"The train went to Harrowboro. And where the train goes, the industry follows."

There is the Congregational church, bright white, black door, as if it knows the souls of men contain both. A chestnut horse lolls his head from a stall at the livery. He stares across at the steps of the church, then swings his head and whinnies.

We stop at the general store, its porch and stairs boasting tin tubs and rakes and a hand plow. Mrs. Emmet's is the next door over. A cat, matted and soot gray, settles in the shade of a washboard. It hisses once at Toby, then pushes its head to his palm.

"Don't touch that." Cathy hurries to catch up to him. She grips his wrist. "Now you'll have to wash your hands." She pulls him to the water pump near the store's siding, forces his hands under the spigot, and then levers the pump until the water belches and flows. "You can die from touching a cat like that. You don't want to die from that, do you?"

I pick up the stick he abandoned for the poor cat and bring it near. Toby's scarlet now, his mouth a line of white.

"Oh, don't go into a snit." Cathy steps back from the pump and shakes water from her skirt. "You know what happens then."

He blinks. Holds his arms straight to his side and waggles his hands. "I'm not in a snit."

Cathy smiles. "Good." She takes his hand. "Put the stick down, Marion. He doesn't need it."

Toby trails after her, waits on the landing as she opens the screen door.

"Go on." She keeps the door swung wide and looks at me. "Are you coming?"

"I'll be right there."

The post office is just two doors down and the letter quickly delivered. Across the street, in a small square park, three women huddle, bonnet to bonnet, then separate and point at various spots on the grass. Another woman lifts a triangle sign and moves it from one spot to the next, obeying the directives of those pointing fingers. She blows out a breath and pulls in her lip, nods and jogs from one spot to another. The sign remains in one spot long enough for me to read. *Honor Your Brother: Future Home for the Statue of the Fallen Soldier, Donations to Orinda Flowers.*

"They're asking for a statue and a fountain." I startle at Cathy's voice just behind me. "Here." She hands me a waxed paper cone of lemon ice, then lifts her own to her mouth and shaves off a bite with her teeth. She pastes on a smile and waves.

The women look but none comes closer; they return to their huddling and pointing.

"I could pay for it all and they'd still be like that." Cathy takes another bite. She turns to me, studying me with those dark eyes. "We have a table. Near an open window. We can watch the fat hens cluck and flap about their statue. And you can tell me about the letter you posted. So secretive."

"It's not. I've requested a meeting with Dr. Mayhew."

"Why? It's done, Marion. The matter is done, except for the trunk. You could have just asked for that."

"But I didn't. You saw her, Cathy . . ."

"Yes. I can't stop seeing it." She crosses back to the general store. Her shoulders pinch, as if she has armored herself.

I follow her and sit at the table while Toby swings his legs and kicks my shins. Cathy glares out the window. Her ice is forgotten, melting and dripping from the paper and over her fingers.

She smirks and lifts her chin. "So much adoration of the dead."

Toby drops his ice to the wood floor. Cathy *tsks* and leans down to mop it up. But her ice drips to her skirt, dark round beads of sugar water. She scrubs the fabric with her napkin, leaving me to Toby's mess.

"You're in a snit," he says, pointing at Cathy.

"Be quiet." She's rubbed the liquid into long streaks on her thighs. Her eyes move from the task to the window glass.

"I'll lock you in the icehouse with the spiders." Toby slaps the sides of his chair and kicks his heels to the legs. He opens his mouth and clacks his teeth.

"Toby," I say, "lower your voice."

"They'll bite your toes and tie you up in leathers."

Cathy presses her hands to fists. "Be quiet." She grabs his arm, jerking him out of the chair, pressing his face to her skirt as she grapples her way to the door and down the steps.

I grab her parasol and come after, reaching for her sleeve. But she jogs down the roadside, Toby's face held tight against her thigh.

"Stop it, Cathy."

"He's a bad little boy." Her jaw is locked; the words come out brittle and sharp.

Toby goes slack. Arms and legs loose, so he slips from her grip and then sits with a thud.

Cathy leaves him there and trudges forward, moving only to avoid an oncoming horse and lumber cart.

I reach for Toby, but he flinches and twists away. "You need to get up."

He scratches the ground with his fingers and remains in place.

Cathy whirls around and strides back. "I'm trying. Can we please just try?"

He breathes in and out. Three times. Then he puts his hand to his knee and stands. He keeps his gaze to the ground. Doesn't resist when she takes his hand in hers.

Her cheeks are stippled red and white. "There, then. We've had our ice."

Chapter Seven

Dr. Mayhew has agreed to meet. And Cathy has asked to join me. "I think it best," she says, tying the ribbons of her silk bonnet. It is pink and edged with lace. Her clothing is as much froth as function. But it is honest. She doesn't mourn. "Toby will stay with Saoirse." Then she takes up the buggy reins and urges the dapple mare on.

The waiting area at Brawders House is empty save for the two of us seated on a bench. It is creams and blues and welcoming here. Great vases adorn the walls, filled with long, curved ferns and a cornucopia of blossoms from the front gardens. The chandeliers are elegant in frosted glass, crystal beads catching the light. The large windows on the back wall are open to the draft. There are no bars here, just metalwork on the windows that is both intricate and sinuous. Shapes of flowers and grasses and birds snake across my shoes. I barely remember this part of the hospital and its polite pretense. But the brick and mildewed stink of the basement is still clear.

The steward, in long, graying sideburns and impeccable black coat, perches on a stool. He has given his name as Northrup and followed it with a weak handshake before pointing us to the bench, mumbling an apology for our loss. He turns the pages of his ledger, each crinkle caught and echoed in the high-ceiling room, each scratch of pen lingering. He stares at me and blinks.

Cathy glances up from her tatting. She twists and untwists the loose thread round her finger. "I found the doctors to be very caring. Not indifferent to their patients."

"So you did visit?"

Her face flushes. She bends to the tatting, biting her lip in concentration, feeding the ivory thread to the shuttle, knotting a snowflake pattern. "I'm not heartless."

"How often?"

Cathy's hands freeze midknot. She frowns and shakes her head, picks at the loops, then abandons them to her lap. "Until she refused me."

I hear voices, just up the wide stairs. Muted mostly, as the doors on both sides of the landing stay shut more often than not. But then one will open, and the voices barrel out and around a nurse with her bobbing cap, the orderly pushing up his sleeves, a matron rolling a metal tray. A blare, a babble, then mutters and thumps.

A door slams above, and a tin or bucket clatters against a wall. I look to the ceiling, as does Mr. Northrup, our gazes following heavy footsteps that come to a sudden stop.

"How much longer?" I ask. My hands shake. I twist the strap of my bag around a palm, then lace my fingers.

He frowns and digs out his pocket watch. "Dr. Mayhew is on rounds. You are here outside visiting hours."

I lean back against the bench, but the curve of wood is not meant for resting. I find myself tilted forward and the edge of my corset digging into the bones of my hips.

There is nothing to do but wait. Watch the man across from me as he writes in his ledger.

"Do the patients come through here?"

He sets down the pen. Stares at me with eyes that are black as night. "This is the vestibule."

"I can see that."

"For visitors. Such as you."

Where, then, did Alice enter this place? With just her trunk and the overwhelming weight of Lionel's lie? Alice stopped speaking at fourteen. One day nattering on about the new black calf, then next day silent. The week after that, the year after that, mute—save our private language of signs and gestures. How did she impart her concerns and fears?

My breath is tight, twisting tighter. I jump from the seat, pace to the front door, and then turn to him. "Where are the patients admitted?"

"Mrs. Abbott—" He lifts a hand and his face glazes into an accommodating pleasantness.

"Somewhere in the back, then." There behind the stairs, a round glass window cut into a door and behind it the basement and the morgue.

"Ah. Mrs. Abbott. Mrs. Snow."

I turn to find a tall man standing too near, causing me to look up at an uncomfortable angle. "Dr. Mayhew?"

"Yes. The exact one." His voice is syrup and honey. He holds a notebook under his arm and thumbs the corner. His hair is thick, flecked with gray, but his wild sideburns are black. I cannot pin his age. His gray eyes are deep set, shadowed by heavy brows. He has seen life—the lines at the edge of his eyes seem as much from heartache as from laughter. His gaze flicks back and forth, and he juts his long chin toward me.

"I didn't hear you near," I say.

"Soft soles. Best for the patients." His thin lips purse, then widen into a smile. "I know why you've come."

He reaches out a hand. I don't take it. He curls his fingers back.

"Dr. Mayhew," Cathy says. "My sister-in-law needs solace."

"Then I shall give it to her." He rolls his wrist and gestures toward a door off to the right. "Let us talk."

The walls of Lemuel Mayhew's office are thick plaster, yellowed from smoke. They are plain adorned, save a large poster on the wall behind his desk. A pen-and-ink of a man, his head diagrammed into phreno-logical parcels and the phrase *Know Thyself* printed across his neck. A fern lounges on a wide windowsill.

Mayhew settles in his chair and leans back. The coils squeak. He stee-ples his fingers and taps them to his lips. "I am as inconsolable as you are."

"Are you?"

"Any loss of life is untenable. But I am glad you've come, so I can share the news in person. We've done a thorough investigation. It's all to order."

"Then how did she get on the roof?"

"The roof."

I roll my fingers around the chair's cushion. "She was under your care. You should know how she arrived on that roof. Since you have investigated."

"Yes, I do. It is . . ." He shrugs, then reaches across the papers on his desk, sets aside the ashtray used as a weight, and flips open a folder. "Mm. Unfortunate. We were, of course, trying to spare you."

"Spare me what?"

"The reports are public, Mrs. Abbott. We must state for the board the doings of the hospital." His chair wheels roll back and forth on the wood floor. "And also consider the family. Miss Snow was a troubled young woman."

"I would like to see."

"See what?"

"The roof. Her room. Her records."

"The report of her death will be public. The treatment records, however, are sealed."

"Then anything that can explain to me why my sister is dead."

He blows a breath through his nose and closes the folder. "Your brother says you were a nurse during the conflict? Are you still?"

"No."

"Duty for the cause, then."

"Dr. Mayhew—"

"Do you recall some of your patients, how they screamed all night of battle? *We just need to take the hill'* or *'Get 'em again.'* Over and over, that mewling cry."

"What does this have to do with Alice?"

"When they died, did you write their folks of those nights? I don't think you did. I think you instead gave them succor and told them their son had died in peace."

"I don't know your point."

"My point is that your sister had much the same horrible nights. I think she wished them to stop."

I swallow. It is like gulping a stone. Or the truth. "So she jumped."

"Yes."

Three stories. Four at the apex.

"Why? How?"

His palm glides over the papers before him. They crinkle and the folds return, though he keeps his hand flat like an iron. "I think when someone wants to . . . end their life, they find a way." He touches the side of his nose, as if we're sharing a secret. "I will never make suicide a part of the record."

"No. That's not right." My breath stutters, and I gasp. "She wouldn't do that."

Cathy rests her hand on my wrist. Her grip tightens as I try to pull away. "It's kind of you to keep that out of public circulation."

"It is heartbreak enough that it occurred."

I twist my arm to release from Cathy's hold. "There were bruises, Dr. Mayhew, that do not . . . Here." I touch my wrists. First the left then the right. "Her thighs. Her ankles. Here." My forehead is hot where I draw the bruise. "How did she get those?"

"We are a progressive hospital, Mrs. Abbott. Our treatments are meant to provide calm. Patients work in the gardens, in the farm. We grow all our own vegetables. Raise our own meat." He gives a sharp laugh. "These patients were better fed during the war than all the rest of us, with our shortages and rations. Better fed. But it doesn't calm everyone. Some must be taken to hand. Other treatments provided. And they work. They do what they are intended to do."

"What treatments?" I lean forward, gripping the edge of his desk. "What treatments?"

"Industry and good clean air on the whole." He smacks his hand on the desk. "I shall assuage you. Come. Look."

We move to the second-floor landing. Mayhew taps a barred window, pointing to the roofs of buildings below. One metal door is locked on our left and another to our right. "Our own gristmill. And there, the herb garden." He puffs his pipe and exhales. "In the spring there are calves. There's a cooper here. Been here since the building opened. We do go through buckets."

"It is all very industrious." Cathy dabs her handkerchief to her forehead.

"The men's wing is to the right. Women to the left. The Owens wing. Charming woman, if somewhat bullish. Ran a school for young ladies. In Munsonville. We are much appreciative of her benevolence."

Cathy nods, raises an eyebrow, and leans closer to the window. "It's so contained to itself."

"Fresh air, responsibilities, and quietude of the mind." Mayhew clamps a hand behind his back and rolls on his heels. "All within this small acreage. In fact, we can't seem to stem the growth. I've got an eye on a further four acres, and a letter in the making to Mrs. Owens."

The lock to the left clinks, and the long handle turns of its own accord. The ward door swings open just long enough for a girl to sidle out. It's the girl from the road, in a gray skirt and apron. She carries a bucket and mop and startles when she sees me. The bucket sways, the water threatening to tip over the lip. "Oh." Then she swings her gaze to Cathy before staring at the floor. Her mouth presses into a tight line.

"Miss Swain." Mayhew clamps his pipe stem.

"Yes, it's me," she says.

"Everything right?"

"Everything's right."

"Well done, then."

She nods and hurries to the stairs, slowing to shift the bucket before stepping down.

"Maintenance. Much to keep an eye on." He points again to the barns and paddocks. "There. A lamb. Ha."

I step forward. I don't care about the lambs or the new roof on the chapel, or the rows of beets and garlic. I see the two brick-clad wings jutting either side of this landing with matching windows of metal grating and whitewashed glass. Meant to let in light but not life.

He peers down through the glass, mindlessly scratching his sideburn. His eyes follow the path Kitty takes along a slope with black ruts and dirt. When she reaches the bricked perimeter fence, the sun catches the metal straps on the bucket. She opens a door in the high wood gate and continues on and out of sight.

I trace the ruts to the building, follow their split around a narrow building set between the wings. Both tracks disappear in shadow, and I wonder: Is that where Alice first was delivered, and the road for her final journey out?

"Do they improve?"

"It is all a matter of the right mix of therapy. Healing the mind carries many complications." He blinks and pulls at his pipe, but the ember has gone out, and with a frown, he tips the bowl of ash and half-burnt tobacco to a heavy brass ashtray near the stair railing.

"And Alice?"

Mayhew's eyes slip to me. "She was, alas, not one of the fortunates."

His gaze stays long enough that I am forced to look away. I make a show of smoothing my skirt. One of the ribbons has come loose. I tuck the string and then lift my shoulders. The sunlight slices through these windows, the only clear ones of the lot, and I squint against it.

Dr. Mayhew pulls a key ring from his coat pocket, swinging it from finger to thumb. Then he clasps it tight in his fist. "Let us visit the women's wing. You have been here before, Mrs. Snow?"

Cathy nods. "We sat on the front porch and had lemon cake."

"That cake is a wonder." He presses the key to the lock, and the metal shivers and tumbles and thunks. One lock, then the other.

"There are thirty-six women on this floor. They will be at their labors. Sewing, I think. Some of the women are quite talented." He pushes his shoulder to the door and leans in. "Mrs. Brighton. I have brought visitors."

Beyond the door are voices, like cat's paws padding around corners; they slip across the doorsill and bat my ankles. A woman in a gray apron and coiled mud-brown hair blocks our way. She twists a rag in her hands. The liquid drips and splatters to the floor. Her eyes are near to black. She doesn't meet my gaze but looks just past my left shoulder.

"This is Mrs. Abbott and Mrs. Snow." Mayhew gestures, palm up. "And this is our Mrs. Brighton."

Cathy's face pales to white.

Mrs. Brighton pushes out her lower lip. She twists the rag and cuts a look at Cathy. "Does she need to sit?"

But Cathy's pallor has now flushed a deep red. She shakes her head and hooks her hand around my arm. "I am perfectly well."

"The women are at sewing."

"As I thought." Dr. Mayhew moves aside, allowing us to enter. "Let us proceed."

Chapter Eight

Mrs. Brighton moves before us, the hem of her skirts brushing the floor. She rolls and squeezes the rag in her hand, and then clears her throat. Ahem and ahem.

I am hit by the smell of the room now: the sweet, flat stale of breath and sourness of body. The arch of lye and menses and soap and too much lemon verbena spritzed to the air.

I press my handkerchief over my nose, but the odors have latched to the fabric, weaving themselves tight.

The room is like an elongated hall, the length exacerbated by the planks in the heavy timber floor. The walls are a white that assaults, and the metalwork on the long single window leaves shadows of concentric circles. Deep, inset doors line the facing walls, and benches without cushions sit between each. The women are in groups of two or three, in curved cane rockers, feet and heels pushing the chairs forward and back. Their hair is plaited, pinned up tight to the head. Old and young. They are intent upon their needlework.

Mrs. Brighton jerks her head for us to follow. The murmurs stop. Now there is but the matron's shoe step and the swish of needles to fabric. Each woman we pass is dressed much as Alice, in rough cotton, though here and there I see a touch of colored lace at the collar or cuff. Each woman's dress bears a number stitched across the left breast.

"Keep to your task. A busy hand promises a productive day." Mrs. Brighton sways down the hall on wide-set legs that give the impression she's on a boat at sea. She looks over her shoulder. "They'll eat you up, if you let them."

I turn to see what Dr. Mayhew thinks of this, but he's not paying attention and is crouched in front of a woman of middling age, with his hands curled over his knees.

"Hello." He gives a dip of his head, smiles. Her shoulders tense and then drop. Her eyes careen around the room, as if she wants the comfort of anyone else. Her doughy cheeks pale.

"Hello," he says again.

A string of a girl sitting near taps her cheek with her index finger. Then she smacks her chin before repeating the pattern. "Della Campbell. She's Della Campbell."

"Yes. Thank you, Agnes." Mayhew bends toward the woman and lifts her chin. "Can you say hello, Della? Are you all right?"

I watch the woman's mouth yaw open and shut. Her needle never stops, in and out it goes, piercing and repiercing a square of red cloth. There is no thread. Just the needle and the pricks of blood where the thread should be.

"She's quite well, thank you so much," Agnes says.

He lays his hand to the crown of Della's head, as gentle as one would touch a child, then straightens and walks on. "She would benefit from the ice, Mrs. Brighton."

"Yes, Dr. Mayhew."

The needles whisper their journeys through squares of fabric. There a calico. There a plaid in green and blue. There a piece of black serge. Not one with thread, not one with a useful item to hold at the end of the day and admire.

Cathy's fingers are like iron around my elbow, and my lower arm tingles with the threat of numbness.

"Can you let go?" I ask.

"Oh." She stares at her hand clutched tight, then drops her grip.

Mrs. Brighton and Mayhew turn to another door. Another room.

It is a dormitory of beds. Twelve beds. At least here there is light, though it is flat white from the paint on the glass. On each bed, a plain wool blanket. To the side, a nightdress hung on a single knob. A writing desk next to each. On one, a brush. Another, a book with a torn spine. Three beds down, a tin cup with a sprig of white flowers.

"Why is there no thread?"

"It's a therapeutic tool, Mrs. Abbott." Mayhew pinches the lip of a tin cup on one of the bedside tables and slides it from the left side to the right. "A meditation, if you will. A way to strengthen the mind."

Mrs. Brighton looks as if she will speak, then clamps her mouth.

"Not even thread."

"Scissors come as a privilege," she says.

My breath stutters in my ribs. I want to turn the beds over, grapple and search the mattresses, the corners of the pillow casings, the folds of linens for all that has been taken away. But I keep my fists closed tight, crushing my purse.

"Where are their trunks?"

"They are stored for safekeeping." The doctor turns in a circle and beams. "We provide all the necessaries."

I press my lips tight and bite down. "Was this her room?"

"One very like it," Dr. Mayhew says.

"But not hers. I asked to see *that* room, Dr. Mayhew. And why she has bruises all over her body. And how she ended up on the roof. That is what I asked."

His hands come up to placate. "Now, Mrs. Abbott . . ."

There's a thrum from the hall, the muffled pound of slippered feet to the boards. Then another.

"This is what happens." Mrs. Brighton makes for the door. "This is what starts. This is why there are visiting hours. Now, I'll be . . ." She leans into the hall. "Eyes to the ground."

Mayhew grips my elbow, pulls me tight to his side, and ushers us out to the hall. The stamps are louder, cacophonous and ringing.

A hand clutches my skirt and pulls at me. Agnes. She pats the top of her head, then points a finger to the ceiling, before poking her finger again to her cheek. "Once up there, you don't come back."

Mrs. Brighton clears her throat—*ahem*—and stares at the woman until she drops back to her seat. Then she turns to speak to me, lips thin, mouth too small. "You've upset my girls," she says and shakes her head.

Dr. Mayhew corrals us to the landing. "Another time, ladies. Another time." And the door clangs shut.

It is not just the women locked behind me that have taken up their voice. Across comes the rumble and pound of the men, caterwauls and drumming.

Cathy bites her bottom lip. She blinks and then stares. Her skin looks made of wax.

I am shaking. I stride back to the closed ward door. "You've answered nothing." I slap my hand to the wood.

On the floor below, Northrup scrambles from his desk to the bottom of the stairs. "You must come down now." His attention turns to someone just to his left. He nods and gestures up the stairs to us.

Mr. Stoakes peers up, out of his coat, his vest loose and collar unbuttoned, as if he's just been interrupted from his noon meal. He takes the stairs, his eyes on mine, and I see the gold flecks amongst the pool of gray and the steadiness one needs to keep a deer from panic.

"It's all right," he murmurs, a soft hand to my elbow and another to Cathy's.

"Don't touch me." Her voice is sharp. She twists away, then grips up her skirts and starts for the stairs. "I want air."

Outside there is sun, bright through the neat rows of trees and dappling the lawn. The pebbled road has been raked neat. Cathy sits with the reins in her lap. The mare shakes her head to drive away the flies.

I turn from the buggy, back to Mr. Stoakes.

"Will you show me?" I ask. "Where she fell."

"Why?" Cathy asks. "Why do you need to see?"

"It's just around the side," Stoakes says.

We walk the edge of the road. I can't look at the building straight on. Instead I watch his boots, square-toed, scuffed, heavy of heel. Not soft soled like the doctor's.

The building casts a sharp, black shadow. We leave the groomed front lawn for bare rock and hard soil. The roses here are untended, the leaves a sallow yellow ruined at the tips by rust and pocks of black. The bushes vine and twist and crawl the wall as if they wish the inhabitants to look down and acknowledge them. But the grated windows are blank, and the rose blooms are drained of color.

"I think she found a way into the attic, then up to the cupola." He steps forward, picking a petal from the rose hedge and rolling it between his fingers. He runs his gaze along the roofline. "We'd find her all sorts of places. She had a knack with locks."

"My brother taught us how to pick them."

He nods and flicks the petal. It sticks to his thumbnail, and he swipes his hand to his vest to unsettle it. "She would have been better not to have learned that."

I return to Cathy, step into the buggy, and fold the step. It is quiet. Just Cathy's breath followed by mine. Just the sharp saw of the cicadas amongst the tree limbs.

Cathy chews her bottom lip. Nods once. "Do you have your answers?"

The buggy jolts forward. "It's not enough."

"Let it be enough." She flicks the leathers. Clenches her jaw and keeps her gaze forward. "Let her rest."

Chapter Nine

"You can't just run off like that." Lionel wipes his napkin to the corners of his mouth, then makes a show of smoothing it back to his lap. "Leaving Saoirse to watch Toby—she's practically dead." He waves his hand and lifts his fork and knife. "What purpose does it serve?" He cuts a thin slice of beef tongue and forks it in his mouth.

"Let's stop." Cathy's plate is full—the tongue is layered with globules of aspic she's scraped from the Brussels sprouts. "Please. It's all over. It's over."

Lionel pushes his glasses up his nose and shakes his head. "I forbid you to go again."

"You can't forbid me," I say.

"I can. I will."

"Lionel." Cathy touches his wrist, but he yanks his hand away.

"If you're in my house—"

"It's my house too," I say.

"No, Marion. It's not."

I drop my dinner fork to the china and push the plate away. My stomach churns and buckles. "He said she killed herself. She'd never do that."

"Keep your voice down." Lionel glances at the ceiling; Toby's room is directly above.

"I know she was ill. God, I know more than anyone. But not that." I take a breath, then another, but my chest tightens. There is the roof and the broken branches and the keen sweet smell of her body that I can't wash from my skin. "I think they're lying. Doesn't that matter to you?"

"Enough." Cathy smacks her hand to the table. Her eyes narrow, and her expression is like ice. "Stop talking about Alice." She stares at her water glass, then grips it and takes a drink. "Stop talking about her. Everything always comes back to Alice. God." She slams the glass and stands, the chair tipping back and smacking the cabinet behind her.

"Cathy." Lionel's voice is low. "Pick up the chair."

"Don't tell me what to do."

"Pick up the chair."

Her hands tremble as she rights it. She sits with a thud, spreads her palms on each side of her plate, stares at the salt box and candles grouped between us.

"There." Lionel leans back and looks at Cathy. There's a wariness to his gaze, as if he expects her to throw the chair across the room and then her wineglass, just for good measure.

She stabs a Brussels sprout and shoves it into her mouth, chews and swallows with a grimace. "I visited Maud Harper yesterday. Of course, she wouldn't come here. No one comes here, and that I will lay directly on Alice. Anyway, that's not here nor there. Her son—you know him, Lionel. Joshua. He was in your class at St. Albans, remember? He has gained a clerkship with Senator Cragin now."

"What's his wife's name again? Maisy, Mary . . ."

"Martha. Martha Quinn."

Lionel snaps his fingers. "That's right."

"They've got luggage and boxes scattered everywhere, and Maud's in a stir as you can well expect . . ."

A shadow flits across the mirror. I turn to the window behind me, certain someone has crossed the yard, but it's only my reflection, shimmery and floating in the whorls and bubbles, that stares back.

"Are you all right?" Cathy asks.

"I thought I saw something. I think there's someone there."

Her napkin snaps and waves as she presses it to her lips. "It's probably Elias. He comes to take Saoirse home."

My heart thumps in my ears. "Yes. That must be it." I settle back to the table. "That's all it is."

Lionel stares at me. I've seen the look before. He's given it to Alice.

Lionel's too tall for my bed, but he stretches out at an angle anyway, his feet hanging over the side. He taps the corners of his square-tipped boots and pummels my pillow before crossing his arms behind his head.

"I'd like to finish brushing my hair," I say. "It's late."

"It's all so neat and tidy in here. Everything in its particular place."

"There's not much to neaten."

"Still. One of your more . . . abiding traits."

His teeth bite down on a cheroot, unlit: one small accommodation since he's taken over the bed and left me to sit at my desk. He wiggles it back and forth before abandoning it to my nightstand. My little brother who's grown tall but not grown up.

"You make it sound like a flaw."

"That would be your lack of humor."

"There's not much to laugh at, is there?"

"Or the way you cut your meat into tiny pieces before you eat."

I run a finger over my brush and pull a long strand from the bristles. "What do you want, Lionel?"

He glances at the closed door. "Close the windows."

"It's too hot."

"Just for a minute."

I reach for the latch. Just past the pond, a glow of light moves through the trees, and then it's gone. The pond and woods are black again.

"Are there squatters," I ask, "in the woods?"

"Did you see something?" His eyes slide to the window, then back to me. "I wouldn't worry. It's just a few of them. They've got a camp up Barrow Rock."

"How many?"

"I don't know. A few. They're back from the war, I think. Just not ready for home."

"You need to shift them off."

"They'll move on when they move on."

"They shouldn't be there."

"They aren't doing any harm. Leave it alone, Marion." He juts his lower jaw and grinds his teeth. "You never leave things alone."

"Is this about Alice?"

"It's about Cathy."

"Of course it is."

"Don't start." The bed squeaks as he swings his legs off and paces to the door and back. "You always . . . I don't want Cathy upset, that's all. This is her house now."

"As evidenced by the wallpaper."

He stops midway across the room and stares at the paper with a frown. "You can change yours if you want."

I tip my head. "I don't want to upset her."

He pushes his fingers into his hair, then rubs it into a muss. "You can't change it, actually."

"Oh?"

"I can't afford it. Not right now."

"But all those contracts."

"For bullet casings. And belt buckles. Do you have any idea the stockpile I have of US Army buckles? Half the contracts haven't been paid. I doubt they will be. And Alice—the cost of her care at that place—and the floors and bonnets and . . . and wallpaper." He sinks to the bed. "I've no work for the men. There's too many of them home, and I've got nothing for them. We're living on credit. Just for now, until I can retool the machinery and . . . I have a few ideas in the fire. It's nothing to worry about."

"Then I won't."

"Today upset Cathy. I need you to not upset her." He sits upright and rubs his thighs. "You can do that, can't you?"

"I want to lodge a complaint. Against Brawders House."

"Why? Why would you do that?"

"Because it's right."

"What's right is to say Alice had a short illness and died. That's what's right. That's what's kindest, isn't it? To her? To the family? You know that's what's right."

I keep my eyes on the brush. "Where did you tell people she was?"

"A sanatorium, for consumption. Cathy thought that best."

"But it's not her place."

"Yes, Marion. It is."

"Can I ask you something?" I hesitate; I want to ask about Toby. If he's seen his son as I have, silent chatter to no one, hearing nothing in return.

His sigh is long. He removes his spectacles, rubs a knuckle to his eyes. His lids are red rimmed and shadowed. I think he knows what I won't ask. What we've both had bite at our own heels—that we, too, are like her. But he doesn't need another hole in the boat right now.

"Never mind."

"And Cathy?"

"I'll try not to upset her. She's been nothing but good to you."

"And the money? You won't tell her about that?"

"It is temporary, isn't it? Because I don't think she'd like something more permanent."

There's a rap on the door. The knob turns. Cathy's in her nightdress and shawl, her hair braided to her scalp. "Don't you hear it?"

Lionel shakes his head and puts on his glasses.

"There's someone at the door."

"Now?"

"You'll need to answer, Lionel."

He crosses to her, then slips past, down the hall.

Cathy steps into the room, her back to the wall and shoulder pressed to the wardrobe. She looks at me. "Are you all right? From today, I mean."

"Are you?"

"I don't know."

Two voices in the vestibule. Too low to make out what is said, but it's short. When Lionel returns, his eyes flick to Cathy, then to me. "They've brought her trunk."

I swallow, but it is like sand.

He slits open a thin envelope with his thumbnail, removing both the letter and the key to the trunk. He chews at his bottom lip as he scans the paper.

"Read it out loud, Lionel." Cathy moves to me, her hand to my shoulder, as if she is guarding me from some horrible news.

"Dear Mr. Snow."

Lionel scans the page, then continues.

"Please again accept my deepest condolences for the passing of your sister. Our investigation has found all procedures were followed by ward attendants. We believe Alice Snow was—as she had proven in past situations— unnaturally adept at easing and opening locks, and was indeed successful that evening in her unfortunate goal. Thus, the inquiry is satisfactorily concluded.

"We will, in condolence, waive the last three months balance from your account, and I personally would like

*to contribute to the headstone. Pls send said bill directly
to me.*

"*I do hope you will think of your sister's time here
and know she was well looked after and is missed by the
attendants and staff.*

"*Respectfully yours—*

"*Lemuel Mayhew.*"

He looks to me, eyes bruised with remorse. "I taught her how to do it. I didn't . . ." He stares down at the key in his hand, then tosses it to the bed, as if it will singe his skin.

"Well, there is our answer," Cathy says. "It's a generous offering."

"An apology would have helped more. All I wanted was for him to tell the truth. That they made a mistake. I wanted him to say, '*Someone didn't do their job, Mrs. Abbott, and I am sorry.*' That is worth something. I just want him to say he's sorry."

Dr. Lemuel Mayhew wants rid of me: he thinks the bribes for silence and the trunk's return will be enough. It sits now at an angle to my wardrobe. The key with its four-clover bow and braid of lavender ribbon rests in my palm. I squeeze until I feel the edges bite my skin.

The candlelight skates and tumbles across the leather straps and brads, falls into the scrapes and tears. Toby's snuck down from his room and now kneels in front of the case, drumming his fingers on his knees and pulling the hem of his knit drawers. Then he scratches under the collar of his undershirt. "Is it really hers?"

He stands, runs his hands over the buckles. Bends down to investigate the rivets and pokes his finger in the lock. He steps away, crossing his hand behind his back, splaying his feet in a wide stance, cocking his head just like Lionel. He closes one eye to peer up at me, just like Lydia did when she wasn't certain of something—an algebra equation, a hat, if Lionel meant it when he asked her to wed or if it was a horrible joke.

I reach for him, a quick caress of his neck, then brush my knuckles to his shoulder. I bite my lip and stop myself from saying, "You look so much like her." Because Cathy is right. She's the only mother he's known. And that is enough now. No need to muddle that up with his loss of Alice, who loved him as fierce as he loved her.

"Do you know Alice wrote me of you?" I give a quick nod. "She said you were very, very clever."

His face flushes, and his mouth opens in a small, pink *O*, for this pleases him.

"What else?" he asks.

"Hm. You are good at your times tables." I cross my hands and roll the key between my fingers.

"They're easy."

"Or you're smart."

"You were repairing the soldiers," he says. "Alice said you used a lot of green string and sugar glue."

My eyes prick. I can see her bent to a notebook, one she carried everywhere, making a quick sketch to give to the little boy, and her fingers trailing the arrows and figures and explanations. Where are all those notebooks she so assiduously wrote in? Her only method to tell us what she wanted, save the grimaces and stomps of her foot, and the way her eyes would narrow and go sly when she teased. Broad gestures that embarrassed Father, that confounded Lionel, that Benjamin ignored.

"We would have been happy for that string and glue," I say. "Did she give you it? The picture?"

Toby frowns and shakes his head. "She liked to draw." He curls his fingers over my fist, prying at the skin in search of the key.

I pull my hand away. Tighten my grip. My stomach sours. I don't know why. It's only clothing in the trunk, perhaps a bauble or two; what did she really own? Maybe all the notebooks are stacked within.

Maybe her child's primers. Or the astronomy book she used to confirm her plottings of the sky.

"I don't think I can open it yet."

Toby's jaw sags in disappointment as if I've kept a present from him. After all, isn't that what this is to him? Just a bigger version of the toy box in his room. It contains treasures. It contains everything I have left of Alice, and I am not ready to go through it and give value to the treasures and the trash.

"Go back to bed."

Turee
Doctor Lemuel Mayhew
Brawders House

Dr. Mayhew—
So Alice is worth three months of fees and a granite stone. And we are meant to be grateful. Am I to assume her bruises were of her own device and phantom sewing needles magically available for her lock picking use? I demand to see the investigative report and have a reckoning from you as to every action taken that evening by your staff and where it all failed. My sister should be alive and instead of writing this letter, I should be writing one asking for her release to my care.

Respond directly with a time and place to meet.
Marion Abbott

Chapter Ten

All night the sky rumbles its grievances. The air is sharp, electric, restless. As is the household. I pace the parlor, watch the brackish green sky and the whip of the hedge when the wind gusts. The windows cackle and rattle. I check the latches. Make certain they're held tight.

Upstairs, Cathy and Lionel fight. I catch the rat-a-tat of her words and the pummel of his. They stop and start, and as the words gain momentum so does the train Toby rolls around its track. Metal wheels on metal axles that need oil. Round and round it goes.

A glass snaps and clatters in the dining room. As I cross the hall, a shimmer of oil light coats the stairs. Lionel stands on the landing, knobby kneed below the hem of his nightshirt. "What was that?"

"Just a vase, I think. Go back to bed."

He blinks, runs his hand through his hair. "You're up late."

"It's hard to sleep with all the noise."

"You know where the whiskey is. If you need it."

The curtains along the dining room window lift and flutter, then are pulled out to the yard, as if the wind has taken hold of them like a thief.

"I'll close the window. Go back to your . . . conversation."

It was a crystal vase, the shards scattered across the floor and table. I jostle the window, but it won't shut all the way. It's stuck, leaving a gap along the sill. Any candle I light to avoid the splinters will snuff with the wind, and my bare feet won't do in the dark. I turn to my room. The air whisks under my nightdress, is hot breath on the nape of my neck. Another whirl comes cool and damp—the rain is coming.

A spike of light illuminates the patterned hallway wallpaper: the mourning doves stretch their wings, and the irises below bend and ripple. Then it all consolidates again to its frozen horrible design.

I pull my boots from the wardrobe and move to the desk chair to button them. The chair has been pushed away from the desk. It faces the end of Alice's trunk as if it awaits someone's vigil. I turn it around, button the shoes, and don't look back at the trunk.

Saoirse keeps a small broom and dustpan in the closet under the stairs. I push the door so it springs open, grab them up, and nearly collide with Toby. He stares up at me. A yellow toy train car dangles from his hand. His pajamas cling to his frame, the static in the air puckering the cotton against his ribs and down his legs.

"A vase broke. I have to clean up the glass," I say.

He runs the back of his free hand under his nose and nods.

"Are you afraid of the storm?"

"No." He sniffs and rubs his nose again.

"Go get your shoes, then, and you can help me. You can point out any pieces I've missed." I watch his eyes waver between his bedroom upstairs and me. "I'll come with you."

The train has derailed; the cars are strewn across the floor. I find Toby's bedsheets tossed and tangled in the wardrobe, his pillow pushed to the far corner.

"That's where I slept sometimes, too."

"You did?"

"When there was thunder." I pick up the train cars and set each on the round rail. "Get your shoes."

"I'm not afraid of it."

"As you say." The train set's dining car is red. Cast-iron figures with rough-shaped features sit at tables: men in tall hats and women in bonnets. The tables are scored with round plates, and there's a little dog in the aisle.

Toby sits splay legged on the floor and struggles with his boots. Behind him, the wardrobe door hangs open. His suits and breeches are lined on hooks. His shoes and boots sit in a neat row, toes facing out.

I set the dining car on the toy shelf, next to the old magic lantern Lionel and I used when we were young. I move to help him with his laces, but he jerks up. Grabs the wardrobe door and swings it closed. "I know how to do my laces," he says, and takes my hand. "We have to clean up the glass so she doesn't cut herself."

I sigh, because it would be something Saoirse wouldn't pay attention to. Just hobble into the room to wipe down the table for breakfast and slice her hand right open. "Yes. You're right."

Toby's mouth pulls into a wide smile. "Yes, that's right."

I follow him to the landing. There is no light from under Lionel and Cathy's door. Only the repeated squeak of the bed coils and sweeter words from Cathy. I put my hand to the boy's shoulder and guide us down the stairs. "Come on. It's soon to rain."

At the bottom, he grabs a bucket from the small closet. Holds it with both hands. He looks at me again, his eyes glassy bright. I know it's from the strange light coming through the windows. But I can't stop the shiver that skids down my spine.

Toby's cut his thumb. I've set him in the chair in my room, lit the lamp, and pulled my leather aid kit from the top shelf of the wardrobe.

"I didn't mean it," he says.

"I told you not to pick anything up."

"I'm sorry."

"It's not deep." I dip a handkerchief to my water glass and dab the beads of blood. "Just a scratch."

He squirms in the chair as I press the wound edges together and tie a strip of cotton around it.

"Is it terrible?" he asks.

"We won't need to amputate. It will sting for a bit, though."

His eyelashes are starred with tears, but he screws up his mouth and gives a quick shake of his head. "I don't feel it."

"You're very brave." I pat the inside of the forearm, then rest his hand to his lap.

"Did you cut many thumbs off? In the war?"

I move from my kneeling position, rest back against the desk, and cup my chin in my hand. "Not a one."

There's a burst of white light, followed by a clap of thunder that shakes the house. Toby claws the edge of his chair, then jerks his sore thumb away.

The rain comes in on the wind gusts, first like fingers tapping the glass, then in sheets that rattle and hiss. The window latches shiver but hold, keeping the rain out. But the closed-in air steams with the damp of it, as if the water has found all the little crevices and boiled inside the walls.

The lightning comes in pieces. Out the window, the pond is a sulfurous yellow, like smoke. In the next flash, the vapor clears; the rain plonks and pulls at the skin of the water.

Another clap. Closer. Enough that Benjamin's portrait shimmies and tips. I jump up, grab at it before it falls off the mantel.

We sit together, Toby's fingers curled into my palm. A roll of thunder sounds somewhere past the hill, over Barrow Rock. A blue-white light slices along the treetops.

"We needed this rain," I say.

"But not thunder."

"No, not thunder."

Toby hums a tune, and I tap our hands to my knee and sing.

I'll be in Scotland afore ye,
But me and my true love will never meet again,
On the bonnie, bonnie banks o' Loch Lomond.

We listen to the thunder grow fainter, the lightning shimmer far off. Sing "Oh! Susanna" and "Froggie Went A-Courtin'."

The rain stops abrupt as it came. The sky clears, and the moon glows behind a long wisp of cloud.

"Look." Toby points past the main pond to where the shore pinches and turns out of sight.

"There's nothing there."

"It's a Bad One. It's come from the Narrows." Toby's got his hands pressed to the glass. He dips his head to peer around the rainwater.

"Bad Ones don't exist. I told you that. It's make-believe. It's . . ." I let out a breath and take his elbow. His body is rigid, on alert. "Alice made it all up."

But it's Alice's arm I hold, and Alice's eyes round with terror that look at me.

"Nothing will happen, Alice," I murmur. "Nothing is there."

Her mouth moves without a sound. She pokes her finger against my breastbone.

No—it's not her—it's Toby, twisting and pulling his arm free, his elbow sharp to my chest. "Look. Just like Alice said."

There in the water, a dark shape slips the surface. I rasp a breath and lean forward to the glass. It's blurred now, human shaped, then not. I can't tell if it twists and rolls or it's the trick of the waterlogged moonlight. I fight with the window latch, my fingers clumsy and numb, then throw the window open. I grip my fingers to the sill, hard enough that the paint chips under my nails. Toby presses his shoulder to my arm as we lean out to look.

"It's a Bad One. It's come to cut my tongue. Alice said it'd come." His voice lifts into a shriek.

"It's a log, Toby. Just a log." I grab Toby's arm and shake. "Alice told you stupid lies."

We stare at each other, both our breaths shallow.

"There's nothing there."

"She doesn't lie." He whimpers and slips away from me, darting out the door before I can pull him tight.

The morning comes, the sky a faded lavender, the warming earth loamy and rotten. The log has beached in the shallows. I have not moved from the chair. My back and legs are stiff and sore. I leave the window open. The pond laps the shore, the tail of the storm still stirring the water, still slipping through the trees, liquid and smooth.

Behind me, Alice's trunk lies open. I hold her inventory list, written in precise cursive with a diagram drawn below of the contents' placement. All the items are still intact; I can't bear to touch it.

Cathy rakes loose branches and leaves from the garden beds, flicking them to a pile. Toby crouches, intent on an insect or worm that's crawling amongst the detritus. When he's lost track, he scoops a mound into a pan and dumps it into the wheelbarrow. Saoirse stalks the vegetable rows, hands on hips, shaking her head. The tomato plants are beaten and sodden. She shifts the leaves with her foot, then twists off the fruit that's still good. The bean posts tilt and twist into the garlic. The peppers litter the soil like Christmas bulbs flung from a box.

"Would you look at this?" she says. "All a-ruin."

A saw bites into wood; the sound zigs through the trees. Elias must be in the front, and a part of the hedge must be down.

The cicadas are quiet. A bird warbles and is answered by another.

Alice's clothes are folded neat and tidy.

Two dresses, one striped, one plaid. Three petticoats. Three bloomers. A pair of black garters. Two corsets. Her plum bonnet and her peach.

Tomorrow I will go to town and order two headstones from Darius Meek and he will tell me there will be a delay. Too many stones to carve of late, the bodies of townsmen home like clockwork, and the church bells worn down in grief. I will ask for a flat rectangle granite for Benjamin; his name on the left and the right half blank, awaiting mine.

One silver-plated brush of boar bristles to take the tangles out. A wide-toothed bone comb. The hat pin I gave her on her sixteenth birthday—a songbird of green glass and pearl perched on its end.

I will ask Darius for a quartz marker, so it catches the sun and scatters the moonlight: *Alice Snow, beloved sister.*

Three books, wrapped and knotted in twine. *A Treatise on Astronomy. Uncle Tom's Cabin. The Last of the Mohicans.*

The wheelbarrow squeals as Cathy lifts it, pushes it past the shreds of iris leaves and down to the bare roses. She drops the handles and gestures for Toby.

Two pairs of boots: ivory white with black buttons and summer soles. Her scuffed, flat-heeled lace-ups. Five rolled stockings. Two black, two blue, one gray wool with a mend to the toe.

I rest my hand to the paper, spread my fingers over the black ink, then pick at the corner with my thumb.

Alice had been so desperate to go with me, those years ago.

"I have been accepted, Alice. As a nurse. You will return to Turee, just until Christmas. The war can't go on much longer, can it? And think, you can help Lydia with little Toby, and I will retrieve you by Christmas, and Benjamin will be back and . . ." But she'd stomped the stairs to her little room and left me alone in the cottage hall. She would not have it. Note after note written and pushed to my fisted hands, under the bedroom door, taken to the post so I would find it with the mail. *How can you leave me? How can you forsake me?* A postcard with peonies: *Selfish.* Salt put in my tea. Letters from Benjamin, speckled with mud from Fort Magruder, Spotsylvania, Poplar Hill all torn to bits and offered as a puzzle to fill my time.

"I will not have our Union fail," I said. "If I can do one thing—the army needs nurses."

Her pencil ripped into her notebook. She tore the page out. *Not a nurse.*

"I will learn. I took care of Mother."

Take me with you.

"No."

Alice flailed her hands, and her voice came out then in a ragged grunt. She knocked over a porcelain angel that cracked but did not shatter. She kicked it across the front room. It spun and skidded under a bookcase heavy with Benjamin's textbooks and atlases.

Her next note was ripped into the paper and shoved at my chest. *You didn't take care of Mother.*

"Go pack your trunk."

This same trunk. I said it was all agreed: she would live with Lionel and Lydia and help with the child. Lionel came for the night and drove her away in the morning. I did not watch them leave. I had my own valise to pack and my own stage to catch.

So full I was of righteousness. So tired I was of her.

I look back to the yard. Toby's wandered away to the boathouse. He grabs the metal lock and drops it so it thuds against the wood. The door quivers. He does it again but grows bored, and Cathy calls him back.

The locket isn't listed in her inventory, not drawn in the diagram, wasn't on her body when I cleaned her. The locket I see in my sleep. The one she never removed. Mother's once. Alice had purloined it. Snatched it from Mother's jewelry drawer and refused to give it up. And why should she? It was the last she had of her.

Five cloth notebooks, blank. Seven pencils tied with string.

Lionel's gone down now to Cathy, wipes the dirt from her cheek and kisses her. He swings his hat and Toby grasps for it, catching the brim.

I turn the paper over: *This is the property of Alice Louise Snow. June 1864. If found, please return to Marion Abbott specifically. Turee, NH. Otherwise destroy.*

My ears fill and roar. I crumple the words in my fist. But the words slip through the paper and between the list of corsets and boar's-bristle brushes. Each letter chained to the other and wrapping up my wrist and elbow. I lurch from the chair, throw the note on top of the clothing she never needed.

Today is Thursday. Cathy takes callers in the afternoon; she'll sit in the parlor, perched on the edge of the settee and wait and hope this week someone will come. No one has in the weeks I've been here. Lionel will ride into town this morning, sit at his broad owner's desk, and mull what the hell to do now there isn't a war and the orders for bullets have dwindled away.

Cathy rests her hand on the rake handle and looks up. "I could do with help."

I grab up my straw bonnet and wave it out the open window. "Coming." My voice rasps rough and odd. I turn away, tie the knot of the hat tight to my throat. I close the trunk lid and click the lock. "Coming."

Chapter Eleven

Turee Jun 6. 64

Marion—
I have chosen Brawders House for Alice. It is close enough
we can visit on occasion and is assuredly more congenial
than the public asylum in Concord. The doctors are con-
fident the environment and facilities will improve her
mental unease.
    We all want the best—
    Lionel

Near Petersburg, VA Aug 20, 1864

Brother,
We have been hard maneuvered by the secesh, and rein-
forcements have come too late. All soldiers exhausted and
myself bone weary though brightened by the sewing tack
and two aprons mailed August 1. Cathy is kind to think
upon me and you, too, for the box of cheroots to pass to
the men. They send a large huzzah.

I have received no letter or word from Alice, though I have written some twenty letters. Out of guilt or kindness I cannot say but certainly out of worry. She is not so able to incorporate such change.

My dreams are troubled often by her crying. Even in the midst of all this chaos, I cannot elude the tears.

Have you visited? Can you send her word I love her? Can you ask if she has received my letters? I sent in July 1 dollar and a small porcelain of a dog that looked much like Old Harold. Can you find out if they have been received?

I am at empty pockets here. Could you send 4 or 5 dollars—I will return when my pay is received.

Marion

Turee Aug 28. 64

Sister—
Enclosed find 5 dollars. It's a gift not a loan.

Toby is into everything, a curious boy and running Cathy ragged. Sometimes he looks too much like Lydia— it is like a fist in the chest. I can't tell C—of course. She's been a blessing, really, keeping all spirits afloat. I cannot be anything except in her debt.

Alice refuses our visits. Perhaps later, Dr. Mayhew says. Letters are held in trust until she is further well. I have much confidence in her treatment.

Kylie Humphrey is missing. Bill Hardis got shot in Richmond and is now home to rest. Did you tend him?

Let this war soon be over.
L—

Dry rivulets snake the surface of Alice's grave, smooth and glittery with crushed mica, the leaves and twigs brushed to a pile at my feet. I have ordered the stone and the one for Benjamin, though he rests under oak and moss somewhere in the South. I sent the good doctor the receipt for both. Lydia's tombstone is simple gray granite, an arched top with chiseled peonies to each corner. *Wife & Mother*. Father's and Mother's tucked into the stand of woods, shadows dappling the rectangle fence surrounding them. Farther still, under the brambles and ferns, other relatives lie with stones laid flat to the ground, words sanded by frost and the passing of time.

I lay a fistful of black-eyed Susans against Lydia's stone. Another bunch atop Benjamin's. The rest for Alice, placed above her heart. Her favorite flower, both plain and showy. We planted the front yard of the cottage full with them, so they waved in the sun, and everything glowed a gold yellow. The bees moved from flower to flower, at first one or two, then too many to navigate the walkway without fear of a sting. Maybe it was her way of guarding the house from whatever scared her. I didn't ask. They were pretty, and it was amusing watching the schoolboys hop and shriek their way past them.

Dr. Mayhew responded to my letter; I pull it from my skirt pocket to read again, as if the words will change. As if his words will be less unctuous, the meaning less dismissive.

Brawders House, August 10, 1865

Dear Mrs. Abbott,
Your grief over your sister's passing is deeply respected. It is always a shock when a family member succumbs to their own demons. The confusion of emotions and thoughts are chaotic at best, and thus I can only tell you that they will lessen, though not fully dissolve, with time. It is, truly, the finest medicine.

Our reports, though you may wish them of a different
nature, stand as is.
    Respectfully Yours,
    L. Mayhew

I cannot accept his answer.

"What happened to you, Alice?" I kneel, press my ear to the soil, close my eyes, and pray for a susurration of words. Speak to me in death, since you would not in life.

A snap of a branch. I sit up, brushing dirt from my ear. I squint at the figure standing behind me. The sun glimmers bright around the boy, outlining him as if he were cut from paper to be framed in the hall. He holds a bow in his fist, the tip dragging by his feet.

"Will you teach me to shoot?" He thumbs the strap of the quiver, shrugging it up his shoulder and then gripping it so it won't slide off. He strides around so I see him properly. His lips are rosy and pursed, his cheeks swathed in freckles. He tips his head and waits for me to answer.

"You should ask your father. Or Cathy."

"No, just you."

The quiver knocks the ground as he drops to his haunches. He reaches out, touching his fingers to my cheek.

Then he stands and walks across the graves, over the mounds and into the furrows. He stops at the edge of the woods. "Come on."

"I don't have a bow and arrow."

"Doesn't matter."

"These are the Sentinels." Toby sets his bow to a fallen log, pulls the quiver strap over his head, and clambers over, his heel catching and stripping bark. He runs into a small clearing bordered by red maples and dark pines. "Come on."

I lift my skirts, follow him to the clutch of trees, and stop at the view beyond. We are on a steep bank of smooth rock, and below slips the black water of the Narrows. I take a step closer, but Toby grabs my skirts and pulls back.

"You can't ever go past the Sentinels."

I stare at him, not knowing what he means. But then he points to the tree by my right. It is just a tree. He points at the next one, then the next—five in all—and says, "You don't see."

"What am I supposed to—"

"Here." He touches a dark line a few feet from the base, a gnarled scar. "And there." The next tree, and then the next. There's a glint of color in the knot closest to me. A bit of pearl lodged in the wood. A round red bead. The teeth of a key. I move from tree to tree. Buttons and hairpins. Jewelry clasps and cufflinks. The green glass wing of a dragonfly.

"I thought I'd lost that," I say.

"We were doing a new tree," Toby says and leads me to a sapling. "Mama gave me a penny for candy, but I put it here." The gash is recent, not seeping, the curve of the coin just peeking out. "You need to put something here."

I take a breath. This is Alice as she really was. Teaching a boy magic and how to keep safe.

"Do you have something?" he asks. "It's very important to give something to the tree."

"Yes. Yes." I grab at the buttons on my shirt, twisting one on the cuff until the thread snaps.

Toby pulls a pocketknife from his vest pocket and clicks it open. He stabs the tip to the tree trunk and digs out a hole. "Alice promised we'd do those four trees too. And the one in front of the house, but Mama had it cut down because it was rotten, so we didn't." He smoothed the edge of the hole, closed the knife, and pocketed it. Then he set his hands on his hips and looked up at me. "You'll need to put it in yourself. That's very important too."

My hand shakes. I close my fist tight, the button warming in my palm. Then I push it to the wood. My thumb is sticky with sap. I rub it along the bark. I want to ask him when Alice changed, when she began to frighten him. Why she held him out the window and did she threaten to let go. Why she took a torch to the glass house. Why she stopped making rings of protection, as she did so long ago for me and so recently for him.

I want to grab him by the shoulders and ask him if he remembers his mother, if there is some amorphous image of Lydia sitting on the edge of his bed at night and kissing his forehead. Someone he called Mother. I want to tell him I know what it was like to be motherless, to watch your mother struggle for air, mouth twisted in desperate agony and a look not of fear of imminent death, but fear of her life hanging on. I want to tell him I could not save her. That I failed Alice, and that I owe her a voice.

I want to say:

My sister didn't kill herself. She loved bees and black-eyed Susans and little boys and china teacups with painted landscapes and shoe buttons and whippoorwills, and when she laughed it sounded like bells.

I want to say:

I am rudderless.

"You have sap on your chin," I say instead.

And he keeps his hands to his hips and nods. "There might be a treasure in Alice's trunk. For the tree. We'll look together. We'll bring it here."

He pats the tree and then my arm, and we walk through the clearing again. He scales the log and helps me over, then hands me the bow. "Do you know how to shoot?"

"Yes."

"Is Mama a better shot?"

"Cathy?"

He shifts his jaw. "Yes. Her."

"I don't know. Probably."

"Will you teach me?"

"If you wish."

With a shift of weight, he's got the quiver strapped across his chest, the feathers on the arrows peeking out from behind his shoulder. He steps through a tangle of browning vines that snap and break as he kicks and twists his boots. "We'll need more Sentinels. They stand guard. So no one gets taken." A finger cocked to the sky. "Come on."

The bow grip is smooth leather. I hold it tight to my thigh and follow Toby under the canopy of trees and through a mire of rocks and roots before we reach the flat stones and sleeping dead again. The flowers have wilted in the heat, the leaves a dull green, petals faded yellow, the center florets purple-black and bulging.

Toby reaches for an arrow, fingering the feathers on each. He chooses an arrow with turkey feathers, pulls it free, and sets it amidst the flower stems on Alice's grave. "She might need that."

A blue jay toes along a maple branch, cocks its head to look down. Its eye is beaded glass, curious and then not. It lifts away with a heavy push to the limb, makes the sky with a flap of wings, and settles on the top of another tree.

There's a brush of movement on the periphery of the gravesite, a darker brown than the bark and the brush. Not the delicate snap of twigs from a deer. Heavy steps that slow and stop. A man holding a rifle, barrel hung to the ground. I grab for Toby's shoulder to hold him still. "Who's there?"

But the man remains still. His straw hat is stained dark at the rim, his hair worn long, tucked behind his ears and touching his shoulders. He peers out at us, his eyes a flat, muddy brown. His boiled-wool vest is shiny along his chest; his canvas trousers bag and pool at his boots. He shifts the rifle.

"Who are you?"

He lifts a hand as if to greet us, then drops his arm. "Just looking for work."

"There's none here. You might try Widow Humphrey, up the road."

"I might," he says. But he doesn't move.

"Come on." This time, Toby doesn't lead. He wiggles his hand into mine, his thumb as tacky with sap as mine, and we take the path side by side back to the house.

"Was that a bad man?" he asks.

"No," I say and waggle his hand in mine. "Just a lost one."

"I can show him all the paths."

"I'm sure you can." I glance back; the man has moved on. "Will you help me with Alice's trunk?"

Toby pushes out his chest and takes a bigger stride. His lips slide into a smile, as if he knew all along I would ask him to help. "No time like now."

"Yes. No time like now."

Chapter Twelve

Cathy lifts Alice's plaid skirt from a peg in the wardrobe and runs her thumb over the embroidered niceties along the cuffs and shoulders. There's an ornate design of wildflowers along the hem. "Lydia's work. I remember when she did that, I do. For Alice's birthday. The first year you were away at the war. Alice gave her a watercolor of what she wanted."

She hooks her finger under one of the wide ribbons that run from the hem and up the skirt, stopping to pull a cord that peeks from the waist. The fabric accordions, just enough to lift the skirts a few inches from the floor. The better for Alice to run in the woods.

"Clever."

She sits on the bed, smoothing the silk of a corset I've removed from the trunk. "This stitchwork. It's close to art. Look."

The thread is nearly invisible, as if the stays are weaved into the fabric. The ribbon lace shimmers a pale pink in this corset, a brilliant yellow in the next. "We can rework it for you."

I turn from the trunk to reach for the corset. The fabric warms under my palm, through to the spring of the metal stays, as if she might inhabit the clothing. I don't want to wear it. It was Alice's; it holds the shape of her.

Cathy takes it from me, rolling it to the side so it sits snug with the other. "What's next on the inventory list?"

Toby holds the hat pin to the light and touches the tip of the song-bird's wing. "Can I have it?"

"What do you need a hat pin for?" She lifts a chemise. There's a tear under the arm. "To the mending basket, then." She tosses it to the basket by the rocker.

I hold out my palm to Toby for the pin. Give him a small nod it will be safe.

Cathy tips her head. "We should also rework the skirts." Her gaze runs down my own dress. "You're not so far off in size. Take a bit in from here. Dye it black, though I think you could get away with violet soon. And the lace collars, you should keep those. She did have a talent for that."

Toby scratches the edge of the trunk's open case, his nail curling the leather strap, then squats down and peers inside. "Can I have the lantern slides?"

"What slides?" I ask.

He holds a box high over his head, and I take it from him. A square box. Ludlow & Pine's *The 7 Wonders of the World* etched around the statue of the Rhodes Colossus. I open the top. Seven glass slides sit in velvet, with handwritten cards serving as a cushion between each.

These weren't on the inventory list. I wonder if she added them at the last minute.

"We'll need to have a magic lantern show," Cathy says. "We haven't done that in ages."

"Alice painted over the wild animals. On the Africa set," Toby says. "Except the wildebeest. I did that one."

"She repainted them all. Those, and *Cities of the World*. And *The Presidents*." Cathy tilts her head to read the slide box. "I haven't seen what she's done to these, though."

I close the lid and move it to the desk, then kneel by Toby. He pulls the books out and sets them by his side. He looks again and reaches for the journals.

"No." I grab them and stand.

"Let me see," Cathy says.

But I hold them and riffle the pages with my thumb first. All blank, the paper still stiff and new.

"Can I have the books?" Toby asks.

Cathy blinks, and stares at him as if just remembering he was in the room. "They're not picture books."

"Then this one." He points to the astronomy book. "It's got planets and stars."

She leans over to look at the cover. "Hm. Well, I suppose . . ." As she straightens up, her eyes flick to the trunk. It is empty. "We're done. I'll have Elias clear it away."

This can't be it. There's so little. The skirt and tops. A brush and mirror. A few books. The pin and box of lantern slides. *The 7 Wonders of the World.*

Elias will take it to the barn and stack it with all the other forgotten things. The broken furniture and outgrown toys. Mother's rocker and Father's smoking stand. Lionel and Cathy will breathe a sigh of relief; nothing to remind them of their part in this.

I grab up the inventory sheet. "No, there's still the locket. Where's her locket?"

Toby slams the lid. He bites down on his bottom lip, pearl teeth on skin blossomed red. "Agh," he says. Then lifts the lid and drops it again.

"Toby. That's enough."

He makes a noise. Doesn't move. He stretches his mouth into a grimace then clamps his teeth. Clack they go. "Where's her locket where's her locket? In the ground with the worms and bones."

Cathy claps her hands in front of his face, startling him to silence.

She grabs his hand and yanks him to the door. "That's it. Go to your room."

He holds on to the knob and plants a foot to the frame. His whisper is like a whistle of air. "The Bad Ones took it."

She pries his fingers and marches him down the hall.

"Mama's in a snit."

"Mama is not in a snit."

Clomps up the stairs. Thuds across his room.

Where is the locket? I want her locket, with the intricate pen-and-inks: Alice on the left, me on the right. I am already losing her image, the vital ebb and flow of her smiles and pouts. How she shook her hand at me for attention and stamped a foot if I didn't give it. I want to touch the warmth of her skin, which was rough on the back of her hands from the sun and soft as a whisper at the nape of her neck. I want to brush her hair, then plait it and pin it with wildflowers. I want to snap at her for not helping in the house and then make Indian pudding to soothe her hurt.

But it's her still, dead body I see.

I glance to the trunk and the lining of sea-blue silk patterned with carriages and tall ships. It sags in the middle of the lid and is loose along the bottom. Where's the locket? Maybe. Just maybe. The lining tears easily. I tug it from the glue and rip along the stitches. Run my palm over the rough wood, then pick at the corners of puckered fabric and the brads that won't give.

I turn to the mending basket by the mantel. Dig out my etui. I grab for the scissors, shaking them from their case, and slice through the silk—for the locket could have fallen in a seam, couldn't it? Wedged itself in a corner or under the bottom casing?

There's nothing but lint and a split wood button. I sit back. Stare at the fabric strips and the yaw of the trunk. I hurl the scissors; they smack against the bed stand and slide to the floor.

"What's all this?" Cathy stands in the doorway. I didn't hear her descend. She closes the door. Snick. Soft and calm. Crosses her hands at her waist and settles her shoulders. Her eyes stop on the trunk, on me, on the window glass and the swing of the willow branches outside. She kneels, taking my hand. Doesn't look at me, just caresses the top of my hand with her thumb. Her fingers are dimpled and soft. She swallows, squeezing my hand too tight before returning to the caress. "It's all put to rest now," she says. "Haven't we put this to rest?"

"I can't." My words strangle then, and I can't stop shaking. I press my palms to my face. I won't cry. It does nothing.

She hooks my hand, takes it up again in hers, then pulls me to her and rubs soft circles on the back of my neck. "It's only us now. We are a small family; we must look out for each other."

She is alone, Lydia wrote, *and does not wish to join her family in Ohio. This wretched war! It marks us all. She weeps and sits often with us, and we feel Paul close at hand when we gather thus.*

"I know what it's like to lose people." With a raise of her eyebrow, she smiles and stands, smoothing down her skirt and picking lint from the folds. "Let us be like real sisters."

But then she seems to realize she's been too forward. She steps back and bites the inside of her cheek before rummaging in the skirt pocket to pull out an envelope.

"You have a letter. It came earlier, but you and Toby were so adamant about the trunk . . ."

Mrs. Abbott is written in neat letters, overthought like a schoolchild, with a dollop of ink wiped from the final *T*.

I unseal the flap and remove a note written on rough paper.

> *Mrs. Abbott,*
> *If you could met at the Trademan's Inn, on 3rd St, H'boro*
> *Monday 730am—I would be most aprecitive.*
> > *Respectfull, Kitty Swain*
> > *—Pls respnd 5 Fayette if you can't. I am a friend.*

I push my fingers to my breastbone, blow out a thin breath, fold the note back to the envelope and into the pocket of my skirt.

"What is it?" Cathy asks.

"Nothing. Just a note from an old acquaintance. A nurse I knew in Baltimore. She's in Harrowboro." I swallow, then continue to lie. "She's asked me to visit."

"Oh. Well. A friend."

"Yes. Could I take the buggy? Next Monday?"

Cathy picks the scissors up and sets them to a pillow. "It's my calling day."

"No, it's all right. I'll take the coach."

She nods and taps her fingers to her thigh. "Where do you know her from?"

"Baltimore." But I am afraid I've stumbled on the word. "Her name is Maddie Leavitt."

"Well." Cathy steps close and runs her hands down my arms. "There you are. You must see your Maddie Leavitt, then."

Chapter Thirteen

There's a rumble of men's voices in the back garden, a cough, the acrid curl of pipe smoke. I shift the curtain. Elias's pointing at the mounds and ruins of the glass house, then he jerks a thumb over his shoulder toward the boathouse. The other man's back is to me, but there's something familiar in the way he stands so still, in the brown canvas trousers crusted on the bottom with dirt. He wipes his neck with a bare hand and points to the boathouse. Something familiar. But then he and Elias amble away out of my sight line.

A knock comes on the door, tentative, as if the owner of it is worried he'll wake me.

I pull a shawl from the wardrobe. "Who is it?"

"It's only me."

"Toby."

"I have something to show you."

"Can I change first? I'm still in my nightdress."

It's quiet then, save for the bump of what I suspect is his everpresent bow against the wall.

"Toby?"

"Do you have trousers? They'll be helpful," he says.

"I don't."

I hear him sigh and scratch a nail on the doorframe, as if he's thinking. "It's all right. I'll make sure you don't get caught up on things."

I smile. "Five minutes, then."

Pen and paper. I dip the tip to the ink. The bottle is near empty. Enough, though, for this.

> *Kitty Swain/5 Fayette*
> *I will meet.*
>   *—M. Abbott*

Cathy's out by the laundry tubs, directing the laundress to the week's work. The woman looks too thin to lift a sheet from the line, but she stands listening to Cathy, holding a full bucket of water and nodding. She is new; Cathy isn't sure if she'll keep her services or find someone else to take on the weekly wash. Her light eyebrows raise and lower not necessarily in time with Cathy's commands. Her hair and skin are so pale she is nearly luminous. Only her hands, crackled red and knob knuckled give away her age. She slops the water into the laundry tub and drags a sheet from the basket nearby.

"*Ja,*" she says. "*Ja.*" And hums and warbles as she dunks in the rest of the whites.

"Hallo, Ingrid," Toby says.

She cuts a look to him. "*Guten Morgen*, Tobias. Mrs. Abbott."

"More bluing this time." Cathy leaves her and approaches us. Her hair has come undone on one side and looks to tumble out in a mess. "How many times can I tell her?"

"That man . . ." I gesture to the barn.

She slides a look that direction, then back to me—dark eyelids and pale skin a sign she's not slept—and keeps walking toward the kitchen. "He won't be here long."

Toby and I pass the barn. Elias is alone now, mucking the stalls. I amble over to him. "Fine morning."

He doesn't stop the scoop and flip of manure. "Fine morning."

I hook my arms over the rail. Toby puts a toe to a board and pulls himself up. "We have a hired hand?"

"Ayuh. We've that boathouse and all the rest of it to clear out."

"Who is he?"

He straightens up, tossing the pitchfork to the wheelbarrow. "Amos. Amos Searles." He pushes the wheelbarrow through to the main barn and to the next stall. I follow the rail.

"Where's he from?"

Elias looks at me and scratches the whiskers along his jaw. "Should ask him yourself, I think. I'm not for saying what isn't mine to say."

I sigh. "Fair enough. It's just that I've seen him in the woods."

"Nothing wrong with that." He picks up the pitchfork and turns to his work. Keeps his back to us as he tosses the straw.

"I'll ask my brother, then."

"It was the missus took him on."

I push away from the fence and give a quick touch to Toby's shoulder. "Come on."

He trails after me as I walk to the road and make the turn to Turee. "You're going the wrong way."

"A small detour, Toby. To town." I raise my finger to my lips. "I need to mail a letter."

"But the postman comes here at eight o'clock."

"I'm aware. But it's after eight, and he has been and gone. This is a special letter that needs to go today."

"But I want to go to the forest."

"We'll go after. I promise."

He nods and shrugs his bow over his shoulder. It drags a line in the dirt, and he stops to adjust it.

"You need a bow your size." I put out my hand. "Here, I'll carry that. I have an idea where to get you one. That's why we're going this way too."

I glance back out the window of the small post office, watching Toby play in the triangle park. He's on one knee, eyeing an imaginary arrow at the poster board for the *Future Home for the Statue of the Fallen Soldier*.

I slide the letter across the counter and wait for the receipt. "It will be there tomorrow?" I inquire.

The postman taps the coins to the wood counter, then drops them in a square box. "Tomorrow. First light."

The day warms, though the sky is a low gray. No shadows in the woods as I follow Toby. As if all the trees were cut out of paper. Toby's jacket is brilliant red. He holds his bow by the leather grip.

"I thought we'd get you a smaller bow." I've been given the honor of carrying the quiver. The hard leather bumps against my back. The ribbon from my hat catches under the strap, and I pull it loose and retie it. "I thought we'd go to the Runyons'." Her boys are near grown; it's worth a visit to see if they kept, or ever had, their own bows and arrows.

"I want to show you the fort." He slaps his knee in frustration that I'm not following right along.

The path we take skirts the pond and then narrows and twists on itself. I wish I'd taken his advice to wear trousers, for the walk is riddled with juts of rock. I envy his surefootedness and keep my eyes peeled to the dirt.

He's like Alice: more at home wandering the woods than cooped up inside.

The cicadas' saw is loud enough to mute our steps along what has become no more than a deer path. The light is deep green and brown; we pass between tumbles of boulders and crawl under trunks of trees that have lain long enough to grow others along their backs.

I catch a glimpse of something bright above my head. A ribbon is tied on a limb, and the brass button weaved to it has caught a shaft of light.

There's another. Then another.

Toby stops in front of a hedge of wild buckthorn that backs to the boulders. He kneels and slips between the mass of branches, disappearing, then reappearing, this time on hands and knees. "It's still here." And he holds out his hand.

"I can't fit through there." I pull out my skirts and let them drop.

"Take off the underthings. That's what Alice does. Then you'll fit."

I glance back the way we came and can scarce make out the path, though there's a glint of the water in the Narrows. Black as mica. Other than that, it seems that if I squeeze between the brush and stone, it's safe enough to shed the layers. Each petticoat a relief to lose, until I'm only in my overskirt and shirt, no longer stifling in all the material. The cool air from the undergrowth twists up my bare legs.

He takes the quiver and the folded clothes from me, then scrambles through the hedge. With a shift of my shoulders, and a wince at the tear of cloth along a shoulder seam, I just fit through the bushes and find myself in a small cave—a triangular space constructed from the collision of the boulders above. The space is quite long, with a pierce of sun at the far end. I can't raise my head fully, but keep it cocked to the side, and sit down on a small rag rug that is gritty with fine silt.

Toby crouches in front of me. He lays the bow and the quiver of arrows near my hip. "This is the fort," he whispers. The words don't carry any farther than the space between us, the rock dampening the sounds rather than echoing them back as I would expect.

He crawls farther into the black and drags back a wicker basket, then tips back the hinged lid. He looks up at me with wonder, then digs into the crate and presents each item to me.

"What is all this?"

"It's for when we need to hide." He shrugs. "Or sometimes just to nap."

"You and Alice?" My foot has gone to sleep; I shift it out straight.

A tin of yams.

Two tins of tomatoes.

A can of pudding. A square one of loose black tea.

Two mugs.

Can opener.

Four bottles of cider.

Two boiled-wool blankets.

He unbuckles a rucksack and removes a wallet. The leather is cracked and scored with Father's initials. He unsnaps the coin case and takes care with removing the contents.

Three bullets.

He sets them in a line on the rug, closes the wallet, and gives it to me.

Then he reaches again and lays a small pistol at my knee.

A derringer.

Snub-nosed, the barrel engraved with vines. I stare at it, then pick it up by the wood grip. Turn the barrel to the wall and check to make certain the chamber is empty. "Where would she get this?"

He shrugs.

I think back to Father, to his adamance on keeping firearms from the house. Just a pistol locked to the top drawer of his bed chest. I'd only seen it used when his horse shattered a pastern. "You will watch," he said. "There is no cruelty in mercy."

His hand shook as he put the nose of the gun to the horse's head. Then his hand steadied, and he locked his gaze with the animal's and shot.

I shift the gun back to the rucksack. Push it to the bottom, under a soft wool scarf.

Toby takes up the wallet. Puts the three bullets to the case. "You can't tell anyone. It's only for emergencies. No one else can know. Now you know, but she said you were supposed to. In case."

"She talked to you?"

"Yes."

"Aloud?"

I can't breathe. My stomach twists as I look at him. I reach to grab his sleeve. "What did she sound like?"

"Like Alice."

"Did she talk to anyone else?"

He twists his arm until the shirt fabric pops free, then starts to pack everything away. "She didn't get here the last time. We weren't fast enough. Mama caught us and Alice got in trouble. And then Papa took her away. He said she would be back soon, but I knew it wasn't the truth."

"How . . ."

"She said you'd come and not to be afraid."

"Not be afraid of what, Toby?"

"The Bad Ones. From the pond."

I shake my head, so frustrated at Alice's obsessions. "She thought they were in your room. You were escaping. Out the window."

I blow out a breath. Alice thought she was saving him. By dropping him from a second-floor window. Alice was a danger.

He drops the crate's top and slides it back behind a pile of stones. "You can't tell anyone about the fort."

"I won't."

He sits back on his haunches, rummaging in his trouser pocket for his knife, then holds the point to the tip of his index finger. "Blood swear."

"Oh, Toby—"

But he makes a quick slice, curling his finger toward his palm to keep the small bead of blood balanced on the tip. "Blood swear."

I shift forward on my knees and take the small knife. With an intake of breath, I cut my own, then hold it out to him. We touch fingers, then I pull back and blow on the cut to dry it. "That stings."

He sucks on his finger, nods, shakes it in the air. "That's so you remember it."

Chapter Fourteen

We walk away from the fort along another path, this one well traveled, used to move a cart from the woodlot to the Runyons'. Brittle leaves and bark husks line the sides. Toby stomps through them and then runs to the other edge to do it again.

I press my thumb to my fingertip where we made the blood oath that Toby no doubt has now forgotten in the glee of crushing leaves. He runs ahead. Stops when he reaches a certain distance from me, looking back and waiting until I am closer before charging off to stamp and twirl again.

He stands at the fork in the path between the Runyons' and our own house.

"This way," I call and point down the way to the Runyons'.

We follow the stone fence, passing fallow land, then a low-slung barn for Abel Runyon's dairy cows. The smell of slop and hogs comes as we trek past the central pens and round to the front of the farmhouse proper. It is solid plank wood, long and low, house flowing into barn.

I brush a leaf from Toby's hair and knock upon the front door.

Essa Runyon answers, leaning one shoulder to the doorframe. She bounces Frederick Hiram up and down upon her hip and looks over my shoulder from the farmhouse steps to the road. "Something wrong with the sheep?"

"No, not at all. We were just, well, my nephew and I wondered if—"

"Ach, Freddie." She winces, tugging her hair from his fist and then swatting his arm. "You know not to pull." Then she looks at me, her eyes narrowed to near slits in her wide face. "Did you get where you needed?"

My skin flushes hot as I recall how she and her husband had found me stumbling along the road. "Yes. I did."

"Good, then." The baby's bare legs swing round and kick into her thighs. She slides him to her other hip and looks down at Toby. "You're Lydia's little one."

Toby snaps his attention from the baby to her.

I put a hand to his shoulder. "This is Toby."

"I knew you when you were a mite. You still are on the smallish side, aren't you?"

He fingers the grip on his bow. "I'm eight."

"Well, you are, aren't you. Been a long while since a Snow came for a proper visit." Frederick sticks a finger to her ear. "Might as well come for a sit, then. Give me a conversation that's more than blubbers and burps." She pushes the door wider and ambles back inside. "You can leave your bow and arrow at the door."

The kitchen, like the rest of the house, is dark wood with low ceilings of hewn beams. One square window with square panes lets in a modicum of light but no air.

Mrs. Runyon lowers Frederick to a rocker bed and pushes it with her toe. He wiggles his fingers and watches her with his black bead eyes as she opens an icebox and takes out a glass jar. "Got plum preserves." I take it from her and give Toby a quick wave to take a seat on the bench.

She grabs a stack of plates from a shelf and sets them to the gingham tablecloth. "Hope you like biscuits."

"Thank you." I sit next to Toby, back to the window, wishing it open. "It's been a hot summer."

"As summers are." She clatters the teapot on the stove, then opens the cast-iron door to poke at the log. "We'll have some coffee, then."

Toby stares down at the baby. "He's very large."

Mrs. Runyon tips her head and barks out a laugh. "That he is."

"We wonder, Toby and I, if you might still have one of your boys' old bow and arrows. And if we may borrow them."

She stretches her mouth in thought, then nods. "Going boar hunting soon, Toby?"

He frowns. "No."

"They'd be on you before you got the arrow nocked." Then she puts her palm to the table. "It'd be you I'd serve here instead of the hog." Her laugh is broad and loud enough to stir the baby. He smiles, pink gums glistening, then shrieks and bellows. Essa clamps her mouth and stares at him until he quiets and sticks his thumb to his mouth to chew.

The room is almost too hot to sit in. Essa serves the biscuits, a heap for each plate, and then pours the coffee into our mugs. Toby's looking both sallow and red. He picks at the biscuit in front of him and pushes the crumbs under his thumb and across the last of the preserves on his plate. Frederick is asleep, one finger to his cheek and his mouth moving with some dream. Essa leans forward, elbows on the table and cup in her hand, nothing fancy about her. She bites at her lip and pulls it through her teeth. She's one of the plainest women I've ever met, but it suits her, as if she never wanted any fuss and bother.

"The boys?" I inquire. Tommy and Samuel. They would be fifteen and sixteen now. Lucky enough to have escaped the war.

She takes a drink of her coffee and puts the cup down. "Out at Widow Humphrey's with Abel. She's got those New Hampshire gilts he's been eyeing. Good stock."

"Hm. Yes."

She stares at me and leans back in her chair.

I press my hands to my chest. "I confess I don't know anything about pigs."

"No. No, I think not. Not a Snow thing to be knowing about." She takes another drink and studies Toby. "There's rabbits out back. In the hutch. If you want to give them a visit."

"Can I?" he asks.

"Of course."

"Just out and to the right," Essa says.

He scrambles from the bench seat and is out the door. Frederick gurgles and arches his back, then smacks his lips and is quiet.

"Only time he sleeps. All night, I've got to walk in circles to keep him from shattering all our ear drums." She toes the rocker again, and we watch him twitch his fingers, then settle to sleep. "None for you?"

"I couldn't." It is the easiest answer.

"Well."

I smile at her, then return to watching the baby.

"Toby looks just like his mother. Dainty fine, like he'll break."

"He doesn't remember her. That's what Cathy says."

"Mayhap what she wishes. But he was old enough. He'll remember."

"Yes."

"Hard thing that. Such an accident. And Alice finding her. No one should go to the Narrows." She squints at the small window and then drinks the last of her coffee in a gulp. "But your Alice was a good one with the boy. Never saw such attention. They weren't near ever apart. Come by for the rabbits. Just wanted to pet them. Asked for a rabbit's foot once. To give the babe. She was never without that boy. Abel saw them in the woods sometimes, and that boy'd be tied up tight to her like a papoose. And then . . . well, we had that fever come through, and the boy was sick, wasn't he? Alice too."

"I remember."

"I think your brother was at wit's end by then. Just one hard thing after another. Can't fault him for finding another wife." She blows a long breath through her nose. "Abel took over some medicine I'd mixed, and your brother was nice as could be and so grateful we'd stopped. Said we didn't need to look in anymore, they were on the mend. And next time, that woman over there turns her nose at us. Tells us it's not our concern." She straightens in the chair. "And I've said more than brings good graces. It's just . . . Lydia came often to look in on us and . . ."

"You were kind to bring the medicine."

"Most people were afraid, you know." She slides the biscuit plate closer to me; when I pass on another serving, she covers it with a cloth. "Thought if Alice touched them, they'd be touched the same. Can't change old ways, can you?" She points over my shoulder to a small sketch tucked in a frame of braided twigs. "Alice drew that up there for us."

I stand and move closer to the sketch. Essa, with the boys hanging off her lap, sitting at the same table we sit now.

"She gave that in trade for the rabbit's foot. She's made me too pretty there, but she got the boys just right."

"Would you consider visiting me at the house? And perhaps ask the other women? It would mean much to me. To Cathy. We can all start anew."

She lifts and drops a shoulder. "Well. I suppose we should. Would be Christian, wouldn't it."

The door swings open and thunks against the wall. Toby's shoulders are hunched tight and his breath shallow.

"What is it?" Essa turns in her chair.

"They're dead."

The chair scrapes the floor as she stands. She rushes to the landing, then stops, a quick touch to his shoulder. "Stay and watch the babe."

Essa holds her hand to her mouth and stares at the hutches. "I fed them this morning." She spins around to take in the yard. One thin trail of blood in the dirt. As if the fox killed them all and only chose one for a meal. The rest lay tumbled atop each other, the red streaks on their fur already dry from the heat. She looks at me. "I just fed them."

Toby's arrow flies true and lands with a thunk in the straw. I clap, then shake his hand. "Elbow up. Does the trick, doesn't it?"

"And thumb to cheek."

"Yes. All clear?"

He nods from his perch on the front step, and I move across the driveway to the bale set to the stump of the old tree. Better here than across in the field: at worst he'll only lose another arrow to the hedge rather than an arrow to a sheep's rump. I tug the arrow free, cock it under my arm, and hop down from the stump, careful to keep clear of the roots that travel the yard. The arrow slips to the ground. Just as I bend to retrieve it, another arrow whizzes past my ear. I scramble away, turning just as it hits the bullseye. The shaft quivers and slows.

"Toby, stop."

But his mouth hangs open and his bow is on the ground in front of his feet, just as I taught him.

"Well, look at that."

My gaze snaps to Cathy leaning out a second-floor window.

"I haven't lost my aim." She rests her chin in her palm and gives a smug smile.

"You could have hit me."

"I could have," she says. "But I didn't." Then she grabs the frame and pokes her head out. "You need to practice from many angles, Toby. Did you see that?" Her cheeks flush and she lets out a light laugh. "I'm going to try again. So, stay clear. Stay clear!"

Another arrow flies from the window, a dark shaft against the bell of sky. It lands within a hairsbreadth of the first and is followed by a *hurrah*.

"Don't move from the stairs." I bound up and into the house. I catch Cathy moving from Toby's room across to her sewing room. I take the stairs two at a time and round onto the landing. She leans the bow against the wall and sets three arrows atop a long table. Then she flicks back a linen curtain.

"What the hell are you doing?"

She glances over her shoulder at me and dips her hip like a coquette. But she doesn't answer, just pulls up the window before grabbing an arrow and maneuvering the bow out the window. She nocks and aims. "Stay clear!"

By evening, Lionel has joined. A happy trio mangling paper targets. Lionel stands just to the side of Cathy, his hand caressing her arm, his whispers making her blush. Then his hand drops down her bodice and pauses on her backside before stepping away to let her shoot.

She is better than good. She is better than Lydia. Showier, annoyingly so. Lydia was patient and quiet, never curtseyed nor flounced.

Lionel's eyes are half lidded as he follows her movements. He smiles and swaggers near to her, then away, wooing and flirting. It takes Toby jumping and pulling his father's arm to garner attention. But it is given extravagantly, with Lionel intent on every word his son says. A hand cupped to the back of the boy's head and thumb circling a caress.

I wander the dining room, window to window, just out of view of the happy family in the yard. The sun is near to set, the sky a dusty purple as the last of the day burnishes the tips of the trees and the rusted weathervane on the old barn across. A pop of red bursts from a silver maple. A scarlet tanager. Cathy lifts and aims, following the arc of the bird as it crosses the yard and grazes the hedge.

I step to the glass and rap. She turns, arm and arrow still aimed to the sky. She says something I can't hear and pivots away, releasing the arrow as she moves. It slices the outer edge of the straw and drives into the dirt, the acceleration enough to bury half the shaft.

She makes a pirouette, hand twirling, and bows deep before strutting to the arrow and then pulling and tugging like a mime before giving up. With a pout and drop of her shoulder, she places her palms together and pleads for Lionel to help. He gives her a kiss, leans to the arrow, and pulls it out.

Then he jogs to the windows, cupping his palm to the glass and peering in at me. "Come out," he calls.

I pull up the window and spread my hands to the frame. "Best five out of ten at forty yards?" I ask.

"Make it sixty." Cathy's already measuring off the yards with long strides to the road. "Then we have a game."

"I think we might be in trouble," Lionel murmurs as he watches her mark the way. "Whatever you do, don't make a bet."

Chapter Fifteen

Cathy won't let us forget she beat us. She swings her foot in church, fanning herself before turning to me with a twist of a grin and mouthing "I won."

I smack the side of her thigh, point my nose to her psalm book. "You're in the wrong place."

Her eyebrow arches and drops. She flicks the fan and gives great attention to the sermon.

Toby sits between her and Lionel. He is taken with the flood of light on the high, arched beams. His mouth hangs open and he points his finger to various streams, following their shape along the white walls and across the dark wood pew boxes. Lionel nods off, the book slid to the side and the spine tucked between his leg and his son's.

It is my first sermon in years. Reverend Howkes, aged to near dust, does not project from the pulpit, and fumbles his notes as he speaks of Lazarus of the Four Days. I watch the bob of heads of those seated in front of us, the arcs and flutters of the women's fans and the men's handkerchiefs. All of it useless in stirring the thick air. The reverend sweats; it rolls down his long forehead, and he blinks to keep the sweat out of his eyes. Were I more Christian, I would sympathize with his plight in losing his notes, and thus forgetting his long-winded story. But I am not more Christian and so do not.

I am instead aggrieved by the heat and Cathy winning by a point and the derringer hidden away in a rucksack. Tomorrow—after meeting Kitty Swain—I'll remove the gun. Put it in the farthest corner of a drawer. I flick my fan, then drop it to my psalm book, setting the whole of it to my lap. There won't be that to worry on. My shoulders loosen and I settle against the pew.

The air glistens with motes of golden dust. I tip my own head and follow the ceiling beams to the strong white columns of the meetinghouse, each one cut from a single tree. The windows are bubbled and warped.

We sing without accompaniment, voices tremulous in the heat, feet shuffling one to the other, turning the pages in our books as one. Somewhere behind us a child bellows and shrieks. Toby cants forward to look at me—for indeed there is not a voice as loud as the Runyons' Frederick Hiram—and blows out his lips and lets out a braying laugh. It transforms then into a peal of joy, and his head tips all the way back to take in the brilliance of light. He bites at it, as if he can eat it all up: the song and Frederick Hiram's colicky yells and his father's complicit grin and Cathy's earnest off-tune soprano.

I think, *We move on.*

Cathy is right. We must move on, or there is no family at all.

Perhaps it is best to let it be. To send Kitty a letter and make my pardons. *We are moving on,* I will write, *because—*

I stare at my hands. Turn them over to trace the heel of my palm and the small scar from falling off a low limb of the front tree I'd started to climb to retrieve Alice, who was far too old to do so. She lay on her belly three branches up, arms and legs flailing like a capuchin monkey, hair tangled with grass and bits of leaf.

"Serves you right," she said. "For trying to catch me."

I sucked at my palm, tongue surprised at the metallic taste of blood, and stared up at her. "I'll wait."

"You can wait all night; I don't care."

"I don't care, either."

"I'll climb to the top, and then what will you do?"

"I'll call Lionel."

"He won't come," she said. "It would ruin his suit."

"Then I'll wait until you're bored."

"I won't get bored." She swung a foot, catching my shoulder. "I don't get bored."

"I'll wait anyway."

"Nothing will happen."

"Something might."

"Mother's dying."

"Yes."

"Papa doesn't see her anymore." I heard the rough scrape of her shoe on the bark as she changed positions. "He sleeps downstairs."

I closed my eyes and pressed a hand to my mouth. My breath was warm against my palm. Mother was bone and skin; her lips thinned and curled against her teeth, her eyes sank and turned away from the world. Morphine no longer gave comfort. The doctor no longer gave hope.

I wanted her to die. Every night, my final prayer was for her to stop living. Stop suffering. Stop.

"Can't you fix it, Marion?"

"No."

When the air grew chill, she reached down and took my hand. "I was afraid you'd gone."

"I won't ever."

But I did.

With a squeeze of my fist, I follow the reverend as he descends the pulpit steps, one finger digging at his sweat-discolored collar.

I will meet Kitty Swain.

The meetinghouse echoes with the doors to the pews opening and latching shut, with murmurs and thuds of books to the backrests, with the rustle of skirts and then the clank of the front doors as they are opened to release us to the common yard.

Orinda Flowers passes our pew, her jowls bumbling around as she nods to us.

Cathy steps close to me, her arm pushed to my back. "Mrs. Flowers. How is the fundraising? For the statue?"

But Orinda has passed by. Cathy lets out a hiss and says, "And your stupid fountain."

The churchyard slopes from the meetinghouse to Sumner's Brook. The grass is sharp and crackles under our feet as we amble to the buggy, one in a line with the others. Lionel has gone ahead. He checks the horses, busies himself with the traces, straightens out the reins, tests the brake.

Toby holds my hand, and he hums and blows out his lips, then trills and hops. One foot three times, the other one six. Then again in the same pattern.

"Please stop." Cathy taps his arm.

He spins around, letting go my hand, and glowers at her as he walks backward. Toe, heel, toe, heel. He's egging her on. I see the challenge in his eyes, hard as flint. And it hits me like a flash that he knows she is not his mother. Because just at the edge of that flint is the frayed edge of loss.

He opens his mouth wide. *"Wah wah wah."* Then he lifts his hands as if he holds his bow and mimes shooting her with an arrow.

She flinches. Her cheeks blush. We are just upon Orinda's carriage, and she has watched the entire event.

"Good Sunday," I say to her but do not slow.

Cathy drops her gaze, as if she is most interested in the tips of her shoes as they peek from her skirts, though her eyes sneak glances at those we pass. "Good Sunday," she calls, loud enough to catch the attention of each group, to receive a lift of a hat or a nod from under a parasol before the groups close into themselves. And close us out.

It is the taint of the Snow family. It is a familiar feeling. Like living inside a bell jar.

Toby's been sent to his room. Cathy locks his door, then crosses the upstairs landing to her own room and draws the door shut. I glance at Lionel in the parlor, already napping, his legs hooked over the arm, a newspaper sprawled on his chest, a snore that will grow louder as the afternoon lengthens and warms.

I continue down the hall, undoing my collar buttons, fanning myself and making my way to the yard to find a breeze. My shoes clatter down the steps to the kitchen, glad for the sound of it. Plates and bowls are stacked on the center table, an empty milk jug, forks and spoons. All in preparation to bring upstairs for the afternoon meal.

I push open the back door, trail the steps to the kitchen garden, and lift the pump handle. The water splashes on the ground, and over my scooped palms. I dash it to my face. It's cold and I flinch as the water slips down my chest. I shake my hands. The water beads catch the sunlight and fall in dollops and drips to the dirt. I look beyond the kitchen garden, following the neat rows. Out at the boundary is the proper garden.

Mother tended both Blush Noisette and tea roses, pearls and pinks. Snipped and arranged throughout the house in summers and pressed between the covers of books to remember in the chill of February.

Lydia added a wooden bench under the weeping willow. Planted gardenias and camellias, a lilac bower. In winter, the camellias bloomed in wild cherries and pinks, and at Christmas, Alice and Lydia and I littered the house with bowls of blooms. The bench sits there still, but the camellias have been removed, the bower taken down. Dahlias and black hollyhocks. Delphiniums and tree mallow. The willow branches tangle and scrape the ground.

The pond glistens mahogany and black in the eddies, slurping around the roots and juts of rocks. Out toward the center, it's coated with water striders, spindled legs splayed and knotted, thousands upon thousands.

I cross my arms over my stomach, dig my nails to the backs of my elbows and walk past the kitchen garden to the front of the house. My foot catches on a loose stone in the path. I stumble and right myself. Turn to peer behind me at the barn and the closed door. Listen to the muffled sound of Lionel's chestnut gelding, the constant saw of his teeth to the boards and the rounds of the mare's quick kicks to her stall.

My eyes snap up to the low roofline of the kitchen and the windows above and stop at Toby's window. The one that needs a post to stay open. The window is closed, the glass reflecting the sun.

I see it: Alice leaning from the upstairs window, her hands tight to Toby's wrists and his feet looking for any purchase on the roof below. To run away and to take him with her.

She didn't want to kill him. She weaved the spells of the Sentinel trees and kept him away from the Bad Ones in the pond. In her twisted mind, she wanted only to save him.

"Something wrong with the window?" Amos stands just by the side of the barn, white shirt buttoned to the neck, pressed coat and trousers. He turns the brim of his hat in his hand. He's clean-shaven, sharp of jaw, his smile light and his step lighter as he approaches.

"Nothing's wrong."

His gaze holds mine, and when I try to look away, he makes a quick *chook* to catch my eye again. He points a finger. "The boy's room."

I touch my throat. My pulse scatters and jags. "There's nothing wrong with the window."

"All right." He puts on his hat and nods, as if he's answered a question that no one asked. "Good Sunday to you."

He passes close enough I must pull in my skirts and step back. He twists to face me but doesn't stop on his way toward the front yard. The smile is still there. He makes another *chook* and glances at my hands still gripped to my skirt, at my hands curved into my thighs. "I said Good Sunday."

"Yes. Good Sunday."

He lifts his hat and bows, feet crossed and arms spread. "And tomorrow's a Monday, and on and on it goes."

Chapter Sixteen

"You're up early." Saoirse stokes the stove in the kitchen and doesn't turn to me, just gestures for me to hand her a bundle of kindling.

I take it from the wicker and give it to her.

She pokes the new wood until it catches. Then she stands, flicking the towel tied to her belt. She takes in my traveling gear. "Where you off to?"

"I have a meeting. In Harrowboro."

"Mm. Taking the coach."

"Yes."

"Not waiting for Lionel so's you can have an easy ride in."

"Saoirse."

"Going through the kitchen door and not the front."

"Cathy knows. I'm not sneaking out."

She raises her hands. "All right." She ambles by me, reaching for two mugs and setting them on the table. The lid to the tea box rattles as she jiggles it open, spooning leaves into the iron teapot, then snapping the tea lid closed. She pushes it back to the shelf and drops into a chair, then taps the cloth for me to sit.

The steam from our teas twists and circles after she's poured it. "Amos says you want the upper windows looked at."

"I didn't say that at all. I don't want him up there."

"He said you said specifically—"

"I said nothing of the sort. Keep him away from the windows."

She lifts her mug and frowns at me as she blows on the tea. "I'll send Elias, then."

"There's nothing wrong with the windows." I gesture to the kitchen door. "The coach." Give her a kiss on the cheek. She startles with surprise. "I'll be back on the three forty-five."

The light on the road is hazy this early. The mist lifts from the packed soil, low and thick. It will dissipate by midmorning, burnt off by the sun. But now it whirls around my skirts, coils around the tree trunks, curbs against the embankments. It floats atop the mill pond in Turee and scatters on the bridge to the livery. The coach sits out front, the four horses in their traces and blinders. They paw the ground and shake their heads, pull at the bits, anxious to go.

The coachman has already taken to his berth, no patience for those who come late. I hurry across the way. A passenger in a tall beaver hat leans from his seat to keep the door held for me, then takes my hand to help me up.

"Are you to Concord?" he asks.

"Just Harrowboro." I perch on the bench, hands under my thighs.

The coach lurches forward. I have a sharp stab of doubt. Perhaps this Kitty will not appear.

The man who helped me to my seat now proffers an open candy tin. "Sugared ginger," he says, and as I take a piece, he smiles as if it's something we share in a secret. But he smiles just the same as he passes the tin to the other passengers and settles his gaze out the window for the rest of the trip.

The liveryman hands me down from the coach. "You sure it's the Tradesman you want?"

"It is."

His expression is leery as he hands me my return ticket, but he doesn't stop me. If he did, I would ignore him anyway.

I pull on my gloves and settle my bonnet, for the sun is already sharp. Then I lift my skirts to avoid the worst of the ruts in and out of the livery behind the Phoenix Hotel. The manufacturers that block the river have been awake and belching soot and flame for hours. Two streets over, the church bells ring on White's block. A passing cart, heavy with grain, slings gravel and dust from its wheels. It is disorienting here. And loud. A different place from the one I left, rougher now.

The inn occupies a narrow slit of building on Fayette, just off the main road, between a market and tin shop, three doors down from the corner. Kitty Swain waits at the entrance, pacing and twisting her hands over and over. She shifts a knit purse from one hand to another. Her dress is a plain brown, no petticoat to fill it out, turned twice at the hem. Even from across the street, I can see how she tucks her face away from passersby.

I wait for a long cart of logs to trundle past, then cross the road. Just as I make the opposite side, a man steps from the market. I drop my parasol, watch it flip and land, watch his shoes as he dances around it and collides into me. He reaches out and takes hold of my arms to keep us aright.

"My absolute apologies—"

"I wasn't paying any—"

"Mrs. Abbott." He releases my arms, steps back to pick up the parasol, and holds it out. He smiles then, boyish and pleased with himself. "It is you. I noticed you across the way, and I thought, well, there is Mrs. Abbott. And here you are."

"Mr. Hargreaves." I take the fan. Tip my head. It is the new Head of Latin. Benjamin's brightest student. And his replacement.

He stares at me, and I think, as I have before, how he wears suits too severe for his features. The simple collar and dark-gray cloth seem meant for another figure, not his with his soft cheeks and lips and ash-blond hair curled at the collar.

"What a wonder to see you here," he says.

"Is it?"

"Ada and I were just . . . well, how are you? I mean—"

"I'm sorry to have missed you when you've called at the house. It's so very far away to come call."

Mr. Hargreaves fiddles with the chain of his watch, and his cheeks grow red. "Yes, well, Ada's fam—"

"How is the cottage?" I ask.

"Snug. Cozy. I don't know how you all managed to fit. With all Mr. Abbott's books and Alice and such."

"We managed."

"Yes."

"And your wife?"

"She's at Mrs. Brown's Academy now. Teaching Roman history. She was always keen on the Romans." He tilts his head and gives a quick *tsk*.

Kitty is no longer by the tavern door. "I must go—"

"Will you come see us this afternoon? If you are not too taken with other calls? Catch up and all that."

He is too young to be headmaster. No matter that he mimics Benjamin in dress. Leans forward with that same conciliatory visage that has been honed to perfection over the centuries by headmasters and parsons and meant to con all sorts of confessions from their followers. It looks ridiculous on Mr. Hargreaves. A sear of anger cuts my ribs.

"Another time, perhaps." I step back on my heel and move to take my leave.

He stops me with a hand to my forearm. "Will you give my regards to your sister? She was always kind to me when I stopped to confer with Mr. Abbott."

"She is dead, Mr. Hargreaves."

His face blanches. "My God."

"It was a sudden illness."

"Will there be—"

"We have buried her. She wouldn't have wanted a fuss."

"No. I suppose not."

"May I take my leave? I only have a short time here in Harrowboro."

"Of course, of course." His hand slips from my arm to my wrist, then drops to his side. "She was so very young."

"Good day, Mr. Hargreaves."

"I am so . . ." He shakes his head and tips his hat. "Ada would be ever so grateful to see you."

"I will leave a card next time I am in town." I continue, stopping at the door to an auction house. Mr. Hargreaves strides off; I wait until he has made the corner, has turned with that purposeful lean to his figure, and then I continue to the Tradesman, with hope upon hope Kitty Swain has not fled.

The tavern door is heavy and scrapes the floor as I push it open. The room is narrow, with a low ceiling and the smell of stale beer and sweat. The windows are shuttered; the light itself comes from the glow of pipes and the sputter of oil lamps hanging from the ceiling. Round tables crowd the room, each holding two to three workmen. Whatever words were uttered now drop from their mouths and fall to the floor.

I remove my gloves, let my eyes adjust to the dim light. I feel gazes on my back and waist and hips. Feel them touch and move away. I think the tavern goers are inured to the colorful class of girl, and not the staid black of my wear.

Kitty stands near a table by the back stairs and waves me over. When I approach, she squints up at me and her face brightens. "You're here."

I roll my gloves, click open my purse, and drop them in. "Yes."

"Yes. Yes, you are." She holds her hand out to me, and her grip is tight when I take it. "I'm Kitty Swain."

Her skin is dry, calloused along the pad. I want to hold it longer, for it feels so much like Alice's, rough, overtended with soap, nails red at the bed from biting.

Then she pulls a chair out for me. Drops in the one across. "I didn't expect you. Not really. No one listens to me, so . . ." She ducks her head to her shoulder. "But you are here."

"Why did you write me, Miss Swain?"

"Kitty."

"Kitty."

She sits back. Fidgets with her hands. Cuts a glance to the barkeep, then back to me. "I'm in the kitchen. Most times. Others, I get sent to clean or whatever is needed. Mrs. Brighton says I am very good at doing what is asked." She purses her lips, as if someone had just forced a lemon in her mouth, then shakes her head. "But sometimes what I'm asked to do and what I *should* do are at odds. And that pricks at my conscience."

"What were you asked to do?"

I see the black flecks in Miss Swain's eyes, the rim of red on an earlobe. She spreads her hands on the table and leans forward like a doll hinged at the hips. "It's what I was asked not to do."

"Which was?"

"I promised I wouldn't say, but I can't promise a lie."

"Kitty—"

"I saw her fall."

I pull in a breath. "What?"

She drops her gaze to the tabletop. "I like to walk the paths at night. Before matron does evening reading. No one saying, 'Kitty, do this, Kitty, do that.' Just me and the stars and the quiet."

"What did you see?"

"No one goes on the roof. But that night, I saw a shape, and I thought, *There's someone up there, standing right on the edge. It's Alice.*

And I thought, *No that's not right. It can't be Alice.* But it was. And I said, 'What are you doing up there?'" She points, as if the roof of the asylum is just beyond my shoulder, her eyes narrowed on some figure only she can see. "She looked behind as if someone else was there and talking to her, and then she was over the edge . . ." She hugs her arms to her chest and rocks. "Her arms spun round like windmills, and I laughed. I shouldn't have, it was terrible, but that's what I thought then. How silly, as if she'd catch the air and it would all stop."

My heart knocks against my chest. "You saw her fall."

"The sound when she landed. It was . . . I still hear it." She blinks and stares. "I ran up quick as I could. She was so still . . . I sat down right by her and held her hand. She liked her hand held, it gave her . . . Mrs. Brighton came running, and then so many others. But I kept hold of her hand all the time until they took her away."

"Was she still alive? When you found her."

"She made such horrible noises. Such—" A sob rasps out of her. She drags a handkerchief from the waist of her dress and holds it over her face. "She was my friend."

My hand trembles as I touch her wrist and wait for her to gather herself. She folds the linen in fourths and smooths it on the table.

"Kitty," I say. "How did she get up there?"

Kitty looks up. "I don't know." She bites hard on her lip.

"Did she pick the lock?"

"There's a metal plate on the third-floor doors. On the inside. You can't pick your way out of that. It has to be unlocked from the outside."

My mouth opens and shuts.

"You can't get out of those rooms." She reaches to me.

"You're telling me—"

"Mrs. Abbott, I don't know what happened. She was in a terrible state, but I can't see it, not jumping like that. No. We always said to each other, *One can hope.* Someone else had to be up there."

"Who?"

"I don't know. I don't know." Her hand trembles. She dabs a napkin to her lips. But she doesn't stop talking, and the saliva smears and glistens on her chin. "She wasn't herself that last week. They had to tie her down to stop her screaming sometimes. I was only allowed a visit once."

A jagged chill scratches its way under my skin. I cannot move. My arms and legs are lead heavy. I fear the floorboards will crack under the weight. "What did they do to her?"

"What didn't they?" Kitty looks at me askance. "Trying all sorts of ways to keep her . . . contained. That's what Mrs. Brighton says. But she took Beatrice's passing hard."

"Beatrice?"

"Beatrice Beecham. She was on the same floor as Alice, they liked to sew together. And then she went to the ice treatment and didn't come back. Apoplexy. That's what Dr. Mayhew said, and that you can't ever know when one will come. And Alice beat her head against the wall until her skin split, and Mrs. Brighton and one of the wardens took her to the third floor."

My legs shake as I stand and lurch away from the table. "I need to see Dr.—"

"Don't tell him I came here. I'll lose my job. I can't lose my job."

I push my way through the room, past knees and elbows. A lunch pail kicked to the side. I wipe at my eyes and stumble toward the livery.

Kitty follows, matching me stride for stride. Not touching me nor stopping me. She follows me into the shade of the livery entrance, slows with me. Steps behind me as I stumble to an alley and bend to the wall and am sick.

She hands me her handkerchief to wipe my mouth. Turns her head to look away as I spit up sour saliva. I press my palms and forehead to the sun-hot brick. Rake in breaths. Swallow back bile. My skin chills and I shiver. Then I blow out one long breath and step back. "Who had the key to that door?"

"Miss Clough. She's the third-floor matron. But she swears it wasn't her. She's a good one, Miss Clough."

"I want to see her." I grab her arm and pull her close. "You take me to see her."

"They won't let you in."

"You get me in to see this Miss Clough, then."

"You're hurting me, Mrs. Abbott." Her eyes go wide, as if she's spotted something just beyond us on the street. "Please, Mrs. Abbott. It's my morning off, I need to get back before they know."

"Did someone kill my sister?" I flash to Alice's hand in mine, so lifeless, the nails ragged and worn. "Help me. Please."

I loosen my grip. Kitty rubs her wrist and pulls at the cuff of her shirt. Then she steps back and digs into her handbag. "Here." She shoves a package at me, solid edges like a book, wrapped in brown paper and twine. "This was Alice's. I kept them for her. I have to go."

"This Miss Clough—"

"It'll have to be at night. When there's just the small staff. I'll send you word." She reaches to me, then stops. "Oh!" Then she jerks away and jogs farther down the alley to the river. She slows, looking back to me. "We both need solace, Mrs. Abbott. I think we both do."

I step out of the alley. The light is a sullen yellow. The wind gusts and pummels my bonnet against my cheek. I grip the parcel tight and wait for the passing of a milk van. The mule's ribs poke its skin and mud-cracked hair. I cross the street, lifting my skirts to avoid the dirt and oil and horse dung. I don't know where I'm going.

Someone killed my sister.

Chapter Seventeen

The Phoenix Hotel lobby is cool. No one pays attention to me. The bench I sit on is curved, tufted with green velvet much used and sheened. The desk clerk has pulled over a small table, has gone to the trouble of bringing me a spritzer of soda water, and I nod at him and take a sip. The spritzer is flat. I pretend it isn't. I pretend instead I am just a woman sitting in a hotel lobby because the weather threatens rain and thunderstorms. I am the widow people give wide berth or too much sympathy. I watch the comings and goings of the people up the stairs, boots and button-up shoes, carpetbags and leather carrying cases. The bell ringing for the bellhop. The room keys jangled and delivered. Comings and goings.

I've set the package on the table. The twine is knotted twice. It won't unknot, so I pull the string to the edge and shrug it off to the seat. A book. Thin, the cover a cheap, blue cotton. The pages crinkle along their edges, as if left in the rain.

Open the book. The words won't bite.

I flip quickly. There's no rhyme or reason to the lines of words and the spattering of sketches. Nothing dated. Alice's handwriting is precise, as it always is—she worked hard at it all those years ago when I taught her. Nothing misspelled, and she was proud of that, studied the word lists I gave her from my old textbooks. My learning of sums and the

French Revolution, embroidery and beginning French, passed on to her in the corner of her room we'd turned into a study.

She's come again. I can't look at her teeth. They're big as the windows. Marion would call her Mary Mule.

"Oh, Alice." I run my thumb along the paper and the indent of the pencil marks.

Kitty's eyes are green glass. Sometimes I want to shatter them. On and on there's always hope. When?

A sketch, then, in pencil. A view of the trees from the women's porch. I recognize the smokestack poking above the leaves. She's drawn in creatures hanging and grinning from branches. Knob kneed. Long nailed. Some with hair aflame.

Today ice. Toes still numb. Lemon cake.

Another sketch: A widow with a veil so long it pools at her feet. She holds a single lily and stands over a grave small enough for a babe.

A page torn out. The ragged edges traced with curlicues. It is Kitty in profile, clear cheeked and smiling. She is almost pretty, and somehow Alice has caught the light from the window.

I will be a good girl.
Box. Mrs. B said not so long this time, but she was wrong. 1,786 seconds. I counted. Sent complaint to Dr. M.

My breath stops at the image on the next page: A girl on a chair, thick leathers. Ankles to chair legs, wrists to the arms. Chest belted tight. Head trapped inside a square box, a lock on the side. A cat lying on top with its paws slung over the edge and its eyes staring direct into mine.

My hand quivers as I hold it to my mouth. The leather straps. The bruises.

"What did they do to you?"

Kitty angry at me. Why can't you behave.

He watches. Everywhere. He's everywhere. His eyes are like marbles. Mrs. B says I'm a tall taler.
Lemon cake. Mrs. B showing off. Ladies sing like cats but terribly righteous. Smell like verbena and shoe polish.

An empty page.

Another picture. A cat. Or not a cat. Parts of a cat and none make a whole. Whiskers in a line as if they'd been plucked and set to a table. A haunch of fur and then muscle, then the bones of the foot, each claw separately drawn. One ear mangled. Along the edge: *HARPER R.I.P.*

Kitty agrees. We'll be better and then we can meet in real life and have creams and cakes.
Not wanted.
Beatrice is dead. She was strapped under the ice and they all laughed when she had a fit.
Mrs. B says STOP MAKING THINGS UP. I made it up in my head, she says, and that I'm too bad a girl and she said, "You tried to murder that little boy."

LIE LIE LIE LIE LIE LIE LIE LIE

Beatrice Beecham lies under the earth, one too many soaks in the water. Say a prayer for the dead and drownd and tell her visitors she died of the plague.

LIE

I know the truth. It's scratched on my eyes and I won't ever ever stop seeing any of it. I was there. I saw. He laughs and hums as we freeze and drown. Our calm time.

I am very cold. He watches me—says I am worth nothing but the dollars he's been given.

I think soon I'll die

Complaint to Constable. Kitty to take.

BOXthedemonsfoundthewayinscratchscratchscratch

Dr. M says the 3rd FLOOR & Kitty cries that's the end then

Where is my trunk it was here it's not here?

Tomorrow. It is murder

I want to go home

Nothing after. Blank page to blank page until the last. And another handwriting, not neat. Kitty's.

Alice Louise Snow. R.I.P.

She was my friend.

I close the book. But the image of Alice in the chair, head locked into a square box, is burnt in my vision, and no matter if I close my eyes or stare at the brass doors across the lobby, I see it. See her.

"She was afraid of the dark," I whisper.

A man laughs in the bar, his head tilted back, mouth open, big teeth. He slaps his stomach and then the bar top.

"She was afraid of the dark."

"Mind if I steal this?" I look up at a man in brown twill. He picks up the facing chair and swings it toward a group of young men across the way.

I don't answer, but pull on my gloves and bonnet, pick up the book, then grip the table and force myself to stand, to walk to the lobby.

The police station jangles with voices. People mill around to wait out the summer storm. I have to bend close to the desk officer to be heard. He cocks his ear toward me and rolls a pencil back and forth on the desk.

"I wish to see the constable."

"He's not here. He's engaged elsewhere." He twists the pencil a different direction and rolls it under his palm.

"Then I will wait."

"He won't be in until very late tomorrow. He's gone to Keene."

There's a boom of thunder. Laughter bubbles and bursts. The pencil is shifted again, ready to be rolled. The man looks past me to the next in line.

I grit my teeth and slap my hand to his. "I want to make a complaint."

Snow & Son Brassworks is silent. No hum and whir, no windows rattling and molds thumping and the constant outflow of candlesticks and chandeliers. Bullets and belt buckles.

My parasol is for sun, not the rain now bloating the clouds.

I shake the lock. Stare down the street for any sign of Lionel. Any sign the business has a life at all. Any chance I can ride out the weather here and return home with him.

But there's no Lionel. I cup my hand to the glass to peer inside. Machinery and wood boxes stacked haphazardly between casting machines. The belts hang loose from the ceiling. My eyes track the stairs to Lionel's glassed-in office. The door is ajar but the room is dark.

A shout from the woolen mill startles me. All around, workers cross from the woolen mills to the depot. Hand carts piled high with packed parcels.

The sky tints green yellow, and a gust picks up the cotton dust from a delivery door. It swirls and eddies and coats my vest and skirts. Then the door is pulled shut, as are the others along the street.

"No stage going out this afternoon. That sky's waiting to take a punch." The liveryman rests his elbows on the wood counter, narrows an eye, and peers past my shoulder. "You'll need to wait for the seven-thirty coach. It might be held up in Concord. Can't be certain about that."

The ties of my bonnet flap as a gust blows through the building. I grab the brim. Behind me, the horses shift and stamp in their stalls.

"I won't take the horses out in this," he says.

"No, of course not."

"You might wish to take a room for the night."

But I don't have money enough for a hotel.

He tugs at his mustard coat, then reaches for the shutter and closes me out.

The rain comes heavy now, sheets that turn to steam against the brick and stone. I stop under an awning. The water pours from the corners, spattering the dirt and churning it to mud.

School Street. Houses tucked behind gardens. The rain pounds the flowers and tumbles over the black iron railings. There's a hiss of light. I jump at the immediate crack of thunder and leapfrog across the street, skirts lifted, shoes and boots soaked enough that it doesn't matter if I avoid the puddles or wade right through them. Another flash and crack. I take my handkerchief from my shirtwaist to wipe my face, though it is as sodden as the rest of me, then rap on the dark-blue door of a familiar plain cottage.

Mr. Hargreaves answers, looking out at me in surprise.

"Mrs. Abbott."

"I'm afraid I am adrift."

"We are delighted you changed your mind." Mr. Hargreaves shifts forward on the settee and offers me a cup and saucer of tea. He smiles, and tips his head. "Ada is quite beside herself."

I look at Ada—or what I can make out of her between the peacock-feather vase and the multiple busts of Caesar and Shakespeare and Bacon on a litter of stands in the front parlor. She is slim shouldered and quiet, currently feeding seeds to a pair of goldfinches in an ornate wicker cage. She sits on a stool between the birdcage and an upright piano. The rest of the furniture is laden with student workbooks and tomes of various natures.

They have painted the walls. No longer the light peach that held in the sun—for didn't the cottage want always for light? Now it is an aggressive puce. The settee itself is much the same tone, the curtains and their tassels a sickly mint, and all of it seems to pall. It is 3:00 p.m. The wall clock clangs the time. "You have put your mark on the cottage," I say.

"Do you like it?" Ada's gaze is that of a teacher; she won't give up the attention until I've answered the question and she is content with the response.

The calico dress she has lent me is too tight at the neck, pinches my armpits. The cotton petticoat is too short in length. But they are dry, and it's the first time in so long I've worn anything with color. It's almost too much, this weave of bright-orange flowers and green threads. "I like it very much."

The answer suits. Her lips play at the corners, and she relaxes in the seat. "We thought, why not?" She gives a shrug. "Why not?"

"It's inexplicable," Mr. Hargreaves says.

"What is?" I ask.

"You. Of all the people I thought I would never see—though I do think of you and Benjamin often—it would be you. On the street." He crosses his feet at the ankles. Shakes his head, then wipes the corner of his lip with his knuckle. "All so terribly grim, though. Poor Alice."

Ada makes a small noise and pinches another serving of millet for the birds. "Poor Alice."

"Ada teaches one class at Mrs. Brown's, on the Romans." Mr. Hargreaves raises a finger. "On Lucretius this week. Is that not right?"

"Theodosius." She stands of a sudden, and sets the cup and saucer to the piano top with a clink. "Theodosius. It's much too early in the term for Lucretius. The girls would rather contemplate the blue sky and the state of their hair ribbons."

Mr. Hargreaves leans back, resting the cup on his chest. "Not everyone is as serious a scholar as you, my dear. Of the girls, that is. Or even the boys."

I look toward the back of the cottage, to the high-walled garden beyond the dining room, and imagine past it to the playing greens of the school. The missing of all this sits like lead. Benjamin at his desk, Alice in the garden. A simple pattern to the days. It is a lie, and I know it. Benjamin at his desk with the door shut. Alice in her turret, the door locked from the inside. Sometimes the three of us passing in the hall and sometimes else a dinner with guests and Alice flitting to each with a drawing of a posy as a gift. Sometimes that. And others marked with all our silences.

"Are you staying for supper?" Ada asks.

"Of course she is. Of course. It's much too horrible out there." He slaps his knees and leans back. "We've left the blue robins." He points to the ceiling. "All those little blue robins Alice painted on the ceiling of her room."

I shake my head. "Why would you keep them?"

"They're pretty." He half rises. "Would you like to see?"

"I'll take her." Ada flicks bits of seed shell to the cage and makes a kissing noise at the birds. Then she takes up my tea by the saucer and sets it to the side table. She tilts her head and waits for me to stand. "You know the way."

Alice's old room with its six walls and windows, a turret built by the occupants two generations before, is musty, empty of furnishings save a sleigh bed and a mattress used now for storage. Old boxes and trunks are stacked atop, a glass lamp without a shade. The blue robins on the ceiling to keep watch over it all. I can't look too closely at them; there's something off about each: a missing beak, a dragging wing, a black eye painted on the blue breast. The wing feathers are blurred, as if she'd caught each of them midflight, capturing the flutter and flap and their valiant attempt to escape.

She was better here. Carried herself, most of the time, as any young woman would. Rising with the first light, dressing in simple calicos or wools, her thumb stuck in whatever book she was reading. A romance. A treatise on the heavens. A train schedule. Sitting at the morning table with Benjamin and me, the sun through the window burnishing the copper in her hair.

Each morning, she ate two poached eggs. One then the other, then cut her toast in diagonal fourths and ate those without butter, from left to right before washing it down with milk. The napkin lifted from her lap, pressed to her lips. Folded once and again as she turned to the window glass and watched the light on the garden hedge.

And I thought—because I always did, over and over—Alice is well. Alice is beautiful, composed like a Danish oil painting, a still life. Well and whole.

But I was burnt by that beauty. It shattered like porcelain, the cracks discolored and fragile where I'd worked so hard to glue it tight.

Ada moves to a window seat, shifting aside a leather hatbox so she can sit. "This is an odd room." She gestures to the walls. "Nothing to anchor anything on."

"Alice liked it." I move to a window across and slip back a lace curtain. The wrought-iron table still sits in the corner of the garden, two chairs tucked in and a third pulled to the far side with a watering can on its seat. The irises have buckled the brick, but the zinnias are bright and full. The garden wall the extent of our world. Benjamin forbade us from stepping past the gate. "It is too much a risk," he said. It was, he meant, too much a shame.

"I'm so tired of wearing black."

Ada picks lint from her skirt, keeps her gaze on her hands. "I am a member of the Ladies Aid Society. We visit the women at the asylum. Every third Thursday."

I turn to her. "So you know."

"Your sister was well cared for, I think. Content. She liked to tat; the lace she made was marvelous. I never mentioned to the others. That I knew her." She pulls in a breath, gives a half smile. "I hope it will console."

"They say she jumped off the roof."

"Oh." She searches the room, struggling for words.

"It's not true. I've made a formal complaint."

"Cathy must be beside herself."

"Cathy?"

"She visited. Quite often. To read to Alice." Ada touches her chin and frowns. "I'll need to write her."

"I'll deliver it," I say. "No need for the post."

Downstairs again, Ada signs her name to a black-framed condolence card. Thomas takes the pen, bends to the paper, and adds a postscript.

The birds, both fat, peck at their feathers. The smaller one has plucked the feathers from around its neck, leaving the skin bare and wrinkled. I toss in seed, but they stare at me and continue their preening.

"Did you know Beatrice Beecham?"

"Who?"

"She died just before Alice."

"We only visit once a month. Perhaps—"

"Never mind." I take the card and slip it to my bag. "I will be sure to deliver it."

"Are you sure you won't stay the night?" Thomas asks. "The weather is still on the move."

"No, thank you, that's kind. I can make the last coach out." I glance at the grandfather clock near the stairs. Too late to look again for Lionel. My purse is on the table in the front hall. On the floor sits the carpetbag Ada has folded my widow's weeds to.

"Still slightly damp," she says.

"I appreciate—When was the last time Cathy visited my sister?"

Ada blinks. Her gaze slips to Thomas, who is smiling, all big teeth and vanity. "I don't remember. Last month, I think."

"July?"

"I think." She presses her palms together, fingers pointed to the floor. "Or perhaps the month before."

Chapter Eighteen

The coach is overfull. My legs are pinched between a knobby knee and a wood crate marked *Wilkins*. The tobacco smoke is thick enough that the open windows do no good to shift it from the tight space, so it curls itself around our necks and shoulders. The woman next to me—a tiny thing with braided rounds of white hair looking close to toppling from her head—wrinkles her nose and then sneezes.

Outside, the road glimmers with pools of leftover rain. The moonlight spatters its reflection in through the wet leaves of the trees. The air is gummy, and the mix of it with the smoke makes my stomach shudder.

I tighten my grip on my reticule. A corner of Alice's book pokes the soft of my inner arm.

I want to go home.

"Where is home?" I whisper.

The coach hits a rut. "Wouldn't find a road like this in Concord, no, you wouldn't," says the woman next to me.

The other voices ripple, and discussion begins on the various grades and soils of New Hampshire roadways. They don't stop yapping as we make Turee. The stable boy pulls the step and doesn't help with the carpetbag. It's passed hand over hand in the cabin and dropped to the dirt.

I hop to the ground. My legs and back still feel the sway of the ride; I press my hands to the small of my back to stretch and gain land legs.

The carpetbag is swiped from in front of me. "Come on."

"Lionel."

He tramps to the road, not slowing his long strides. His beaver hat catches the lamplight on the mill pond bridge. It bobs in time with his steps.

I shrug my purse across a shoulder and jog to catch up. "They've lied, Lionel."

"No." The muscles in his jaw tense.

I grab at his linen coat, bunching the fabric and twisting it to get him to slow. To stop and listen.

"I said no." He yanks his elbow up to free it from me, then shakes out his arm.

I run sidewise, move in front of him, and push my hand to his chest. "Where were you today?"

His green eyes flick to me, then up again to the road. He twists his torso to elude me.

"Where were you?"

His boot hits a puddle, splashing mud along the hem of his trousers. "God damn it."

"I needed you, I needed to see you. Where were you?"

He stops. Grips his fingers to my arm and pulls me so I'm on the tips of my toes. His teeth are bared, lips taut, the whole of his face quivering. Then he shakes his head and keeps walking. His fingers dig as he half pulls me down the street.

"Let go of me. People will look." But there weren't people, only the fields and the white-headed sheep.

He leans forward, doubling his pace. His Adam's apple slides up and down, stretching the skin of his throat.

"They killed Alice." My arm's going numb under his grip. "Did you hear me?"

His step stutters. He drops his hand from my arm, wiping it on the side of his thigh, and makes a noise in his throat.

There's a flash of movement from the turn to the house: Toby careens around the hedge and rushes toward us. "Auntie."

I push his hands away when he tries to grab on to me. "Leave us, Toby."

"Not now." Lionel takes a breath and leans down. "Go get a treat from Saoirse."

"Do what your father says."

The boy flinches, as if I've cuffed his ear. When I reach in apology, he smacks at the top of my hands.

"Toby. Enough." Lionel drops the carpetbag and lifts him under the arms. His legs dangle, socks slipped to his ankles. He squirms and kicks, red cheeked and thin mouthed.

"Do something with him." I brush past them and make my way to the front door.

"Where are you going?" He sets Toby down and follows me. His shoulder bumps into mine as he elbows past me in the hall, blocking my way. "You lied to Cathy. You said you were going to see a friend."

"Move."

"I told you not to—"

"I want you to see something." I shove him away, scramble around the chairs in his office, then grapple in my bag for Alice's book. "This is where we sent her, Lionel. We sent her to her death. You and me." I circle the desk, pushing bills and diagrams to the side, then set her notebook on the leather. "Someone was watching her. And Kitty said someone was on the roof. Alice turned around and—"

"You need to settle down."

"I won't."

There's a quick movement; Toby slinks around the doorframe and plasters himself to the wall. Lionel sees him. He takes a step back, palm out, as if he's keeping his son from me. "You're scaring the boy."

Cathy is now in the room. "I can hear you all the way in the sewing room."

"It's not just negligence, Lionel. She knew about another woman who . . . She sent a complaint to the constable. So at least give me the courtesy of looking at this."

He lifts his hands and looks over my head at Cathy. "Do you have any idea what she's talking about?"

"You need to stop, Marion," Cathy says. "You're sounding like her."

"They're lying." I pound my fist to my thigh. "Listen to me."

"Get Toby out of here," Lionel says.

Cathy takes the boy by the hand and leads him back to the hall. Bends to whisper something in his ear. Pats his head. Then she closes the door and leans against it. "Marion."

"She knew she was going to die."

She presses her lips together, bites the inside of the lower one. "Where would you get an idea like that?"

"I met with Kitty Swain." I turn to Lionel. "But I think your wife told you that; she read my letter—you read my letter—which is why you met me so rudely at the coach."

Lionel's gaze flicks to Cathy, then he startles when I thump my fist to the book. "Here. Read it."

He pinches a corner and opens it. Not to the first page, but to the page with the cat. His cheeks pale. He turns another page. Back to the first.

"She knew she was going to die." I stab my finger to the page. "Look." Then I twist the book around, flip back to the picture of the box with the lock on at the temple. "Look. The bruises she had were directly from this device. I'm sure of it. This—*it is murder*. Maybe she saw something. I'm certain she did. Beatrice Beech—"

"And maybe she killed the poor cat and cut it up just to draw pictures of all its parts." Lionel turns the book to Cathy.

"I don't want to see it," she says. "She wrote things like that all the time. What in here is different from anything else she's written?"

"Kitty said her door was opened. She was pushed off that roof. And she was locked in a box before that. Those bruises I saw, they're directly from that, I'm sure of it. She's afraid of the dark, Cathy, you know that. You don't leave someone in a box who's afraid of the dark."

Lionel snaps the book shut. "You need to leave things alone."

"Something was going on, Lionel. She writes it in here. She sent a complaint."

"Delivered by Kitty," Cathy says. "Or so she states. What a marvelous imagination for a dull girl."

Lionel laughs. Puts his finger on the journal and slides it back to me without another look. Then he takes a ring of keys from his trouser pocket and unlocks a cabinet behind him. He grabs a handful of papers, all folded in thirds. Official blue paper with numbers inked along a top edge. He pulls out another handful to drop on top of the first.

"Why don't you look at this. Before you believe her." He clears his throat and unfurls the nearest, shaking it and holding it out. His eyebrow lifts.

"*A party of seven Confederate rebels stole three bushels of corn from the feed barrel in the barn. Proof: Milk taken from milk cow. Proof: udders. Proof: Cobs on property.*"

He folds it and sets it to the side.

"*Runyons of Turee, Post Road, continue to enter my room and wake me hourly. Proof: Always leave a crow's feather on the pillow. Three included.*

"Or, how's this: *Lionel Snow (brother) has poisoned the wood warblers. Proof included: 1 bottle of lye, 1 bottle of whiskey, millet stirred with above. No bird song.*"

My stomach drops. "How many?"

"Twenty-seven. You're not innocent, either. She submitted a complaint that you smothered our dear mother with a hand pillow. Embroidered with spring peas."

"Why do you have the complaints?"

"Constable Grent was kind enough to return them to me so I didn't go bankrupt paying fees for delusions. Thus precluding the need for a ridiculous investigation."

"She never did that when she lived with Benjamin and me. I don't . . ."

"Maybe Benjamin intercepted them all."

"He'd have told me."

"Would he? Or would you have taken them—believing them true, even if it was about you murdering your own mother? Would you have walked that down to the station and filed it yourself?"

"Of course I wouldn't." My skin prickles with sweat. I swipe the back of my hand to my forehead, hold back the clatter of memories. "Those are fantasies."

"So is this book," he says. "I'd like to have a talk with the woman who gave you this and filled your head with some inflated conspiracy."

"I believe her."

Cathy twists to face me. Her lips are drawn taut. "Your obsession is ruining this family."

"She wouldn't be dead if she'd stayed here. She didn't deserve—"

"Enough." Lionel's face is purple with rage. "Stop defending her."

I fist my hand, then stretch it out. "She couldn't get out of that room without someone opening the door. Someone obviously did. She knew it was going to happen. She knew it." I point to the notebook. "It's all there. It's . . . someone had to have pushed her. She wouldn't have . . . She's telling the truth. I'm sure of it."

Cathy twists the book toward her, lifts the cover, then lets it drop closed.

"What if I'm right?"

She gives a nod, then moves next to Lionel. She stacks the papers, runs her palm down a side to straighten the pile, then sets the papers on top of the notebook. "So, someone at the hospital took it into their head to let a patient run free. Sorry. *Pushed* a patient from a roof. To what purpose? I mean, really?" She lifts her palms. "To what purpose?"

"I believe Kitty. I believe her." I look toward my brother. "I would have taken care of her."

"How?" Cathy asks. "You have nothing now, Marion. She'd be right back here and it would all be as much chaos as it was before. She killed herself." She lifts a shoulder and drops it. "It should have been expected. She tried once before."

"When?"

She crosses her arms and bites at her lip. "She was in the greenhouse. When it burnt. Barricaded herself in with the pots and stuck something in the lock. Poured oil from the lamp all along the floor. If Elias hadn't come from the barn . . . I don't want to think what would have happened."

The cabinet drawer scrapes as Lionel opens it. "Give me the book," he says. But it's in his reach, so he grabs it up and drops it to the papers.

"Please listen."

Lionel locks the cabinet. "No more, Marion. Take one moment to see your sister as she really was."

I push aside the chintz curtains in Toby's room, tug the roller blinds until they lift and open with a snap, then pull up each window. The stump of the old tree looks like a wound in the yard. It's split in places, dark fissures where the tar has been painted to stop more growth. The roots that once fanned across the ground have been lopped. Still the dahlias rise, inky purple and ruby, the flowers the size of dinner plates.

"What would you like me to read?" I ask, then step around the toy train track and move to the side window.

He rolls the top edge of his sheet between his chin and neck.

I push the windowpane with the heel of my hand to unlodge it. This is the window Alice held him out. Below is the kitchen. The roof sags just near the far edge and needs new shingles. The frame slams shut the moment I turn from it. My heart jumps at the noise.

Toby's lashes flutter as he blinks, then he rolls the sheet once more. "You need the pole."

"Where is it?"

He presses his chin to his chest and shrugs.

I flick the curtain back into place and kneel at the low bookshelf. "Now, which book would you like me to read?"

"*Five Weeks in a Balloon.*"

My finger drifts across the picture books to the Jules Verne. "Is it a good tale?"

"Oh yes. It's got condors and Timbuktu and they fly in a balloon and hunt the tantelopes."

"Well, then. I think a few pages." I hold it up. My skin is clammy, fingers cold, though the room is still stifling. I'm overtired and the thump of my pulse echoing in my ears is deafening. I force a smile, as if everything were all right, and an antelope hunt were the height of excitement for the day.

He turns on his side to give me room on the narrow bed, plumping the pillow and then resting his head on his arm.

There's enough room to sit with one leg stretched out and the other bent with my foot to the floor. I lower the oil lamp's flame and settle the book to my lap, opening to the bookmarked page.

"*'No; it is a swarm.'*"

"*'Eh?'*"

"*'A swarm of grasshoppers!'*"

"That's Dr. Ferguson." Toby yawns and pushes his knees against me. He pokes at different flowers on my borrowed skirt.

"*'That?'*" I continue. "*'Grasshoppers!'*"

"*'Myriads of grasshoppers, that are going to sweep over this country like a water-spout; and woe to it! for, should these insects alight, it will be laid waste.'*"

"You don't read as well as Papa."

"I haven't had much practice. Reading to children."

"That's all right."

"Should I go on?" I shift my hip to alleviate a twinge and drop a hand to his head, combing my fingers through the fine hair.

"*That would be a sight worth beholding!*"

"*Wait a little, Joe. In ten minutes that cloud will have arrived—*"

"Did someone hurt Alice?"

I bite my lip. Keep my hand to his hair. I shake my head and stare at the stags and deer leaping across the wallpaper. "I . . ."

He turns away, curling tight, knees to his chest and fists to his eyes.

"Toby, I—"

He swings an arm out and knocks the book shut, then squeezes himself into a tighter ball. His shoulders quiver and the edges of his shoulder blades poke his nightshirt as he breathes and desperately tries not to cry.

I rub my palm to the book's cover and curl my fingers to the edge. Then I set it to the bedsheet and rest my hand on his arm. "Would you like your papa to say goodnight?"

He stills, then nods his head.

The bed creaks as I rise. I lean over him and kiss his cheek.

"We were going to run away," he whispers.

His skin is hot as I press my nose to it. "I'll send your father in."

"Not Mama." He twists of a sudden to look at me, and when I try to stand, he tugs my sleeve once. "She doesn't believe you."

"No."

"I do."

Alice took an oil lamp to the glass house. All night this image has played in my head, and I'm afraid to return to the nightmare that made me wake sweating and trembling.

Alice carrying an oil lamp. Setting it to the narrow space between garden tools and clay pots. It's spring. There are footprints in the soil. From the house to the barn and into the little house. The steam on the glass is perfect for tracing hearts and boats with sails and daffodils.

She unscrews the lamp. Drizzles the oil along the walls, then in a circle around her skirts.

She douses the packed dirt, and it's just May; there are seedlings in the pots. She's brought a box of matches. Now she opens the box, makes a choice. Closes the lid and puts the box to a shelf. Looks up at the house—at who?—takes a breath and strikes the match on the closest pot. The phosphorous flares bright blue and white, makes her blink, and she has one moment of doubt.

She blows the match out then. Is careful to wait until she can pinch it without burning her fingers. Her eyes lift and stare through the glass, directly at me. "There you are," she says, and her voice is as light as it was when she was a child. "I've changed my mind."

But the door is locked when she reaches for it and she doesn't remember doing that. There's a brass bolt blocking the keyhole and a thin hiss of flame whispers as it slips closer. She spins around, looks for the start of the flame. It licks her skirt. A red tongue. Then it bites.

Turee, Aug 17, 1865

My Dear Ada—
It was so very kind of you to lend me togs so I might make my way home without discomfort. I am very glad to have made your acquaintance, and hope we may become new friends.

I was hoping you may do me a tremendous large favor. Could you please—when you make your next visit to Brawders House to give comfort to the patients—find for me a young employee there named Kitty Swain and

*present her this note, I would be in your debt. She is quite
remarkable with a patterned birthmark cross her cheek;
she may be serving the cake. I put my faith in you to hand
this to her directly. Her grief over my sister is delicate, and
I would beg no fuss or attention be made.*

*Could you please bring her response to Turee? We—
Lionel and Cathy and I—invite you to spend the afternoon with us. We would be delighted for you and Mr.
Hargreaves to call on us. Cathy is insistent on enjoying
your company. And I can return the dress and luggage you
provided me when I was in need of it.*

Yours in Friendship,
Marion

Turee, Aug 17
Kitty Swain—Brawders House

Miss Swain—
*I expected a swift note of return on arrangements to visit
the person we discussed at our last meeting. This is an
imperative.*

*Please respond directly to Mrs. Hargreaves with date
& time. She will find you.*
Marion Abbott

Chapter Nineteen

It's too hot inside the house. The curtains hang listless. The windows are thrown up, but there's no air to catch. Saoirse has made a tray of cold meats and fruit, but there's too much fat in the ham and the fig is overripe. None of it appeals, and I push it around the edge of the plate.

"A bullseye. You are improving, Toby." Cathy twists a spoon to her fig and scoops out a bite. She runs her tongue over her teeth, dislodging seeds, then sets the fig and spoon to her plate. "I hope you didn't kill any sheep." She cuts a corner of cheese and takes a bite. "Lionel?"

Lionel shakes his head and doesn't look up from his plate. He came home while Toby and I were in the field, stopping his horse long enough to watch Toby miss the target by a foot before giving the horse the reins and allowing it to walk them to the barn.

"No, thank you, Cathy," she says.

"No, thank you," he mutters.

Thunder rumbles but doesn't approach. Just lurks like a mongrel dog at the edge of the woods. Toby has picked the seeds from his fig and pushes them into a triangle with his fork.

Cathy takes his fork, then the plate, and drops them both with a clatter on the serving cabinet.

"I want that," Toby says.

"I don't care." She flattens her skirts under her legs and sits again.

"Give him his food." Lionel's on his third glass of wine, and his words are flat.

"No. He has to behave. You need to learn to behave." She slides the food platter close, picks up a small bread plate, and forks two slices of ham to it. Then she tips the salt box over the meat, pouring enough to coat it white. "Eat."

Toby glares at the plate she's pushed before him. He sticks out his bottom lip.

"You can't give him that," I say.

"It's not your business."

"You'll make him sick with that much salt."

Lionel makes a noise, half sigh and half groan, then turns in his chair to look out the window and ignore us.

"I don't want it." Toby clicks his teeth, then lifts a piece of meat, letting it hang between his fingers before throwing it across the table. It lands on Cathy's chest, then falls to her lap.

Her face is stone. Only her chest rising and falling gives hint to her anger.

She picks up the ham and lurches from the chair, rounding the table to him. When he tries to tumble to the floor, she grabs his upper arm and twists him upright. "Do you want to go to the icehouse? Because I'll take you there. I swear to God, I will."

She takes him by the shoulders and pushes the boy against the chair's back. She grips the ham and pushes it at his mouth.

"Stop it." I grab the meat and toss it back to the table. "There's too much salt."

"He'll be civilized and eat his food."

Lionel watches her, takes a drink of his wine, and looks back out the window. Then he slams his fist to the table.

Cathy jumps back and gawks at him. "What was that for?"

"I won't have it." His jaw clenches tight as he stands and shoves his chair to the table. "I should never have . . ." But he clamps his mouth and stalks from the room, slamming the door to his office.

The only noise is Toby clacking his teeth. He's eaten the ham.

Cathy looks down at him, her smile smug. "Good boy."

"Drink your water," I say.

"Stay out of it." Her voice is sharp. She runs her hand over his hair. "Now you're a good boy. We'll have a magic lantern show tonight. Just for you."

I can't stay in the house. I stride instead across the road from it, out from the claw of the light, to the dark of the field. The moon is just tipped over the trees edging it. Thin sickle, not much light. The road ribbons to black in each direction. Far out I hear cowbells. Near in, the grasses bend and slip against each other with a whisper of wind. Something moves in the grass, just to my left. The movement sharpens into a group of sheep.

All the windows in the house are lit now, upper and lower floors, and the long single floor of the kitchen and storerooms. It's like a dollhouse: Saoirse walks through the kitchen, is shrugging on a shawl. Cathy sets something on the dining table, stops in front of the mirror, then walks through to the parlor. Lionel's there; he's holding out the magic lantern, his shoulders bent as he sets it to the piano top and wipes the lens with his handkerchief.

Cathy stops by him. Holds out a piece of paper. He turns his back to her. Opens the lamp casing and removes the small bowl for the oil. She takes it from him and bows her head as she reads and walks out of the room.

On the floor above, Toby looks out the glass. It's not his room—he's in the sewing room. His window is blank.

When Cathy returns, she hands Lionel the bowl, now full, ready to illuminate the room. He steps close. Kisses her shoulder. She melts into him, for one moment soft, and then back to the business of preparing the magic lantern. She says something to Lionel, her lips pressed to his ear.

He's not paying attention, though. He's looking out the glass at the dark, too, and startles when she touches his hand to remind him of his job.

There's a swing of two lamps from around the back of the house. Elias coming for Saoirse, and the hired hand, Amos. They stop at the side entrance, then the lamps swing again as they take the road to their cottage and their own evening meal.

No one in the parlor now. Toby's left the upstairs window. I fumble for my watch, tilting the face to the moonlight, just enough to see. I should walk back. Pretend everything is as it should be. Watch the slides of African elephants and marmosets and fleas, and we'll all laugh as if everything weren't broken.

The front door opens, spilling light. Lionel steps out. There's a flare of a match, the orange glow from the cheroot he's lit. He crosses the drive. Fireflies scatter around his figure. The tip of the cigarette arcs as he lifts it, then lets it fall to his side. He stops across the road.

"I've got the giraffe slide," he says. "I know they're your favorite. Unless you want—Cathy said there was another set."

"She can't treat him like that."

He drops the cigarette. Grinds it under his heel. "He needs to mind his manners."

"You don't believe that."

"I do."

"He's lost too much."

"So have I."

"But you're not eight."

"Cathy's trying her best." He shrugs and picks up a loose branch. Carves it into the dirt, then tosses it. The branch skitters across the earth. "You shouldn't have come home, Marion."

"I shouldn't have left in the first place."

"Maybe not." His heel bites into the gravel as he turns back to the house. "Never mind. Come watch the show."

"We're starting with the great gorilla." Toby crawls up onto the settee and then onto my lap. He waves to a sheet tacked to the parlor wall. Just to the left of it, I watch us in the convex mirror. The mahogany frame loops around the distorted reflection that takes in nearly the whole of the room. Toby is enamored with it, as if it is a way to watch others in secret, and his gaze flicks in the mirror between his father, Cathy, and me.

"You'll like these, Marion." Lionel holds a slide to the light, then slots it in the lantern. "They're the ones we had as kids. Alice repainted them." He claps his hands. "Tonight, we shall travel to the dark continent and come face to face with the wildest of earth's animals."

His laugh is forced, and his eyes travel to Cathy, who sits in an armchair with a *Godey's* magazine in her lap. Her chin rests on her fist, elbow to the arm of the chair.

"I brought a chair for you," she says to Toby, and pats the child's rocker by her feet. "You're too big for Auntie's lap."

He shakes his head, digging it into my chest.

"Never mind, then." Cathy flips a magazine page. "Show us the wild gorilla."

Lionel holds a small card aloft and clears his throat. *"The gorilla—"*

"You've got to show the picture first." Toby sighs and drops his shoulders. "Picture first, then Alice's cards."

"Right, yes, of course."

"Alice's?" I ask.

"She wrote new ones," Toby says. "You'll see. They're much funner."

Lionel moves the lantern farther back. The image cast on the wall is blurry, then sharp. A gorilla bares his teeth, staring straight at us. His paws, so like a man's hands, seem to reach from the picture. His eyes gleam bright yellow. His throat is an abyss of red and black stripes. Alice has painted him a monster.

"The gorilla," Lionel reads, his voice low and stentorian, *"is never to be provoked. He is the mightiest of the jungle, can easily take the life of a lion or a wayward duck . . ."*

"A duck." Toby laughs with a snort.

"That's what it says. *He grasps the prey by its throat and squeezes until each bone snaps . . .*"

"This is awful, Lionel." Cathy closes her magazine.

"It's what it says."

"Why can he beat a lion?" Toby asks. "Lions have fangs and the sharpest of claws."

Lionel squints at the card, his mouth pulled into an overacted frown. "Lions don't have thumbs. Thumbs are everything in the jungle."

Toby shakes his head.

I hold in a laugh and force myself to look quite serious. "It's true. It's all about thumbs. Your father is all thumbs."

Lionel lets out a roar behind us.

"That's a lion," Toby mutters.

"No, that's the gorilla. He's going to strangle the lion with his—"

"That's hideous. It's just a big monkey, Toby. It eats . . . fruit," Cathy says. "Heaven help what she did to the ones you have, Marion."

Lionel removes the slide, replacing it with the next. It is a group of giraffes, long necked, reaching for leaves in a tree. Their coats are intricately designed, each a different pattern. The sky is a pale blue, and in the distance is a wide, gold savannah. Along the bottom of the image she has written *For my sister. 1862.*

Lionel shuffles the cards. "*The most graceful of the animal kingdom is our gentle giraffe. It is friends with all the animals of Africa, with the exception of the flea. It is impossible for the giraffe to scratch its neck—a requirement for turning out fleas, and thus, the flea causes consternation to the giraffe, who wishes, some days, for all fleas to take a boat to South America and bother the jaguar on his nightly prowls.*"

Toby turns to look at me. He pulls the cuff of his shirt over his thumb and wipes my cheek. "Don't cry."

I close my eyes and squeeze the bridge of my nose. "I'm very tired. I think I'll . . ."

Toby slides from my lap to the cushion. "Alice likes giraffes too."

"I know." My chest burns; I wrap my arms around my waist and pull in a quick breath. I force myself to smile. "I know."

Chapter Twenty

"It is quite a view." Thomas Hargreaves puts a hand up to cover his eyes from the sun and bends over the porch railing. He flips the flap of his jacket with his other hand.

"It will be." Lionel leans his hip to the rail and continues to pare an apple. The peel twists in the air as he runs the blade under the fruit's skin. He glances out to the pond. "Cathy wants a vista." He points the knife to the posts and boards of the boathouse, now stacked across the foundation of the glass house. "It's a useless structure. No one swims anymore. We'll have a grand bonfire soon."

"More cherries?" Cathy passes a porcelain serving bowl to Ada.

Ada sets her fan to the table and picks out a few of the less battered. "Marion?"

I shake my head and grip the chair arms, rubbing my thumbs to the wood. Ada hasn't made one gesture to me that she's got a letter from Kitty. Instead she followed Cathy all around the house for a tour that included details on every bit of new furniture, parquet, wallpapers, plates, and the stores in Boston and London from which they were ordered and shipped. "So difficult without Paris available," she said when the tour stopped in the dining room. "The blockade . . . well, you know."

"So difficult with a war," Ada murmured. But she oohed and aahed, and Mr. Hargreaves shared a smoke in the front yard with Lionel.

Cathy is well on form today. She wears a frock of insolent reds splattered with pink dragonflies. It is the third she brought down in the morning, begging my opinion, though when I declared the blue adequate and the fabric cool for the weather, she took her own advice and now hovers over the company. She watches Ada so closely as she chews a cherry and spits the pit to a napkin.

"They're late season, but I think very sweet. Don't you think they're sweet?"

Ada folds her napkin and tucks it under her plate. "They are. They are." She tips her head and looks at Toby. "There are three left. Would you like them?"

"They give him gas." Cathy slides the bowl toward her. The base catches the tablecloth, hooking a thread and pulling the fabric forward. With a quick *tsk*, she snaps the thread. "It's so kind of you to call this way. We are far out of the circuit. I know Mr. Hargreaves is busy with the start of the school year."

He swivels to us. "The maddening boys. Isn't that what Benjamin called us?" He lifts an eyebrow. "Maddening boys."

"He called you that, yes," I say. "And other things."

"Which we no doubt deserved."

"Ada teaches too," I say to Cathy. "Roman history."

"Roman history." Cathy laughs and claps her hands to her lap. "That's . . . wonderful. How do you fit that in with all your volunteering?"

Toby crosses his legs on his seat and picks at the hem of his shorts. He rocks back and forth, his chairback knocking the wall.

"Toby." Cathy gives a small shake of her head.

He slows, then shoves the chair back with a thud, lifting his eyebrows in surprise. As if he hadn't meant it. But his smile curls enough to show he meant it.

"Toby." I rest my hand next to his plate and tap a finger. He drops his legs and sits straight.

"Is that a secret language?" Cathy smirks. "Marion and Toby are very close. She's taught him to be a wild child. Or continued the lessons of her sister. So, we have a teacher in the family too."

Ada frowns. "I'm sorry our card came so late. I didn't know about Alice's passing until Marion told me."

"What card?"

I shift in my chair. "I forgot to give it to you."

"Did you?"

I stand, picking up each of the plates. "I'll take these in."

"I'll help." Ada makes to stand, but Cathy stops her with a hand to her arm.

"We'll all leave it. Saoirse will take care of it. Let's just enjoy the sun."

"I think a walk." Thomas rocks forward on his toes and snaps his heels to the wood. "May I escort you, Mrs. Abbott?"

"Of course."

Lionel gives the pared apple to Toby. "Then I will be in charge of your wife."

"What about me?" Cathy asks.

"Toby will take you."

Toby grimaces and drops the apple to the plate. He reaches for Cathy's hand.

"Wipe your hands," she says.

As the men pull out the chairs, Ada leans toward me, then loops her arm through mine. "I think *I* will escort Marion."

"Good," Cathy says. "Toby can go with his father."

Ada is much taller than me. Like a reed. Her arm is light in mine, her fingers drumming my wrist as we follow the others to the garden. Cathy has her head tipped and her attention to Thomas. She deadheads a rose along the way, crushing the petals in her fingers and scattering them to the ground. She hasn't stopped looking at Thomas as she does it. Lionel's hefted Toby to his shoulders, and the boy giggles and squeals as his father tickles his stomach, then bounces him up and down.

Ada slows and runs her hands along a weeping willow branch, then turns toward me. "Do you know what you're doing, Marion?"

"Did Kitty give you a letter?"

She shakes her head once, slow, and glances to the others. Thomas has pinched the stem of a peach dahlia and hands it to Cathy.

My stomach drops. "Nothing?"

"She's an odd girl. I thought she was a patient when we first visited."

I swallow back bile. "No letter."

"Do you need to sit? You're looking quite pale." She maneuvers me to the bench by the gnarled trunk, shifting away the willow branches and letting them settle back like a curtain around us. "There. Better?"

The light is a sea green. As if we are inside a glass bulb. The branches scrape the dirt, stirred by a single breeze. Ada drags her upper lip over her teeth and then releases it. She flicks her fan and waits.

"How goes the complaint?"

"I've heard nothing," I say. "I don't think the constable takes it seriously."

"I wouldn't doubt it. If the complaint doesn't involve cards, stolen horses, or a few bills dangling just within reach, it drops to the bottom of the list."

"How would you know that?"

"Follow the crimes that never get to court, Thomas says. He's very keen on justice. Or the blind eye it's given in Harrowboro."

"Where are you both?" Thomas calls from down near the pond.

"I'm overheated." Ada raises her voice enough for it to carry. A teacher's voice with its stolid edges. "We'll be down soon." She twists the fan and flips it back. "Nine p.m., Kitty said. It's the shift change. There's a thick patch of woods along Bow Brook, just at the turn from Pleasant. A Mr. Stoakes will meet you there."

I blink in surprise.

"Wednesday night." She lifts her chin to fan her exposed neck. "We were meant to sing chorales with the women last Thursday. But only a few were brought down to the dining hall. Everyone was too careful. Dr. Mayhew sat with us. Not his usual custom. He's a friend of Thomas's. They meet at the Reform Club sometimes. They're meeting Wednesday night."

"When Mr. Stoakes will be in the woods."

"At just that time." She peers up through the tangle of branches, then at me. "Are you certain there was wrongdoing?"

"Yes."

"Hm."

The willow branches slip and bobble across the ground and are dragged up in Lionel's hand. "Telling secrets?"

Ada snaps her fan shut and sets it to her lap. "Women always have secrets, Lionel." She smiles and sways so our shoulders touch. "But no, we were just solidifying plans for her visit to us. I'm trying to induce her to speak to the girls in my class. She can talk about nursing and other such adventures. I thought I'd ply her with dress shopping first."

"Oh. Well, of course." He blanches as he looks at me. "Do you need a new dress?"

"Even widow's togs can be fashionable."

"I'll just look, Lionel."

"Get what you want."

"It's all settled, then. If you're certain, Marion." Ada stands and moves next to Lionel. "I'm so glad you came to escort us. I'm a bit peckish for those cherries."

After the walk, the Hargreaveses take to their buggy. Ada reaches down for Cathy's hand and then mine. "What a pleasure to see you all. And you—I'll see you Wednesday." She pulls on her gloves and drops back to the buggy seat. Her skirts billow and settle. "You'll give the girls a fine lecture, I am sure."

Thomas flicks the reins. The skin ripples across the black hair of the horse's haunches, and the Morgan jitters to the side before moving off at a trot. Toby runs alongside, trailing his hand through the hedge. Mr. Hargreaves stops at the end of the drive, then lifts his top hat as they turn to the road. Ada twists back to wave. She holds my gaze, her smile dropping, and she gives one final nod before they are off and away.

Lionel swats a fly from in front of his face. "Still maddening." He rubs Toby's head and turns to the house. "Checkers?"

Toby nods and traipses after him.

"Thank you," Cathy says. She watches the road, the lift of dust from the wheels of the buggy.

"For what?"

"Them. Company." She takes her handkerchief from her skirt waist and dabs her forehead and the back of her neck. "You don't know what it's like."

"I do. Only Benjamin's students came to the cottage. Just for their study nights. We had no other company. He forbade it."

"Why?"

"He was ashamed." The buggy is out of sight; the dust clings to the air. "I know what it's like."

"But you have a new friend now. Who invited you, and not me, to visit." She paces to the door, then back. "What did I do wrong? Really and truly?" She pulls in a deep breath, blows it out, then lifts her palms. "Does anyone see *me*? Or do they just see a second-rate second wife?"

I press my lips tight.

"What is it you want to say, Marion?"

"Nothing. I don't want to say anything." I step past her.

"So you'll shut me out too."

"I'm not shutting you out." My foot catches on the front step. I right myself and turn to her. Her shoulders are clutched tight, and she pins me to the steps with a stubborn look. Her loneliness rolls off her in waves, and I think how hard it must be really. That she is looked at askance. That the Turee gossip is like a noose. I've seen her perched on the settee, awaiting cards that won't come, ears perked to carriages that won't stop. "I know how hard it's been for you. I appreciate—"

"I stayed here after Paul . . . I don't ask your love. Just some modicum of respect in my own house."

"It was my house once too." I push open the front door. "The cherries were rotten."

"I'll only be gone the night." I roll my stockings and place them in the open leather case.

Toby's got his arm hooked over the arm of the rocking chair and kicks the floor with his heel.

"Did you have fun at checkers?"

He shrugs. "Papa let me win. He thinks I don't know. But it's easy to tell when he's lying. His eyes go like this." And he bugs his eyes and then blinks and bugs them again.

I laugh and smooth a chemise to the case.

"What are you doing there?" he asks.

"I'm visiting Mr. and Mrs. Hargreaves."

"I know, but what are you *doing*?"

"I'm going to talk about being a nurse. On Thursday morning."

"At a girl's school?"

"My old school."

"What else?"

"Oh . . . looking at dresses. Feeding her birds."

"She has birds?"

"Two."

"What color?"

"Yellow. With black wings. They're pretty."

He wipes at his mouth. "I want a bird."

"Perhaps when you're older and can take care of it yourself."

"I want a dog. Mama hates dogs."

"Does she? Hold the corner of this skirt, will you?"

He reaches to clasp it, and I take a brush to the bombazine fabric. It rustles with each stroke.

"I think you should wear pink."

"Pink doesn't suit me."

His nose wrinkles. "Where are you really going?"

My back tenses, but I continue to pack. Here the skirt. There the wallet with the few dollars Lionel has provided. The blue jay feather. "I told you."

"But it's not the truth." He bangs his heel to the floor and wraps himself around the chair's arm. "You're a bad liar too."

I kneel down to him. Move the hair from his eyes with a thumb. "You need a haircut."

"Where are you going?"

"To find out what happened to Alice."

"Will you be back?" he whispers.

"Yes. I promise. One night."

He reaches to touch my hair, tucking a loose strand to my ear. "All right, then."

Chapter Twenty-One

Nine p.m. Mr. Stoakes meets me at the far field of the asylum grounds. He leads the Hargreaveses' black horse into a small clearing, setting the buggy's brake and looping the reins around a tree limb. The moon is atilt, brushing the ground a flat gray. An icehouse hangs over the pond's lip. Just past it are straight rows of simple stone markers.

"A graveyard." I search for the bulge of a new dug grave, but see nothing amiss.

He nods and continues on.

There are resting places like this flung across the swath of war. Soldiers buried, unnamed, Union or rebel. Those not lucky enough to be collected and identified before the battle moved on. Numbers carved to the wood posts. When the regiment passed one of these outposts, the doctor's horse shivered and stomped. The soldiers took off their kepis, prayers for their own survival on their tongues.

At the paddocks, the goats butt their heads against the fence as we approach, looking for treats. They scrape at the earth. Beyond, in the shadows of the barn, the pigs grunt and rustle loose straw.

Stoakes takes my elbow and guides us past the barn's entrance.

There's no one here. No one in the barn tending the livestock. No one shoveling coal or chopping wood. The lathe is silent, the room empty.

"Right here." He explains nothing more. Then he's around the corner between the shed and the shop, descending a flight of granite steps to a door dug into the earth.

He puts his ear to the thick wood. Knocks. Two short raps. Both are returned a moment later and the door pushed open, forcing us both a step back.

"There you are." It is Kitty. "She's agreed."

"Come on." Stoakes grips the door and ushers us in. A long tunnel faces me, its gas lamps few and encased in metal cages. The floor is worn stone tilting to the middle, and the whole of it is heavy damp and sharp with lye.

Kitty scuttles before us, the lace on her white cap fluttering as she moves ahead. The gaslight flares and dims and flares again. Each time, she is lost and then found, that cap glowing, the brass shoe buckles gleaming.

"You've done good to come," she says.

My stomach tightens and turns. "Is this all necessary?" I ask and press my tongue to the salt and dust on my lips.

"It's how you'll get to the third floor," Stoakes says. "It's left alone during most of the night."

The tunnel ends at another door. Kitty raps and turns to me. She puckers her lips, then spreads them in a smile. She knocks again.

There's a dull clatter of keys, then the door unlocked from the other side. But not opened. Kitty grips the handle and pushes. Then we are through to a room of laundry tubs and drying racks. Whoever unlocked the door has disappeared through another and left it ajar for us.

Stoakes pulls his watch from his pocket. "Last rounds. We'll wait."

Kitty shuffles, clasps her hands behind her back, and sighs. A pin springs loose from her ruffled cap and drops to the stone floor. Her hand darts out to grasp it tight, then she smiles at me and waves her prize in victory before returning it to its place.

The storeroom ceiling is low; I can touch it without much of a reach. Stoakes tips his head to keep from knocking it. Only Kitty seems at ease here. She's taken the stool, crosses her legs like a sailor and stares at me. I clench my hands, though I wish to grab her shoulders and shake her.

"I loved her," she finally says.

"I did too."

It is hot here, the air thick with old meat and oily steam. I push up from the chair and brush past Stoakes to the main kitchen. Three women turn from the stoves to stare at me. Each in the same cotton cap Kitty wears, each holding aloft a wooden spoon, their mouths open in surprise. Like maidens spinning the hour atop a cuckoo clock. But my laugh strangles in my throat as the one on the end, middling aged and purse mouthed, flings her spoon across the room. Brown gravy spatters across the fabric of my skirt and slides in dollops to my feet.

Her doughy cheeks pale. She twists her apron up, squeezing it like a rag. "I didn't mean it." Then she lopes across to me, wiping at my skirts. She is the woman from the ward whom Dr. Mayhew stopped to assess. *Are you all right?* he had asked. But I remember how she shivered.

"It's fine. There's no harm." I step away, but still she follows, grabbing and dragging her apron against the fabric. Her cheeks and neck flush in spots, and the skin is raked with scabs. She shakes her head, quick, as if someone's cuffed her.

"Stop it." I yank at my skirt.

Kitty shushes her, as you would a skittish foal. "Let her be, Della."

Mr. Stoakes reaches his arms around the woman's middle and carries her back to the stove. Then he picks up the spoon and tosses it to a bucket. "Get a clean one."

The woman dips her head and picks and tears at the number—4587—stitched on her chest pocket. "I didn't mean it."

A bell clangs out in the basement hall, a flat, dull sound.

"That's done," Kitty says. She rubs her palms down her skirt.

There are footsteps on the stairs. One set. The door from the main hospital pushed open. A woman enters. Her walk is determined and sharp, and there is no grace to it. She holds her shoulders tight, her neck rigid as metal, her chin forward. She is dressed in plain gray with an apron so starched it rasps against her skirts. She flattens her palm to the fabric to tamp the noise.

She stops directly in front of me.

"I am Harriet Clough." Her voice is like a rasp digging its way through wood. "You are unexpected."

"But I am here."

"So you are." She tilts her head, parses me into pieces and puts me back together again, her expression never changing, save a tightening at the corners of her brown eyes. "What do you want?"

"I want to know who failed my sister."

"I won't be the scapegoat. I did nothing wrong."

"Then show me what happened."

Della starts crying; the other two women return to the pans. They are afraid of Miss Clough. I feel it in the shiver of air, the split second of hesitation before they pick up their rags.

The woman who's accosted me—Della, number 4587—blinks and snaps her fingers against her thigh. Her cheeks blotch with red, and the freckles darken.

Miss Clough reaches out and grips the woman's hand. "Don't bring attention, Della. Never bring attention." She squeezes tight until the snapping stops, and then lets go and smiles. She watches me, aims her voice to them.

"This is Alice's sister. She wants to know about Alice. You'll all stay quiet for me, won't you?"

Her skirts make a sharp shirring noise as she turns to the doorway. "We have very little time. Follow."

We hurry through a worker's hallway of whitewashed brick and high-set windows. The sweet smell of baked bread and the acrid smell of the vinegar used on the floors mix and bite.

The hallway widens, trolley carts line the walls. Wide fabric straps and braces hang from hooks. We step into a room of white tile and black grout.

Like the room where Alice lay on her bed of ice.

But it's not that room. It's large and square with bathtubs and spigots and rolled hoses that clamp to the walls. Seeping lines of rust stain the tiles below the spigots. Four wheeled bins stand in a row, a flat shovel leaning to each.

It is so white. Tile. Tubs. Floor. Ceiling. The globes encasing the gaslight. Towels rolled and stacked to painted shelves. Cotton gowns along pegs, as if their owners had just shrugged them off, just stepped to a bath. All of it save the spigots piercing through the wall. Save the smooth-handled shovels leaning against a wheeled cart. Save that corroding rust. The common bath, I think, except it is knife-edge cold; most baths retain the steam, the cloy of warm water and soap and scrubbed bodies. There is none of that here.

I reach for a strap, roll it to my wrist, flinch at the bruise it would make if pulled tight.

"They bring the women in from there." Miss Clough points to the thick metal door. The paint has been scraped where the long handle arcs, exposing the black iron beneath. "Then it's a wash and an ice."

"I don't understand."

"It's necessary, sometimes." Miss Clough's starched apron scrapes against her skirts as she passes me, stops at the metal, leans her ear to it. She glances back at me. "I don't believe in it, not as much as the doctors use it."

She blows out a breath before listening again at the door. "Bring in a harridan and she'll leave a saint. At least temporarily. Sometimes for good. I've seen it work, bring some ease."

"My sister?"

"Yes." She pushes open the door and waves me to follow. "Sometimes."

"Beatrice Beecham?"

She chucks her head and clicks her tongue. "Yes."

Her apron saws and shifts, echoing in the narrow hall as we sprint to a stairwell at the far end. She lifts her skirts with one hand, the fingers of her other running along the twisted iron banister. We climb two flights. She stops only long enough at the next floor's landing to peer over the railing before proceeding up the next flight of stairs. At the top, the only light comes from a bare pipe and a single blue-white flame.

"There's only two ways in here. Up these stairs or through from the main landing. And only one way to the roof." I follow her gesture. "One flight up."

My heart thuds and then jitters and knocks.

Miss Clough fingers the keys on her waist, frowns, and stares at each. She opens her mouth, then closes it and gives a shake of her head. "I was surprised she was transferred here. It doesn't happen often. Most never leave this floor."

She makes quick work of lighting an oil lamp stored in an inset on the wall. She takes it up by the handle. Her eyes flick back and forth as she stares at me. Then with a shrug, she turns away to slide a key to the lock. Three keys to three locks.

Miss Clough looks at me over her shoulder, puts her finger to her lips, then pushes the door open.

Here there are no benches. No long window at the end of the way. No women sewing. Closed doors, each with a narrow hatch to deliver food or a glance. Paper cards slipped in brass holders just below the hatch's shelf.

Caroline Merritt 3768

Dorothea Ott 3624

Elizabeth Atkins 4669

Another name. Another number. They are behind the doors. They listen. There's a tapping sound to my right. A chatter of teeth and whimper from the left. We pass two rooms, empty but for green glazed walls and single cots. The window is painted white. There is no ceiling lamp nor bedside table. The meager hall light casts most of the room in shadow.

Miss Clough touches my elbow. She tips her head toward another open door and holds the lamp up.

"Her room?" I whisper.

She nods and keeps the lantern high. Her hand shakes. The flame quivers and flares.

I am afraid of her. Miss Clough with her starched skirt holds the lantern to the last doorway they will pass through.

If I take a step under the lintel, will the door slam on me too? I laugh, try to dislodge the thought, but my mouth fills with bile.

She seems to know. Waits with that shuddering lamp. And perhaps out of kindness—or clever in the way one lures a cat—she walks in first.

This is Alice's final room. A floor of oak and walls that stink of bleach and new paint. A metal cot, leather straps neatly buckled across the striped mattress. A pillow bare of covering, discolored along the bottom edge from drool and saliva. The detritus of fevers and deep dreams. The pipe for the gaslight, now idle, caged in a tight weave of iron. An iron plate over the lock on the door. Impossible to pick.

"You see?" She touches the plate, then arcs her lamp, and the glaze of umber light catches on the armrests of the room's singular chair. Here, too, are leather straps. And here, too, are footrests and bindings. And at head level, a box swung open now on its hinges. A round hole for the neck. A cabinet lock and bolt at the temple. Just like the drawing.

I stumble back. "What is this?"

"It reduces the mania."

"She's afraid of the dark." I round on her. "This is what you do?" My voice is pebbles and spit. I grab for her, but she flinches away. Her mouth opens and shuts like a fish.

She waves her hand to quiet me. Because I'm moaning, loud and low, and she wants it to stop. I press my palms flat to my face, push hard against my cheekbones. My knees buckle. "How could you do this? The dark—"

"I gave her a lamp." She stands beside me, setting the lamp to the small side table, so it lights the cot's frame. White paint scratched down to the rust and metal. "I care for these women. I listen to these women."

"But she's still dead."

"Yes, she is."

"So you didn't listen to her."

"She was much troubled. She said—"

"She never spoke."

"But she did. In her way."

"No. Not since . . ." My stomach twists as I look at the woman. "I don't believe you."

"She sang sometimes. Nothing that made any sense—but it was sweet. And it was how she signaled to Kitty."

"I don't understand."

"To say it was safe. They were close. Sometimes it was a warning."

"Where are the complaints she made? About her treatment? About the other woman?" I dig my fingers into my palm. "There are records."

"They'll be long gone. Or changed. Dr. Mayhew will have seen to that."

"But you could make a statement. To the police."

"You signed the death certificate," she says. "An accident. That clears him and this facility of all liability. Everything else will have been dropped down the incinerator."

"Why should I believe you?"

"I have no reason to lie." She grabs my arm. "Kitty has notebooks. She used to keep them for Alice, smuggled them in and out. Before she was transferred up here, Alice made her promise to give them to you. That you'd know what to do."

"There are other notebooks?"

"We have little time." She steps close to me. "The night she died, there was a situation on the second floor. I went down, as we are to do when needed. I locked the ward door. I never forget to lock that door."

"Are you the only one with the keys?"

She shakes her head. "The night watch. The doctors. Even Kitty has a set to borrow when she needs them." Her eyes are glass marbles in the sallow light.

"You don't think Kitty—"

"When I came up again—and it couldn't be more than a few minutes, whatever had happened had passed by the time I got there—when I came up, her door was open." She jerks a finger. "And the entrance. And the access to the roof."

I stare down the hall. The door is shut. There's nothing to see.

"But by the time I'd made it to the roof, it was too late. She'd gone over the edge."

"Or someone pushed her."

"What did she know that she shouldn't?" She peers out, then takes my arm and moves us away from the door.

"Besides Beatrice? Besides the horror of that box?"

"Dr. Mayhew believes in his treatments. His writings on them are well regarded."

"But they don't work."

"Many times they do."

My teeth rattle; I am cold everywhere, my fingers numbing as if held to snow. "My God, I don't know."

"Shh." Miss Clough puts her hand to my mouth. There's a clang and clink of entry locks ricocheting like loose shot. It's answered by a muted pound from the inside of one of the cells. "The night watch—"

Out the door. Down the hall. Ignore the sighs and chitters that seep from the cells. Miss Clough turns down the lamp flame and sets it back to its spot on the landing. She takes the keys to the locks, checks them again.

We leave through the same back passage. There's a thump of a door closing directly below us. She stops, snatching my wrist to keep me from descending, and then leans over the railing to peer in the shaft.

"Harriet?" A woman's voice carries up to us, sliding along the railing.

"Mrs. Brighton."

The second-floor matron. I push myself farther against the wall and hold my breath.

"You're here late."

"As are you," Miss Clough answers.

"One last pass. Check the locks."

"We think the same."

"Mm." Mrs. Brighton follows with that little cough. "Shall we go down together?"

Miss Clough hasn't moved. She remains a statue bent over the railing, knuckles whiter and whiter as she grips the wood. "I'm just heading up."

"But I thought—"

"Good night, Mrs. Brighton."

"Don't miss psalms."

"I would never."

"All right."

"Yes, all right." She shifts a heel. Leans farther.

Mrs. Brighton's footsteps echo as she takes the stairs down. There's a waft of air from another door opening, then closing. Then our own breaths released.

Harriet Clough's words run in circles. They hang in the air and chase around me as we return to the kitchens and the sweet smell of bread. Stoakes waits by the tunnel door. Kitty jumps from her perch on the long table.

"Where are the other notebooks?" I ask her.

Kitty's face blanches. She stares at Miss Clough, then at me. "I don't have them."

"What did you do with them?"

"They were taken."

"Who took them? Kitty, who took them?"

Her hand trembles as she reaches to touch her throat. Her breath comes fast and ragged.

"Mrs. Abbott," Stoakes says. "We need to go." He pulls me to the tunnel. I reach for his arm to slow him.

"Wait." I look back to Miss Clough. Her form is flat like a shadow puppet, lit from behind by the kitchen light. "We need the police."

"No." Her voice is sharp like nails. "Dr. Mayhew is too . . . You haven't been here, Mrs. Abbott. I hope you have another story for your night."

Something catches her attention; she turns away, leaving Kitty alone in the room.

"Kitty. Please. Who took them?"

Her wheeze echoes along the tunnel. "Mr. Snow." She slams the door shut.

I can't move. Mr. Stoakes's voice rumbles from the tunnel walk, and he drags me the rest of the way.

Mr. Snow. My brother.

Chapter Twenty-Two

The Hargreaveses' Morgan horse is jittery, not sure of me, second-guessing his own steps down the road. Even with the two lamps Stoakes has lit and hooked to the buggy, I can't see farther than the gelding's ears.

Fireflies peek and skim amongst the trees. Silent and bright, then snuffed out in darkness. The horse blows a breath, shakes his head. His skin quivers from withers to flank. The crickets and cicadas make him leery, make him fold his ears to his head and push through the night.

Lionel took the notebooks. He lied. How many times had he told me Alice refused to see him? A lie. Are they locked in his cabinet drawers with the one he missed? Now he has the set.

He has her complaints, kindly returned by the constable who has ignored mine.

He didn't want her released. She knew something. And she knew I'd believe her.

It's there, the answer; I can feel it tapping at the back of my head.

The buggy lifts and drops hard in a rut. I loosen the reins, let the horse take his head. He stumbles, then catches himself up on his haunches, pulling the buggy forward in a rush. I plant my feet to the boards.

"Shh. There's nothing there."

But he tears a rein from my hand, the leather slicing through my thin glove. He's got the bit now and yanks the other rein free. I lean forward to grapple for them before they get tangled in the traces and around his legs.

Something spooks him; he jumps, and the force of movement throws me back to the seat. A lamp swings out and cracks against the beam. The candlelight snuffs out. It's all I can do to hold on, my grip to the reins no good against the wild sway, the wheels in the air, then slamming to the roadway. A spit of foam from the horse's mouth splatters on my cheek. Tree limbs brush the buggy top, scratch across the soft roof. There's a keening crack of wood. Something slamming my back. I'm like a doll, tossed to the road, my skirts caught in the churn of the wheel, and I can't pull free. Dirt and stone fly and cut and I twist around, legs splayed behind and shoulder digging a trough in the earth.

I hear myself shout; hear the screech of the carriage as it drags. Hear the hard beat of the gelding's hooves. Then a burst of silver light and pain in my skull. And nothing.

Heavy breath. Warm and hay sweet. A tickle on my cheek. I turn my head. Wince at the movement, at the dizziness and the whirl of the moon and the trees and the horse. His chest heaves. He paws by my ribcage. Presses his muzzle to my arm and I gasp and almost pass out at the pain. I clamp my teeth against it, suck in air and force it out. I try to move my fingers. It's enough. I roll my head to look at the abnormal bend to my forearm, the broken bones pushing and stretching the skin and bulging from the ripped fabric of the sleeve.

My breathing shallows. I stare at the horse, match my heaves with his.

Think.

The fireflies are impossibly bright. Thousands of them. I squeeze my eyes against their glare.

Another touch to my shoulder, gentle.

"I've crashed the buggy," I say, then look up at green eyes and red hair always in need of a cut. Alice nods and touches my cheek.

"I've broken my arm." I twist then and vomit. Spit and vomit again. I roll back slowly, cradling my forearm with my good hand. "You wouldn't have any chloroform, would you?"

She kneels down and runs her hands along my limbs. Every place she touches warms and then ices. I want to ask her . . . something. Tell her to check the horse. Ask her . . . something.

Wood-planked room, like a stall. Straw pallet. Up above, thick oak beams. Spider webs swing in lazy circles. Another pair of hands, these heavy on my shoulders, a calloused stroke on my neck.

"Mr. Stoakes."

"Mrs. Abbott."

There's another man to my left in a loose linen coat. His hair is very black and his mustache is too short on the left side. He scratches his arm and then bends down to me. His fingernails are cut to the quick, and the skin red, raw moons. "I'm going to set your arm."

"No. *No.*"

Mr. Stoakes looks at him and nods once. He rummages on the floor, then brings a rag to my nose and mouth. "Breathe in."

It's all gray now, no edges. Someone's voice is insistent, a bark and babble. A woman in calico behind the man in linen. The words are blue and slide past me. Fall like glass to the floor. Scatter like beads and beetles.

Then a horrible grating pain.

Mr. Stoakes sets a brandy on a table beside my bed. A bed now, not a cot. A white plastered room and not a stall. It's my second drink, and the voices coming from the other room are rounded and soft like butter.

Stoakes tamps his pipe and lights it. He sits forward and helps me take a sip of the drink.

I shouldn't be here, wherever here is. It's not proper to sit alone in a bedroom with a man I don't know. To drink a second brandy and let him wipe the dribble from my chin. I've been undressed, down to my chemise, some other woman's robe slung over my shoulders for modesty. My skirt is still intact, though ripped to shreds where it caught in the wheel.

My arm is in a sling, tied with wood splints; my fingers are purple and remind me of early spring eggplants. The whole of it throbs and aches.

"The bandages need loosening. If they're too tight, then gangrene will set in." I blink and wait for him to answer, but perhaps the words never left my lips, because he's puffing his pipe and glancing at the outer door.

I lick my lips. Wince as my tongue catches on a stitch, pulls the skin.

"Where—" My voice is like crushed stone. I swallow and swallow. "Where am I?" But I think I've asked this before, because his eyebrows lift before he answers.

"The inn."

"Your room."

He shifts in his seat near the end of the cot and pulls a thin blanket up my legs. "My bed."

I wheeze a laugh and run my tongue against the back of my lip. "The horse?"

"Cut on the pastern. It's been seen to. The buggy's axle snapped."

I nod, but it feels like an arrow to the head. He hands me the handkerchief. Allows me to cry and doesn't look away. He crosses his arms over his barrel chest as he leans back. He is larger than I remember from the asylum; perhaps it is due to the narrowness of the room, the small table. Somehow it is comforting.

I wipe my nose, wad the handkerchief, and push it under my hip. "You found me."

"I heard you, more like." The voices outside rise and then settle again. A man and woman.

"The doctor?" Yes, the doctor and his wife. She kept hold of the light when he took my arm to set it.

Stoakes looks toward the door. The chair squeaks as he presses back into it. "I wouldn't call him that."

"Something spooked the horse."

"Did you see something?"

"I last remember you. You lit the lamps . . ." My vision waffles. "No. Nothing else."

"You'll need a tale. The bone man won't say anything. I told him I found you on Jaffrey Road, and that's the only thing he needs to know."

"Jaffrey Road is the other side of . . . It's not my horse. I borrowed him and the buggy. Mrs. Hargreaves. Thomas Hargreaves."

"Do they know where you were?"

"She does. Oh, my God." I try to sit up. My head swims, then feels like it's being tightened in a vise.

He puts a hand to my shoulder and settles me back. "Give me the address. I'll send a boy."

"Did someone kill my sister?"

He doesn't answer. Just rests his elbows on his thighs and smokes. Apple smoke.

"I went to the war to get away from her," I say. "That's the truth."

"Is it?"

"My husband and I . . . There was always Alice in the way. Always. I've always taken care of her. He knew that . . ." But the vision that comes to me is not the cottage or Benjamin but Kitty. Kitty bent to a crumpled Alice. Holding her hand. Listening to the horrible noise of someone not ready to die. "You told me she didn't suffer. But she did."

"Perhaps she did."

"Why do you work there?"

Stoakes knocks the ash from his pipe to a plate, then lays it crosswise. He takes a draught of his drink—a darker liquor than mine. "My brother Antrim got shot at Bull Run. I was right next to him, just pulling at his sleeve to get him to move. If he'd taken one step. But it got him. Here." He points to his forehead, above the left eye. "Didn't kill him. Wish it had. He couldn't stop the deliriums. Mother couldn't watch out, not that, not a grown boy. So I received a deferment. I make sure to look after him now. That's why I'm there. Him and others."

"I'm sorry."

He nods and lifts his chin. "You're shivering."

"Yes." I pick up the brandy, swallow the last bit.

He shrugs out of his coat and drapes it over my shoulders. It smells of sweet tobacco, and its warmth wraps around me. He sits back and lifts up the pipe again. "Just think. You could have been the one was kind to my brother. Wrapped up his wounds and held on to his hope."

"Your brother matters a great deal to you."

"That he does. As your Alice matters to you."

The stark morning light washes the room. Ada's eyes are liquid blue, pulling me in like a mesmerist. She sits on the edge of the bed, her arm next to my hip. She picks at the fabric, her fingers pushing it to the mattress, then winding it up. She is still in her walking cloak, the pin holding the neck tight and leaving a thin red line where it rubs the skin.

Mr. Stoakes was good as his word, had called for her and then slipped us down the back stairs to a cab he'd hired. She said nothing—just stared at me and then gave the driver a tip when we made it across town to the cottage.

I want Mr. Stoakes in the room; I want him to smoke his pipe and let me cry. Instead it's Ada peering at me as if expecting some answer. And the blue robins circling the ceiling of Alice's old room.

"Well?"

"Well, what?"

She jerks straight and lets out a long sigh. "My God, Marion."

My hand throbs; I need to loosen the splint ties, but when I move to sit, it jostles my arm. I hold my breath for five seconds, then let it out and point at the knots. "This needs to be loosened. The swelling—"

She unties the sling, a piece of gingham crudely cut, splaying it on my chest and thighs. Then she pulls at the cotton strips, one at a time, unraveling the knots, then, "Put your finger here." And when I do, she ties the cotton again without shifting the splint, slowing just for me to pull my finger away and give mercy to the ache.

Thomas was here last night. He followed us up the stairs, his hand sliding along the railing. He's waiting for the lie I'll need to tell now because Ada shut him from the room and told him he was no help in the matter.

"Tell me your story again."

"I was visiting a friend." My lip has scabbed. My tongue hits the back of my teeth as I talk, careful to keep my mouth still as possible. "From Baltimore. From the hospital. The war." I try to conjure a name, but my thoughts spread like a fine mist. "Dinner at the Phoenix."

"Good." The feather mattress plumps as she stands and paces along the windows. "You had lamb and mint. Strawberry tart."

"I don't like mint."

"Stewed apples." The window casing groans as she opens it. The outside noises slip in: horse hooves and boys calling and the constant rumble of people living life. "Someone might ask."

"Thomas will?"

"Yes. He will. And Lionel. I've sent a telegram."

"Help me up." I twist and shove my heel and knee to the bed. I want up. I want clothing. I want my brother to tell me why he lied.

Ada assists, pushing and plumping pillows.

"Is he coming here?" I ask.

She nods. Her eyes flick to me, then she makes a fuss with the sheet that slid sideways. "Did you find your answers?"

"She was pushed. Someone took her to the roof and pushed her over the edge."

Her palms smooth the sheet over my legs. She tucks in the lower corners. "My God."

The light flattens and flashes. Black and white, like a train. There—something white and the whinny of the Morgan. But the room returns to the robins and blues, and a knock on the door interrupts us.

"I let myself in." Cathy's voice is muted behind the door.

Ada rushes over, pulling the door wide, holding it open. She says something I can't quite hear. She taps her chin with her thumb, listening. Nodding. Then Cathy has rounded the doorway, stands at the end of the bed. She grips a leather travel case with both hands.

"You've got yourself in a fine mess." She sets the case to the floor, unpins her traveling hat, and lays it atop my feet. Her eyes graze the scrapes and bruises on my face, stop on the stitch in my lip. "That, unfortunately, will scar." She shrugs. "There are worse things. The arm, for one."

"I was out with a friend. To dinner."

She picks up the water glass and holds it to the sunlight. "Just water?"

Ada steps forward. "We've no potions. We're teetotalers. I could bring chamomile."

Cathy's eyebrow lifts and she sets the glass down before bending to the case and unbuckling it. "I've brought clothing. You really do need new clothes, Marion. I've a shawl you can wear over your chemise. Until we're home." She lays out bloomers, a petticoat, a brown twill skirt. "We'll dye it when there's an opportunity, but for now, this will have to do. Can you stand?"

I push my good hand into the mattress to lift myself; Ada holds me under the arm when I stand and tilt too far forward, digging my toes into the rag rug to maintain balance.

"I'm all right."

Cathy is all motion. Here untying the sling, there the buttons of the nightdress, flicking the bloomers in the air as if she's just pulled them from the laundry line. "Was it only you, then? In the accident, I mean. Were there others involved?" She lifts the bloomers up each of my legs and pulls at the waist to fasten them. "What was her name?"

"Who?"

"Step in." She points to the petticoat. "Your friend. You had dinner, remember?"

Ada gives me an imploring look, then picks up the sling and fusses it around my arm. "I'll have you come another time," she says. "For the girls."

"We should contact your friend. Let her know. And your rescuers. I think a note of acknowledgment would be in order." Cathy pins her hat again and gives Ada a peck on the cheek. "Lionel will talk to Thomas about any damages."

It is glaringly bright outside. The buggy is open, the canvas top folded away, leaving the sun to pound at my skin. Ada says nothing as we depart, just stands at the short iron gate. The windows of the houses reflect the glare. I squint against it. Close my eyes. But the sway and bump of the cab and Cathy's silence make me light-headed and nauseous.

The buggy whip sits perpendicular to the road. Cathy's back is just as straight. She takes a route that skirts the town, and I'm thankful for the reprieve from the sun, for the trees are thick and the light dappled.

I can't stop the images that skim across my mind. That horrid box. The ice baths and white, white walls. Miss Clough's starched skirts. Mrs. Brighton's voice echoing in the hallway. I shudder, as if ice water has dripped on my back. My hands and fingers grow cold and numb. My teeth chatter and clack. I know it's shock.

When we turn to Turee Road, she flicks the reins. "You lie as badly as your brother."

"I was at the asylum," I say.

"Yes. Yes, Ada told me."

"Lionel has Alice's notebooks."

"Does he?" She shakes her head. Gives a quick smile and without warning pats my leg. "I think you're the only one who knew how to take care of Alice."

"I met with a matron. The last one—" I gulp back a sob and cover my mouth. "Someone killed her, Cathy. Someone opened her door and dragged her to the roof and pushed her off."

She chucks her chin and doesn't say anything.

"Miss Clough—"

"Miss Clough?"

"I need to see the constable. I want to add to the complaint."

"What complaint?"

"I told you."

She pulls the reins hard and stops the buggy on the side of the road. The wheels roll and crush the cicada husks and leaves. "What complaint?"

"I made a formal complaint. Against Mayhew."

"Why?"

"For negligence. Now I want it for murder."

"Oh, Marion. You shouldn't have done that."

"I should have done it right away. The first day when I thought . . . But now there's witnesses. There were people who saw it all."

"*What* all? What did they see?" She turns to face me. "What have you started?"

"I don't . . . You were there. Last month. When Ada was. She told me so."

"I wasn't." She shakes her head and turns back to drive. Her skin is splotched. She clenches her jaw, long muscles along the bone tensing and relaxing. "Ada is mistaken."

"Cathy."

"I wasn't there. She wouldn't see me."

Chapter Twenty-Three

My legs can't hold me. I fall back to the bed, bones and chest hollow, listening to Cathy's footfalls upstairs, muted steps on the hall runner, the staccato on the wood. Lionel's voice. Toby's. There's a clatter of pans in the kitchen. No one comes to the room for what seems hours.

"Here." Cathy finally returns. She tilts her head, then offers me a spoon, the liquid sluicing in the bowl. She reminds me of myself once, sitting on the edge of a soldier's cot, hip to leg. "Here," she says again.

I turn my head away; the liquid has a sharp smell. She touches her finger to my chin to tip it, then the medicine slides like velvet across my tongue. Her touch is warm as she caresses my throat, soothing it into a swallow. The liquid is bitter and I rub my tongue on the roof of my mouth to get rid of the taste.

She waits.

The medicine's already doing its trick; my lips don't cooperate, are numb and swollen. I want to know what she's given me. But my mouth doesn't work, and I can't formulate words.

She combs back my hair with her index and middle fingers. "You need to let your sister go."

"I can't." I lean back, my head to the pillow and eyes too heavy to keep open.

She puts her hand on my wrist, just at the edge of the splint, and holds her thumb on the skin. Then she leans close. "There won't be a complaint." She squeezes then, sending a radiating pain up my arm. "You won't ruin this family. I won't let it happen." She twists, just enough that my vision sparks and flashes. "I don't care if someone pushed Alice or if she jumped. I do not care."

I struggle against her, swing my arm, and then push at her chest. The sheet has twisted around my arm, pinning it and tightening like a noose. I gasp a breath and struggle up. "Let go."

"Shush, Marion, shush." She reaches over, takes the sheet end, and unwraps with the care one gives a babe. "Shush. You're having a nightmare."

"You were just here . . ." But I don't finish, my words curdling under her gaze.

Her mouth toys with a smile, one side and then the other, and her eyes are overbright, as if she's just woken from a high fever. She picks at the ties on my arm, but not with any attention. Instead, she bites at a loose piece of chapped skin on her lip, all the while staring at the cut on mine. "What did she do? When the door was opened?"

"I don't . . ."

"You said the door was left open. There are only two choices: stay or flee. She didn't stay. Did she? And if she chose to flee, why to the roof and not down the stairs and out to the woods?" Her eyes grow wide and then shift away, move side to side as if she's unreeling a story.

"Three doors. One, then another, then another. Up the stairs. It's a steep roofline, shale shakes. It would take effort to stay upright. You'd need to balance on the cornice. She'd need to be sure that's where she wanted to be. Wouldn't she?"

Her breath is hot and sour sweet. She rubs her lip. Watches something just beyond my shoulder. "Just to the tip of the building, where the ground is lowest, the drop the longest. That's where she stopped. Arms out, and one foot, then the other. Mm." Her gaze snaps back to mine. "Yes. Just as she told me she would."

My mouth gapes open. I can't move.

"Just as she said. Just as she wanted." She pulls at a button on my nightshirt, then stands and walks the hall to the stairs, the white lace of her shawl aglow. She stops at the turn to the stair, her hand resting on the banister. "Good night."

In the morning, I sit on the covered porch in a rocker, brought here by Cathy and Saoirse, with a side table stocked with magazines and a plate of meats and cheeses. Saoirse has made molasses bread, still warm and aromatic. Lionel stole a slice before clambering down the stairs to join Elias and Amos by the boathouse. He waved as he strode backward, then grabbed up a crowbar and called, "It's all fine." Though I didn't know what he meant, and why he wasn't furious about the wreck of the Hargreaveses' buggy nor worried I might have lost my life after it crashed. No, just, "It's all fine," before hefting the crowbar to the wood and levering out a plank. Amos glances up as he crosses with an old rocking chair slung over his shoulder. He's clean-shaven and wears a felt hat I recognize as one of Elias's. His brown hair still touches his shoulders, but there's more shine in it. It's his eyes that give me pause, though, a gray green that remain a second too long. He gives a quick nod and drops the wood to the rest. Then he shields his eyes and looks up at me. "Are you well?"

"Yes, Amos. Quite well."

But if one were to paint a picture, it would be titled *Invalid*. I don't want it; I am restless, and last night's dreams—for Cathy assures me she did not come down from her room—circle and bite and cower away when I look.

I pull the shawl she's brought me, but it's caught under my hip. I drop the fabric. Even were I to get it loose, it would take a half hour to fling it over my useless arm.

"So tell me, nurse, how tight or not shall I make this?" Cathy had come early, when the light was still but a glimmer of violet and the loons made their morning plaintive calls. "And I've brought this for your sling. Much more fashionable."

Certainly. If one were fond of peacocks and fairies, both of which had been printed on the silk. She's gone to town and promises to bring back something even nicer.

Now I drop my head to the back of the chair and follow the lines of the porch ceiling. There's an old spider's web that flutters between two of the boards and the fried paper and pulp of an abandoned yellow-jacket nest in the corner. Yet the long table is covered in a damask cloth, and breakfast was served on porcelain.

Maybe it's true. Maybe Alice chose to jump from the roof. But then why would Kitty be so adamant? And Harriet Clough? I shift my slipper against the wood and recall the hiss of her starched skirts. Brawders House was as paradoxical as this house, with the fine front vestibule and fancy flowered gardens, and yet the paint on the lock plate of Alice's cell scraped by her fingernails. Maybe it's true. Maybe there's only so long someone can abide a place like that before all hope is squelched. If she jumped. *Just as she told me she would.*

If I could just see the notebooks.

"Auntie." Toby clomps up the porch stairs and runs his palm on the railing before stopping in front of me. He closes an eye and assesses me. Then he moves closer and stares directly into my left eye, so I see only the gold flecks in the blue sea of his. He lifts his eyebrow. "I can see your soul."

"Can you?"

He pushes the chair arm so it rocks, and twists to watch the men in the yard. "We're having a bonfire."

There's a squeal of wood yanked from the building below, then the clap of it to the others. The boards that will be saved. Just the posts and rafters remain. Amos climbs a ladder to what's left of the roof and straddles a beam.

Everyone busy or away. I take a bite of cheese, then swipe a crumble from my skirt. Everyone busy.

"Toby, take the molasses bread to the men."

"I want to have an archery lesson."

"Yes."

Amos's boot swings in time with his hammer.

"I'm going to lie down. Take the bread to the men, all right? I want the house quiet."

"But—"

"Take the bread." I stop him with a soft hand to the arm. "Tomorrow. I promise."

The house is curiously still. The curtains in the parlor and dining room are closed against the swampy heat and glare, cloaking them in a russet light. The furniture and curios feel as if they are encased as a fly in amber. A gash of light from the transom over the door brightens the hall.

My slippers are quiet on the parquet, too loud when I hit a loose square. I traipse the hall, peek into Lionel's office. Dust particles hang in the air, too lazy to fall. There's a half-finished cup of coffee on the corner of the desk. The milk has curdled. My hands tremble. I ball them into fists to stop it. Keep my fingers curled around the splint.

I touch the knob of the cabinet to the left of his desk, the one with the complaints and the notebook that wasn't his to take. Still locked. Each of the drawers locked tight. The desk drawers as well.

There's a loud pop. I freeze and wait. Just the house settling.

I kneel, run my hand under the middle drawer, then drop to my haunches when I find nothing. No key tucked away.

If only I'd been as good with a hairpin and followed Lionel's lessons when we were young. I'd thought it dishonest. Raised my nose and marched inside. The good little girl.

My eye stops on the shelf across, on Lydia's photograph tucked near the back. Easy to miss if walking by but directly in the line of sight if sitting at the desk. Lionel rarely talks of her. As if to say her name brought too much pain.

I slip to the kitchen. Find a knife, a thin fillet knife. I clutch the handle, then hide the blade in the folds of my skirts as I leave the room.

But it doesn't help with any of the locks. It's too wide for the lock itself and too thick to slip in the space between cabinet and drawer. I stride from the room, down the hall to the parlor, to Cathy's tall secretary. The shelves are full of curios. They sit behind the paned glass doors, and the knife turns the lock without much effort. I don't know what I'm looking for. I lift up a vase painted ruby and gold, tip it to see the contents, find it empty save a single gold clasp to a necklace. A bluebird of happiness has a place of honor on the middle shelf, and on the lower a tintype of her mother and father in their Sunday finest, him in proud sideburns and her with round glasses and the hand on her lap blurred because she moved it too soon. I've never met them; they trailed their other daughter to the Ohio Valley sometime past. If Cathy receives letters, she does not share the news.

I push the door shut and turn the latch. There is but a single drawer to the desk, though it is wide and deep. I curl my fingers to the handle and give a good pull. The drawer squeals as it opens, the sound like a banshee shriek in the still of the room. I push my thigh against the front to stop it from dropping out.

The household ledger, green leather with worn corners, seated to the left. Two nib pens resting on a piece of cloth. On the cloth, dark ink stains. A stack of blank paper.

I lift the ledger to the desk, then bend to peer into the back of the drawer. One box. I reach for it, hold it in my palm. It is plain maple, oiled and hinged. I set it atop the ledger and lift the lid. Inside is a crushed-velvet bag, the satin strings drawn tight. I pick at the tie with my good thumb, but the knot is too tight. I twist to hold the end of a string with my other fingers, using the weight of my arm and splint, but there's not a way to untie it, and when I jerk, the splint knocks the box to the floor. I grab it up. Push the bag inside and shove the whole of it to the pocket on my skirt.

The ledger holds the normal pages of transactions for eggs and milk, the Mortons' weekly payments. Cathy's handwriting tilts and whirls, but the numbers are precise. Deposits from Lionel. House money. Sewing thread and rush baskets. I flick the pages back from the present, stop on April 5 the last. Run my index finger down the figures and stop. *Buttons 10-.* It is an exorbitant amount for buttons, even for Cathy, and perhaps I've skipped a line, for my head is beginning to throb. I run my nail along the ledger's line, from the amount to the item.

The other figures are as expected, the daily costs marked with care, the deposits from Lionel generous and regular. How many creditors has he borrowed from? Then again, *May 6: Buttons 10-.*

And June 5, the same.

July 7, double. *Final.*

I roll the pages backward, to the first of the year. There are no payments out of the ordinary until the one on April 5. Each month forward, a purchase of buttons and a figure not less than ten dollars.

Each payment nearly a half of the funds Lionel has given for the running of the household.

The thud of a door startles me. I shut the book, slip it back to the drawer. I grip the knife, then cross the room, my hip catching the corner of the card table as I pass by. I drop onto the settee, lie back, grabbing at a magazine and thumbing the pages.

Footsteps approach from the back, up the kitchen steps and through the hall before stopping at the parlor. "I'm trying to read, Lionel."

There's a shuffle of a boot. "It's Amos, ma'am."

My eyes snap open and I sit up. "Amos."

He doesn't step in the doorway. "We'll be setting the fire. If you want to come."

"I thought that was tonight."

"Ready now." His voice is reedy, and his eyes don't stop watching me. He points at my cinched arm. "Which bone?"

"Both."

"Hell of a thing to heal, all right." And then he rolls his sleeve and holds up his arm, showing off a bend in the forearm just above the wrist. The skin is scarred, white puckers. Old scars.

"How did it happen?"

"I left the lid off the well when I was a boy. My father didn't like it. He gave me a whack with a shovel."

I nod and look away. The sun has crawled higher, and the room is darker without the cut of it through the curtains. "No one to set it?"

"No, ma'am. Just me and him then." He rolls his sleeve down. "You don't remember me."

"Should I?"

"You were a nurse. I was Ninth New Hampshire. Came in from Hatcher's Run."

He could be any soldier, I think. Though his eyes are disconcerting; something that would have been remembered. But not in the last year. Not then. Then the men came too fast, and each was a wound to drain and bandage, a face to wash, a final letter to a mother or wife that sounded the same as any other letter I'd written. I'd lost the mercy to care for them. I'd lost the ability to care for the cause.

"I don't. I'm sorry."

He lowers his head and shifts his boot. "Just a case of the Tennessee Trots." When he looks up, he's smiling and his teeth seem yellow in the muted light. "I deserved a medal for bravery. Just getting through that."

"You and everyone else." I shift on the couch. The box I've stolen pokes into my hip. "You were lucky to live. More of you were buried to dysentery than a gunshot."

"It was a break from marching and fighting, I guess." He runs his hand down the doorframe.

"And now? Where's your family?"

"Got none. Just odd jobs to keep my mouth fed." He glances around the room and settles his gaze back on me. "You looking to kill someone with that?"

My eyes drop to the knife I hold tight on my lap. "No. No, I . . ." I drop it to the lace-covered side table.

Amos gives a quick click of his tongue and looks back to the dining room, then up at the arched window in the front hall.

"You can go now," I say.

"Can I?" He arches his brow. He's laughing at me. I'm alone in the room—in the house—and he knows it. He could do anything, steal anything from my person or the room and I wouldn't be able to stop him. He gives a little nod of his head. "It's cooler in here."

My jaw tightens. "Get out."

He clicks his tongue again.

I feel the thump of my heart in my chest and the hammering throb of it down my arm. I grab the scrolled arm of the sofa to push myself up. "Get out of this house. Get out. Get out."

He stands there, hands raised, and looks down the hall. His mouth moves; he's talking to someone, but I can't hear it.

Lionel strides in the room. He puts his hands to my shoulders, maneuvers me to a chair, and pushes me down. "Stop yelling."

"Get him out, Lionel."

Lionel kneels, hands curled over the chair arms, and gives a nod of dismissal to Amos.

"I found her like this," Amos says. "I just came in to see what the matter was."

"Go mind the fire."

My mouth hangs open. I try to breathe, to pull in a lungful of air, but it's caught in the back of my throat. Lionel puts his hand to the back of my neck and tips me forward, head between my legs. His hand rubs the skin in time with my breathing, until my lungs no longer burn.

"Who is he?"

"Shh. It's all right now."

We stare at each other. He moves away, running his hand through his hair. Then he stops and stares down at the fillet knife on the side table. "What's this for?"

"I think Saoirse left it. Such an odd thing to leave in the parlor."

"You didn't bring it?"

"Why would I?"

"I don't know. I don't . . ."

"I might have needed it."

"He didn't—"

"No."

"Good. That's fine." He picks the knife up by the handle, letting the blade swing as he walks out of the room. "Let's get to the bonfire. I'll have a word with Saoirse later."

Chapter Twenty-Four

Toby dances from foot to foot, hand gripped to the bow he won't let go of, eyes glued to the first flames to lick the bonfire. Elias has a hand to his shoulder, keeping him far back. Safe from sparks. Amos tosses an old chair on the boards. He ignores me. Stays to the far side of the fire. The frays of fabric smoke and catch, the flames climbing to the seat and flaring bright as they eat into horsehair and straw. The smoke lifts, smudging the arch of sky.

Cathy stands on the porch next to me, her hand to her forehead like a captain looking at the sea. She smiles like a satisfied cat. "Saoirse swears she didn't leave a knife in the parlor."

"Oh?"

"Not that it matters." She shrugs. "What's more worrisome is you."

"I didn't do anything untoward. That man—"

"I know what you say."

"What *I say?*" I can't abide this. I reach for the stair railing and take the steps to the yard.

The fire is like a wall of heat. The flames twist like sinews, blue and golden orange.

Lionel holds a plank. A cheroot hangs from his lips. "It'll be a grand view soon," he says, then tosses the board to the pyre.

"Did you tell him to leave?"

"I can't let him go. Not yet." He says this under his breath, his back turned to the fire.

Amos catches my eye and grins. He shoves a pole into the flames and steps around the fire, tamping and coaxing. His hair is flat with wax and bits of ash that have stirred in the air and settled on his head. He swipes at an ember and returns to his task.

Toby lifts up his bow and spins, letting out a yell. Then he turns toward us. "No more boathouse." His lips pull back in a grimace. He pumps his arm and yells once more. Then his shoe catches a root, and he stumbles.

I rush forward, but Amos blocks the way. He wraps an arm around Toby's chest, pulling him upright and back. Then he keeps a hand to Toby's shoulder, leaning down to nod at something Toby's said.

I stride around, stepping over the wood and boards not yet added, and grab up Toby's hand. "You'll stay with me."

"He's all right here," Amos says. "He won't come to harm."

"It's too close to the fire."

"You should be more careful." Amos steps close, his eyes on me. Then he scoops up Toby's bow and holds it out to the boy.

Toby's hand is hot and dry in mine. I pull him to me and move away from this man whose eyes flicker with the fire.

"I want to stay with Amos," Toby says.

"You were too close. You could get burnt."

I move toward Lionel, who stands with his arms crossed over his chest.

"I almost fell," Toby tells him.

Lionel glances at him. "But you're all right?"

"Yes."

"Mmm."

My eyes catch on something at the bottom of the bonfire. I can just make out the charred corners and spines of Alice's journals.

"You're burning them." I look at Lionel. "You took them from Brawders House and now you're burning them. I wanted them."

He squints at me, then blinks when the smoke and heat twist our way. "You should have asked sooner."

I drop down close by the flames. Lionel's used the journals as kindling. The paper burns and curls, each page blackening to ash.

The stench of smoke lingers in my hair. The air is oily and tastes of soot.

Cathy wanted a view; but now there's scars in the ground where the boathouse and glass house once stood, and the wide-open space makes the pond seem too big, as if it's been given the freedom to creep closer. The water is black as ink and slips between the bulrushes. The katydids scratch out a song that crescendos and then dips to a silence that is broken only by the lap of the water.

By spring the ground will be filled with new growth, whether water reeds or garden flowers, who's to know? Either way, Cathy will have erased another bit of the past and decorated it to her tastes.

Once there was a boathouse and a rowboat painted white with red stripes. Lionel fished and I dozed in the bow, head to the sun.

Come along, he'd shout to Alice on the shore. *Come along.*

But she'd just wave and return to her drawing pad. Sometimes she sat, still as a statue, only her eyes casting along with the twists and turns of the little boat in the breeze. And other times she took to the glass house for the day, not minding the heaving heat of the sun beating the windows. Once I found her there in a faint, red cheeked and sodden with sweat, a trowel and the shards of a shattered pot by her head. Soil scattered and the seedlings too fragile to replant. It was my birthday. My twenty-seventh. Benjamin had come to call, and he sat with Father and Lionel in the dining room while the candles dripped wax on the ginger cake.

I stood and gave my apologies. "I'll find her."

Father gave a puff of annoyance. "She's too old for this."

"Yes," I said and took my leave to find the spoiled eighteen-year-old child.

"Get up." I toed her leg and kept my fists to myself.

She sat then, eyes glazed, hair matted and tangled in its torn hairnet.

"Why do you do this?" I jerked forward. Grabbed her shoulders and shook her. "You're my prison. Everything I've wanted has been ruined by you. You've taken it all."

I yanked her to her feet. All the while she kept silent, just a high, strange wheeze she stopped with a clamp of her mouth.

Then her fingers were on my cheeks, her palms pressed along my jaw, and she kissed me on the ridge of my brow, her chapped lips against the skin. She stepped past me, head down and hands holding her skirts, docile and alone as she walked the path. Slowed at the stairs and waited for me. Took my hand in hers as we walked up. She sat in her chair and ate a piece of cake. Smiled at Benjamin when he stood and blustered on. Raised her glass of sherry when Father toasted my health and Benjamin's and our soon-to-be married life. Then she stood without warning and walked from the room, her arm slipping away as I reached for her to stay.

"I'm sorry," I whispered. But she made no motion she'd heard.

That night, she didn't crawl into bed with me. She returned to the glass house. And then, when we'd all moved to the cottage, she kept to her own bed in the room with the robins that wanted so much to be free.

I turn from my window. There should be the tick of the mantel clock. But it is still, the hands at three and twenty. I pace from one corner to another. Pick at the ties on the splint.

The cotton cover smells of lavender; earlier, Saoirse slipped some in the cotton rolls and padding before tying the whole together. "Good as new in a few weeks," she said.

The room is lit now only with the one oil lamp on my desk. I stare at the box I've stolen from Cathy's secretary. The top is a burnt image of a sleigh. Two horses, a man and woman, the White Mountains behind them and a scatter of pines.

I struggle with the latch, the box slipping from under my splinted arm and clattering to the floor. I reach for it and pinch it between my knees. Dig my thumbnail to the top to open it and lift out the velvet pouch. I clasp the satin string in my mouth, working the knot until it loosens and I can dig my finger into the bag. The sharp tip of a pin pokes my skin. With a quick glance at the door—locked, is it locked?—turn the pouch and let the jewelry slide to my lap.

It is a brooch. A peacock of scrolled rose gold. Obsidian eyes. A shellac of blue at the breast. Chips of glass dyed garnet and emerald for the tail. I turn it over, looking for an inscription, find nothing but a cheaply set clasp.

It is familiar, in the way of something seen once, perhaps commented on, and then forgotten. Not mine. Not Alice's. Certainly not Cathy's, whose gems were real.

I drop it to the desk and flop back in the chair. Stare at the ceiling and the glow of the candle. When I blow out a breath, the light wavers, then steadies.

My arm throbs. The cut on my lip has scabbed over and itches. My head aches—from lack of sleep, from the fall—from my sister dying.

On the bed stand is the tonic Cathy has generously poured in my mouth and dripped into my tea. A brown glass bottle without a label, a laudanum more opium than brandy.

I grab it up and push the cork against the edge of the table to open it. If I drink it, I will sleep. If I drink it, I will lose myself in terrible dreams. The liquid sloshes against the glass. I unlatch the shutter and pour the medicine to spatter the ground below.

There's an orange dot out near the far side of the pond. I turn down the oil lamp and pull the shutter just enough to watch. The light jigs and lifts. A cigarette or pipe. Yes. There's the flare as it's lifted to someone's lips and the smoke dragged in. Amos. He stands in one place and smokes. That orange light lifting and dropping and then tamped out.

As if he's watching us.

Chapter Twenty-Five

Cathy startles me awake. "You need to get up."

She grips the back of the rocking chair I'd fallen asleep in sometime during the night and stares at me. She's dressed in a hurry, in a summer chintz that hangs loose around her hips. No petticoats. A button missed at her waist. Her hair twisted into a knot.

I rub my face. Wince when my hand brushes and pulls at the scab on my lip. "What time is it?"

She lets out a frustrated breath, then moves to the windows and pushes open the shutters. The light is early-morning peach and violet, the air cool from night.

"What's the matter? Is it Toby?"

She yanks open the wardrobe and throws out a dress, followed by stockings. "The constable."

"What?"

"The constable." Her words are a hiss.

I stand, tugging at my nightdress, fumbling it off, grabbing and pulling the clothing on. My hands shake. "Help."

Chemise and drawers. Stockings rolled—Cathy's hands tremble, too, as she works the garter buttons.

"Arms out," she says and settles the working stays, circling to my front to cinch it up. Blouse and bodice, stockings and shoes. All the while, she breathes in and out and moves me about like a doll and misbuttons both the blouse and my left shoe.

Finally, she flicks the gaudy fabric for the sling and bungles the knot. She yanks the fabric and jostles my arm.

"Lionel?" I query and pray he's left already.

She shakes her head, her hands busy again with the knot. She's rough as she pulls at my hair, braiding and pinning it. "You make this right."

"It's what I've been trying to do all along."

I nod at her to open the door. Then I take in a breath and hold it all the way down the hall. The men murmur from the parlor. My step hitches. There are three voices. All men. Lionel, yes, I hear his laugh, though there's no mirth in it.

I pull and smooth the sling on my arm. Set my shoulders and enter. "Constable Grent. How kind of you to finally choose to visit. I thought you'd quite forgotten . . ." But my words drain away as the men's gazes swing to me. Lionel at the window, his face blotched with anger. Dr. Mayhew stands next to him, his bowler held to his chest. He gives me a perfunctory nod.

"Mrs. Abbott."

Lionel gestures to the constable before clasping his hands behind his back. "This is Constable Grent. Come for you, Marion."

"Why—"

The constable, whose knee creaks as he crosses one fat leg over the other, fans himself with a sheaf of papers. His white mustache flutters and his eyes peek from his cheeks. His gaze is hard as malachite.

"Do you ignore every complaint," I ask, "or just mine?"

The man lowers his lids and curls the papers. "May I ask after your injury?" Then his eyes pop back open, and he looks at me as if anything I say will be misheard or ignored.

"You may not."

He blinks again. "But I may."

"It was a carriage mishap." Cathy has slipped in the room, closing the door. She lurks near the corner card table and taps a nail to the felt. "I don't think that's illegal."

I pull in a rasp of breath; my knees are too wobbly to move. "You never answered my complaint, Mr. Grent."

The constable rolls the papers in his hands. The tips of his fingers are stained brown from tobacco, and a faint stale smell of mildew wafts from his clothes. "I am here now."

"I have more to add. To my statement."

Dr. Mayhew gives a tight, quick smile. "But I have a counter-complaint. Trespassing on private property. Which you did. And in which"—he points his hat—"you injured your arm."

"I was with a friend in town. At the Phoenix."

"I do recognize there is a bit of road that needs repair," Mayhew says, and looks to Lionel, "so have made payment to Mr. Thomas Hargreaves for the replacement axle."

"No," I say.

Grent flicks the papers on his lap and glances at Cathy, then Lionel. "We would like to talk to Mrs. Abbott. Make sense of this complaint. Alone."

Lionel swallows and sulks to the door, taking Cathy by the arm. "I would like to—"

"Alone, Mr. Snow." And Grent's smile is wide as a walrus's. He waits until the door has clicked shut. His smile remains as he watches me. "Will you sit, Mrs. Abbott?"

"No, I'm quite well here."

The sofa cushion wheezes as Mr. Grent settles back. "Mrs. Hargreaves states that you took their buggy. An Abbot-Downing."

"She offered."

Grent's eyebrows raise near to his hairline. "That is not what she has written." Now he unfolds the papers, licking his thumb and flipping the corners until he finds what he wanted. *"I heard a commotion*

in the barn and could not stop Mrs. Abbott from leaving. She persever-
ated earlier upon the grievances she believes were committed at Brawders
House. I thought I had dissuaded her but was not successful in my
attempts."

I step back. My heel catches the doorstop and twists my ankle.
Ada . . .

Constable Grent coughs.

"That's not true, I . . ." But why wouldn't she say that? How else
does she explain to her husband she's mixed up in this, even if only as
a messenger. "Did you read my complaint?"

"Indeed, I did."

"My sister was pushed from the roof of his asylum."

Mayhew turns to the constable. "As I said." He tosses his hat to a
chair and leans against the window frame. "Your sister was not pushed.
I answered that before, Mrs. Abbott."

"No, you didn't."

He purses his lips. Combs his fingers through his sideburns.

"I believe I did. But let me answer in simple words even a woman
can understand. Your sister picked the lock on her door. She evaded the
ward attendant, found her way to the roof, and took her life."

"What were the attendants doing? While my sister snuck her way
from her room, through whatever other locked doors there may be,
without anyone once stopping her and asking what she was doing?
Someone pushed her."

"Our investigation showed all ward attendants that evening had
done their duty. The rounds sheet was duly checked off at appropriate
times. I put much faith in my attendants."

"And yet you all let someone die." I clench and unclench my hands.
Dig my nails into my palms. "I know about the box. That chair. You
strapped her in. I know someone was watching her. She knew. *She knew*
what you did to that other woman."

He stares at me. His words are careful when he speaks. "Your sister was violent, uncontrollable, and delusional. There were necessary precautions for her safety and others'. That included restraints. The mind can fill with too much chaos, and nothing works. Hydrotherapy worked for a short while. I thought we'd turned a corner."

"The ice baths."

"You know of it?"

I stop myself from saying how much I know and what I've seen. Stoakes and Miss Clough both so careful to remind me to lie. That I had never been there, never seen any of it. "I have heard of its use for consumptives."

"The blood slows, the heart calms, the mind cools. I've seen wonders."

"But not with her."

"You can only leave someone in ice so long."

"Did you leave Beatrice Beecham in ice, or tie her down in the ice?"

He crosses his arms over his checked vest, his thumb playing with the chain of his watch. His attention has shifted to the window. I follow his gaze to the front yard. Elias and Amos push two wheelbarrows to the stone fence to make repairs.

Mr. Grent clears his throat. "Dr. Mayhew."

His glance snaps back to the room. "As I stated, your sister was violent and . . ."

"She was murdered within your facility. As was Beatrice Beecham."

"There is no Beatrice Beecham, Mrs. Abbott. She's a phantom. *Be good or you'll go like Beatrice Beecham.* I've heard the women say it; I've heard the matrons threaten with it."

Grent stands. "Mrs. Abbott—"

"I stand by my report," Mayhew says. "And I stand by the well-being of all those under my care, though you may not believe it. Every last one of them. I won't have you sully my work nor that of anyone else who chooses such a career. You have been speaking to staff. I can guess who. And I will call them to court to state under oath that you trespassed on my property. That you disturbed the peace of unstable and fragile patients all under the irrational notion that someone chose to willfully murder your sister."

Blood beats in my temples. "I will call those same said staff to speak for me. Because someone did willfully kill my sister."

"Who?" He raises a palm. "If those staff believe something so untoward happened, then who?"

My mouth dries up. I sift through the memories—Kitty, Stoakes, Harriet, Alice's notes that she was soon to die—all the innuendos that someone had done something. None of them seeing anything specific. A turn of the head. An open door. "I don't know."

"Why did your sister stop talking?"

I take in a breath, dizzy from the change in subject. "She was fourteen."

"Not when. *Why*." His cheek gives a tic.

"There wasn't any why. It was just Alice."

"Your mother died that year. She was ill quite a while. It often runs in the family, but you would know that, wouldn't you?"

"My mother was of sound mind."

"Mm. Miss Snow intimated you smothered the poor woman. With a pillow embroidered with snap peas. And you ordered her to never say a word, or you'd cut out her tongue."

"No. That never . . ."

"Whether it did or not, it's in her records. Which would, by law, be unsealed. In the case of your formal complaint."

"I didn't do anything of the kind."

"But you did something. Most delusions have an element of truth in them. At least I've found that to be the case. Which element that is can be up for interpretation. Usually determined by those with a medical background. Mm. Poor girl. Every morning to wake up thinking, *If I utter a word, my sister will cut out my tongue*."

"That's a monstrous . . ." My legs shake. "That is a lie."

"She tells the truth or she doesn't, Mrs. Abbott. Which is it?"

"You'd drag a lie into court."

"Just as you would drag insinuations. And no one would believe Kitty Swain anyway."

"How dare you."

"Sit down, Mrs. Abbott." He clamps his hand to my wrist and gives a sharp pull. "Sit down."

I drop to the seat. He releases my arm, sniffs, and smiles wide. Then he signals to Grent to hand over the pages, then scours through them. "Yes. Yes. I see that you were thorough in your complaint. Doors and locks and women dropping from rooftops. And then you returned. A matron told you she saw nothing at all because she was downstairs assisting with another patient. Isn't that correct?"

"She was killed."

He tilts his head. "Harriet Clough has been removed from service. She was negligent, as you say in your complaint, and left a door open that should not have been. I am fully disclosing this in front of the constable so you may record it as you see fit, Mr. Grent. Kitty is a half-wit. She was abnormal in her relations with your sister. That information will not leave this room. Kitty has her own delusions, and the only truth in them is she watched your sister fall. But your sister had no delusions that night. She had opportunity to end her suffering, and she did so." He turns again to the window, a frown pulling his lips. Elias works a stone to the fence as Amos chisels another. Then Mayhew turns to face me fully, a thumb hooked in his vest pocket. "Your complaint is as meritless as the ones your sister chose to incessantly write. All of which will be pulled into court, as will you and your brother and the initial reason for Miss Snow's commitment. She held a small boy out a window and would have let him drop to his death. If you wish to drag all of that into court, you will need to be prepared for the questions. Of your own stability and delusions and responsibilities. Do we understand each other?"

Mr. Grent stands next to Mayhew, a hand to his pocket and an expectant look to his face. "Withdraw the complaint, Mrs. Abbott," he says. "Your father was a good friend; there's no need for this to tar the family. And Dr. Mayhew will be most generous in withdrawing his."

I clamp my teeth. "No."

We are silent. Mayhew picks at his watch chain with his nail. Grent lifts a small spoon from a cup and saucer Saoirse must have served on their arrival. He dips it into the cup and stirs. Knocks the rim of the cup and puts it again on the plate.

"What do you say?" He slurps the dark liquid and balances the drink in his hand.

"No."

"Your sister attempted to kill a child," Mayhew says. "She confessed to holding the boy out the window with the intent of dropping him to the ground. She confessed. And I have a witness to prove it. Do you have witnesses?"

I grit my teeth. The walls narrow until they press against my shoulders and push Mayhew closer and closer until I see the veins in his cheeks. "You've turned it all around."

"I think not." His skin flushes, and he pins me tight with his gaze. "Your sister, if you continue, will forever be known as a monster."

My chest caves. All the breath I've been holding is expelled. Unsteady, I grab for the corner of the card table, knocking it into the wall.

He is right; he will win. I have nothing to give, just innuendo and gossamer strings of stories. I have no money of my own to pursue the matter; Lionel would never support it if I did. And to have Alice known as a monster—no. I can't. I won't.

"Constable, to confirm, the clinic has waived the last months of fees, of which the family was in arrears. Miss Snow's headstone was paid for directly by me; Mrs. Abbott sent me the bill." He lifts his own cup and slurps. Sets it down, then takes the papers from Grent and folds them to his coat pocket. "I believe we are agreed?"

I drop my head and nod.

"Then our business is done. I leave you to your day."

Chapter Twenty-Six

"You were lucky, Marion." Cathy and I watch from the window as Grent hops on one foot, the other in the stirrup, as his chestnut horse curves away from him, avoiding the man's weight. Then the man heaves himself up. Mayhew sits straight, hand on his thigh, his pinky ring glimmering against the black serge of his trousers. He looks to the window, to me, pulling his gloves from his chest pocket.

He slips the gloves on one finger at a time. He swings his gaze to the house, smug face, and tips his hat. He's a liar.

The horses' hooves kick up dust as they trot to the road. Elias and Amos don't look up as they pass by. But Mayhew slows his horse and says something to them. To Amos. Receives a shake of the head and a turned back.

Lionel closes the front door and stops in the entryway. He claps his hands. "Well, then. Who wants a drink?"

Cathy stares at me, her eyebrow lifting. "Is it over, Marion?"

"I withdrew the complaint."

"Well, then," she says. "We can finally give Alice her rest."

Lionel busies himself pouring brandies into three glasses. He hums, and then laughs, turning to hand us the drinks. "I can say, that gave me a start, the two of them showing up. Just . . . well, a start. As if I'd done something wrong."

His cheeks are red, a jovial host. He skirts a look around the room and out the window, looking everywhere but at me. "It *is* over, isn't it, Marion?"

I slug down the brandy. It burns the back of my throat. "I'll have another."

Cathy makes a small noise of approval, then lifts up the bottle from the sideboard. She holds it by the neck, letting it swing so the liquor sloshes against the glass, then pours too much. The brandy trickles over my hand to the floor. She lifts the corner of her mouth in a smile. "My apologies."

The bottle is set back with a snap. She raises her glass. "To Alice."

I throw the drink in her face.

She blubbers and spits and blinks. "What are you—"

"You have no right to say her name." I put the empty glass next to the bottle and move to the door.

"You're just like her," she says.

I hesitate, my hand to the doorframe, then lower my gaze to the floor. "I'm sorry. The morning's events have overcome me. I'm not in my right mind."

She throws her glass; it shatters against the wall just by my head. "You should be careful what you say. You might end up just like her."

"Stop it." Lionel steps between us. He presses his hand to Cathy's shoulder.

"Get your hand off me." Her words are low as a hiss.

"New life," he says to her. Then he looks at me. "New life."

I give a curt nod and walk out.

Most delusions have an element of truth.

Not snap peas. The pillow was embroidered with more delicate flowers. Sweet alyssum.

My mother's eyes so hollowed with death. I held her gaze. One slow blink of entreaty. I dreaded this day, no matter how often I prayed for it.

"I can't."

Her mouth spread into a grimace. *Please . . .* Pleading, her voice a tight wheeze. Pushing the pillow at me and *please.*

I took the pillow. "Wait in the hall, Alice."

But she didn't. She spied it all from the doorway.

And after, the pillow still gripped tight in my hand, I turned to my sister. "There is no cruelty in mercy."

She stared at the pillow's tassels. Such a cheerful spring green.

"You must never say a word."

But mercy to one is cruelty to another.

"I'm sorry." My throat tightens against that shame of what I've done. *You must never say a word.* It is my fault. I am culpable for all of it.

A thump to the door of my room makes me jump. "Not now."

Another thump, quieter, like a soft kick to the frame. The light from the hall glows under the door. Two feet in shadow. One foot then resting on the instep of the other. A toe lifting and tensing.

"Auntie?"

I cross to turn the key.

Toby stares up at me. He's carrying the magic lantern, held tight to his belly and chest. Both pockets of his trousers bulge with rectangle boxes that poke the fabric. "You missed dinner."

"I wasn't hungry."

"I thought we could watch a show."

"Well. I see." I glance down the hall to the parlor.

"They're playing cards," he says. "Old Maid." Then he shrugs.

"That's a terrible game."

"It's for babies." He lugs the lantern to the desk, pulling the slide boxes from his pockets and stacking them in readiness. He grabs the matchbox from the floor and hands it to me to light the oil. He turns the machine so the lens faces the wall, then digs through the mending for a petticoat to drape over the rocking chair. But the flicker of light is half on the cloth and half on the wall.

"Here." I move the petticoat to the wardrobe, closing the top of it in the door. I gesture to the rocker. "Now, you can take the seat of honor."

He closes the door, then clambers to the chair. He doesn't rock but sits still with his hands in his lap and legs hanging loose. "I brought *Old Mother Hubbard*. And the one Alice had in the trunk. But not *The Presidents* because I know them all. Do you know them all?"

"I do." I tilt the top slide box to read it. *The 7 Wonders of the World*.

"Do you know the vice presidents?" he asks.

"Have you watched these?"

He shakes his head. "Are they interesting? Because the presidents aren't."

"There's pyramids and great statues and marvelous magic gardens." I can't open the box one-handed. "Can you?"

He pulls off the lid and reaches for the first slide, pinching just the edge. "Can I put it in?"

I nod and take the box, resting it in my lap.

He swings the hinge and slides the glass in place. The image, a bright wash of greens and browns and pinks, spills across the wallpaper. When I turn the lantern, the image flickers against my sleeve. A morass of flowers, the door to a building, open, a man shown from the back, in a tall hat and his hands clasped behind him. Just the shoulder and the arm of a woman clad in pink, the rest of her body outside the glass frame. There is a black "1" at the bottom of the image.

"The Gardens of Babylon, I think." I pick out the first card from the box and tilt it to read in the image's light. But it isn't right; it is written in pencil, the letters so faint I must bend close to make them out as I read aloud. *"ONE: I saw her with him—"*

"That's Papa," Toby points. "By the barn."

I stare at the image on the wall. Lionel. In the shadows of the barn, the gray-and-white muzzle of Cathy's dapple mare. Cathy's hand outstretched. Cathy in pink with lace at the wrist. "It can't be . . ."

I return to the lines of text on the card, scanning the words.

> —and he said no not you I do not want you anymore you've ruined everything. And she said she wouldn't leave and then he pushed her and said he's chosen. Don't come here anymore! He said. But she did come.

Nothing on the card's back.

Toby picks at his lip. "Why did she paint him into the Blableeon Gardens?"

"Babylon," I mutter, then replace the card and pick out the next.

> TWO: We're going for a row, Let's go in the boat, Liddie. And Lydia said—I'm not feeling well. But the fresh air is good, Cathy said, and, Alice mind the babe, you can do that, can't you, Alice? He's napping, anyways. He wasn't, he was on my lap and we were watching the Dragons fly on the water and the red leaves and Lydia said—I have a sore stomach. But I think she was with child. She smelled different but she got up and said she'd walk because they often did in the woods.

I run my finger over the edges of glass, until I find the last card.

> SEVEN: He tied the rope around her chest and said don't let go of that end, Alice, it's dark.

"Auntie."

"Not now, Toby."

"Change the slide."

"Not . . ."

Alice, it's dark. We both pulled and pulled with the rope around a tree trunk to hoist her because of the grasses. Her skirts were terrible heavy with water and—

The light is blank, too bright. Toby has pulled out the slide and grabs for the box in my lap.

"No. Toby, no."

"I want the next—"

"No."

But he has the box and holds it over his head. His mouth curves down and he glares.

"Put the box down."

"No." He tucks it under his arm, thin chest heaving. "I want to see the next."

My hand sweats; I can barely hold the card. It slips away, flutters to the floor. "Give those to me."

He steps back, knocking over the mending basket. I watch his eyes glide to the door. He tenses and bolts. I grab his arm, jerking him back hard enough he can't keep hold of the box. It thunks to the rug, the lid springing open, the slides rolling from the case. Six slides.

His free hand claps against his pocket. He makes a high wheezing noise, and I feel the trembling all the way to his bones. I've petrified him.

"I don't want to see *The 7 Wonders.*" My voice is rock rough. I let his arm go, caress it, then kneel to pick up the box, to gather the slides. One has cracked in two. I find the card I'd crushed and dropped. Push it into the box, then grab it up. "I want to see *Old Mother Hubbard.* Can we see those?"

How wary he is. He knows I'm hiding something. I set the box to the end of the bed, just long enough to push myself up with my good arm. Then I move it to the mantel. Set the box next to Benjamin's photograph, out of reach. I pat the top. "Another time for this."

"Why can't I see those? Maybe Alice painted me on a slide too."

"No. I don't think so."

"How would you know?"

"Because I do."

"I don't believe you."

"Well." I shrug. "You should." I hesitate at the *Old Mother Hubbard* box. "Have you seen these?"

He gives a sharp nod and I release a long breath. No surprises.

"*Old Mother Hubbard*, then."

Chapter Twenty-Seven

How pretty the paintings. Alice has replaced the original slides with a new set of her own design. Her hand so light, the images swirling with movement and color. The faces so detailed she must have used the smallest of mink brushes.

Look at the paisleys on Cathy's dress. She wears a pretty shawl, lemon yellow and patterned with ferns. Her smile is curved and curls around her ears. Lydia's hand rests on her belly. It is flat; it is with child. *Alice mind the babe.* And Alice holds Toby in her arms. In the background, the tree leaves squint and blink and reflect on the surface of the pond.

Slide by slide, I watch. Once, then again. Seven slides, numbers plain and neat on the bottom. Number six is split in two. Six cards. 1, 2, 3, 5, 6, 7.

> *THREE: It was hot the sun was very high up. They went toward the Narrows and they shouldn't have. No one should go in the Narrows, and they did.*

The perspective is from on high, as if Alice were perched in a tree. I yank the desk chair over, clamber close to stare at the slide.

It's our little rowboat. *The Mariner.* Alice has painted the overhang of rock that looks like a gargoyle. All along the stony banks of the Narrows, creatures point with fingers sharp as sharded glass to the little boat and the two women. One dark head. One light. Crinoline skirts as wide as the boat. Lydia's arm hitched forward, elbow resting on the lip of the boat. Cathy seated behind. The oars have been pulled in. Rest neat on either side of the shell. Cathy's arms are outstretched, something taut between her fists.

I replace the slide with the fourth. I don't need the missing card. Not with this image.

No boat. One woman. Arms floating wide, facedown in the water, her head covered in a cheerful hood—lemon yellow and patterned with ferns—tied with three tight knots at the neck.

> *FIVE: Then Cathy came back and walked right past me and said nothing.*

My breath stops. Cathy holds her skirts. They are wet, as are her sleeves. She is in motion, tramping the slope from the boathouse. But it is her eyes that make me clutch my breath. Death sits in them.

> *SIX: Lionel came home and ran straight down to the pond calling Liddie! Liddie! He made me give Toby to Saoirse and he got an oar from the boathouse and a rope and he said, follow me. Liddie he called! It was getting dark. We found her by the steep rock in the Narrows. Lionel pushed the oar in to see if she would grab it but she was dead.*

I hold the left half of the slide in front of the light. The top of her head, the fabric hood snagged in a tangle of roots.

On the right half, Lionel scrambles down the slope to the water.

> *SEVEN: He tied the rope around her chest and said don't let go of that end, Alice, it's dark. We both pulled*

and pulled with the rope around a tree trunk to hoist
her because of the grasses. Her skirts were terrible heavy
with water and muck. And he laid her down. Liddie! he
said & he stared at me. & then pulled at the hood but
the knots were terrible tight. I caught it in my teeth and
ripped it. Her head bounced and swiveled I thought she
would say something but she was dead. Liddie! he cried.
CATHY, I yelled. IT WAS CATHY.

I can't look again. Lydia's eyes, pale blue like Toby's, are filled with surprise. Forever filled with surprise.

And betrayal.

Instead, I turn the card over. *I saw.*

The lantern's lamp sputters; I've burnt all the oil from the pan.

One by one I replace the slides, the cards. Close the box. *The 7 Wonders of the World.*

It's just a story. One of the many delusions Alice so fervently believed to be true.

And even if it was true . . . even if she told, who would listen? Look at the complaints that moulder in Lionel's drawer.

The little boat sits on the sea now, just a dot near the horizon line. It's a dream. I know it's a dream. The boat is blue and white, the horizon deep red, the water glassy smooth. A picnic by the sea, long bristle grass bent to the sand, a lift of rock full sunned, warm on one side, the other slick with shadow.

"Alice is dead," I say, but Lionel doesn't hear me. He's far down the curve of pebbles, his trousers rolled and one suspender loose against his thigh. He picks up stones, turns them in his hand before arcing them to the water and watching the punctures to the sea skin before bending for another rock. His hair is too long and very red; he pushes it from his forehead and keeps his hand up to scan the small cove.

A flight of laughter from the far end, in the dark shade of an overhanging rock, two girls small as dolls who swish their hips as they exit to the light. They move like porcelain figurines, eyes painted bright black, lips brushed deep pink, heads swiveling to look to him and then to each other.

Alice sits on a flat outcrop, hands crossed on her stomach, skirts gathered to her knees. The sun catches the fine blond hair on her shins. She scratches her calf, then settles back down with her head on my thigh. She watches Lionel slice the water with another rock.

Her hand reaches for the slate and chalk we've brought in place of paper and ink. She marks it and turns the board to me.

He's in love with Cathy.

She looks up at me, green eyes flecked with gray. Sometimes the gray darkens and shifts with the light and mood. Her chest lifts and jostles with a laugh.

The wind lifts the brim of my bonnet. Ruffles Alice's skirts and Lionel's hair. The water curls and buckles, sharp edged and annoyed.

"He can't marry her. He's marrying Lydia. It's already settled."

Alice rubs the side of her hand to the board, then jabs her chalk to it. *You don't see. You don't listen.* She bends her knees and cradles the board to her stomach. Then she pulls a strand of her hair, rolls it around her fingers. She shrugs and points to the board again. *I saw.*

"A *hoo*!" Lionel calls from the other end of the cove. He stands on a log weathered gray from salt and waves. Such long arms. Wide hands. Still the smile of a boy shifting under the mask of a man.

There's another peal and giggle from the little dolls at the other end of the cove. The wind waffles, blowing their skirts this way and that.

I button my shawl. "It's getting cold."

"Are you all ready yet? I'd like to get back to my lecture. I haven't finished it."

My shoulders and neck go stiff. Benjamin has ambled over the hillock. I don't remember him coming, but there he is, and Alice's board clatters to the rock as she sits up. Her legs are pimply with goosebumps. She gives a great shiver and pushes her skirts down.

The sun slips behind the dunes, tipping the sky peach, and the boat rolls over the horizon.

I grip my collar with one hand and gesture for Lionel to come back. I call to him. But he's not listening, has his hands clasped behind his head and stares at the water.

"Lionel! Come back."

With a twist he turns his torso to acknowledge he's heard, then points to the empty stretch of sea. "They went in the boat. They went away in the boat."

The earth has settled on Alice's grave, a little more each day. As if it is pulling her deeper into the ground. In another month the leaves will cover it, and a month after that the snow will fall and settle on the gravestone like a wreath. Now there is no stone, no leaves. Just the dried stalks of flowers and the arrow Toby left. I move to the head of the grave, toeing aside twigs and cicada shells, then shove the arrow to the earth, the quill feathers pointing skyward. Something to mark the spot until the stone is cut.

"I see, Alice. I hear. But I don't know what to do." It is certain that should I bring the slides and cards to the constable, he will return them to Lionel who will inform Mayhew—or worse, the public asylum—of my own troubling behavior. A madwoman believing a madwoman. I need a witness.

Saoirse *tsks* and grimaces as she replaces the cotton ties on my splint with clean strips. She leans over the kitchen table, her palm under my fingers, pressing each of my nails and waiting for the blood to bloom underneath.

"You should have been a nurse," I say.

She lifts her shoulder and pinches my thumb. "Not a week here without some sort of scrape or bruise to look after." She sits back. "It looks well."

"Thank you."

The door to the main house is open, as is the door to the garden. But it gives no succor. The air is heavy damp, and nothing stirs it from its sleep.

"May I trust you?" I murmur.

I don't know if she heard. She winds the cotton and puts it to the cabinet shelf, then leans her hands to the white wood counter before grabbing up a towel to wipe it down.

"Saoirse, please."

She folds the towel and lays her hand on it. "I heard you."

"I think Cathy killed Lydia."

Her sigh is long; she stares out at the yard. "You know what you're accusing?"

"I do. Alice saw."

"Child—" Her voice is sharp. She shuts the door to the house, then stamps to the outer door and shuts it too.

"Why do you think she was put in that place? You know her. She's not violent, she's never once . . . She didn't try to kill Toby. She tried to save him. That's what I think. And maybe it was all in her mind, that he was in danger. Or maybe not." I spread my hand to her. "Maybe not. She saw what she shouldn't, and Cathy must have paid someone to, to . . ." A sick dread claws up my stomach. I stand. The chair tilts and falls against the wall. "All that money in the ledger. She wrote *Buttons*. Once a month from the first week Alice was committed. Cathy paid someone to kill her. Because Alice knew the truth. She saw her murder Lydia."

"Do you listen to yourself, child? Do you but listen?"

"I'll prove it. And the constable will listen to you. If you tell him." I reach across the table to her. "Saoirse. All you need to do is watch."

She opens her mouth to say something, but instead swallows and picks up the calico cloth for the sling and folds it around my arm. She is careful with the knot, and her touch lingers on the back of my neck. "You never left things be, did you?"

I weave my hand to hers. "Tomorrow night. After Toby's asleep. Make her favorite dessert."

"What will I be looking for?"

"Her guilt, Saoirse. Her guilt."

Chapter Twenty-Eight

Cathy is suspicious. She watches me over her wineglass, the ruby red of the liquid sparkling from the oil lamp. She has pulled her feet up on the settee, her skirts *(Oh, Cathy, but pineapples and oranges are such a marvelous pattern; I would never think to pair them!)* splayed all around so she looks like a barrel of fruit on the steps of the general store.

Lionel finishes hanging a sheet to the wall. As he moves close to the convex mirror, I see his eyes in the reflection wander to me and then to Cathy. Wary there will be a fight. Does he know what Cathy did? Or is the tale she tells, of desperately trying to save Lydia, what he believes? What makes him able to sleep through a night? This woman committed my sister to keep her from telling the truth. And had her killed before Alice could tell the truth to me.

Her gaze is flat and steady. All I can see is the lantern slide: skirts and cuffs dripping wet as she leaves the boat for the shore. Leaves Lydia blind and suffocating under the hood, every breath a drag of water to the lungs instead of air. Flailing for any purchase on the steep rocks and instead gripped and clawed by roots and river rush.

"You outdid yourself with the meal," Cathy says.

"Saoirse made it. I merely suggested . . ." But here my hand trembles as I pull the clip from the magic lantern and lift the oil pot. It's full. It's as full as it was when I checked prior to dinner, when I checked as she chose a wine. The box of slides sits at the ready. "Lionel, can you?"

I gesture him over with my good hand, give a wave to the other. "I feel so helpless."

"Soon to be healed," he says and takes a match to the wick. His back is turned to Cathy. He shakes the match and murmurs, "Thank you."

I stare at him. My smile is taut. "Sit down. Saoirse is bringing dessert. Your favorite, Cathy. Raspberry Charlotte. And we're going to watch *The 7 Wonders of the World*."

"I've seen it," Cathy says.

"Oh, I don't believe so." I jiggle the box so the lid pops free. The slides tinkle against each other.

"Since this evening comes with Raspberry Charlotte—with cream?—then I'll suffer through this."

Cathy taps her wedding ring to her glass and watches as I take out the first slide. I look to the hall, for Saoirse should be here now. I turn my hand and wipe the sweat from my upper lip with my knuckle. I catch myself in the mirror, face ablaze in red, looking every bit the terrible liar Cathy thinks I am.

Lionel sits in the armchair, resting his chin on his palm. "Toby would like this too."

"He's seen it," I say and turn the slide round and round in my fingers. "And he's already asleep. There's no reason to—"

"Raspberry Charlotte," Saoirse announces. She waddles forward with the tray of cake slices and offers one to Cathy. "The first of the bunch. I added extra sugar and vanilla."

Cathy glances at me. "You spoil me."

"I am making amends," I say.

She digs her fork through the berries and cream, slices the soft cake beneath, and raises it to her mouth. Then, "Aren't you eating any?"

"I'm not hungry," I say.

Lionel takes the other two plates. "More for me, then." He sets one to the side table and the other to his lap.

"If I were a queen, I'd make you eat it." Cathy stabs the air with the fork. A berry slips off to the rug. "Then I'd know if it was poisoned." Her laugh is light. Then she pops the piece in her mouth and chews.

Saoirse stands directly in front of the lantern light. The silver refracts the lamp, and Lionel squints when a beam hits him. "I'll go, then." Her gaze moves from me to Cathy.

"No." I stare at her.

Cathy raises an eyebrow.

"She might as well stay until we've finished," I say. "You're nearly done, but Lionel has a whole other piece."

"Get me another glass of wine, then. And move out of the way. You're blocking the showing." Cathy's jaw shifts back and forth as she finishes another bite.

Now Saoirse has moved to the sideboard. She busies herself with setting the tray just right, with picking up the wine bottle, her look to me as she turns around full of nerves. She presses her lips tight and looks toward the hall as if she'd rather be anywhere but here. As if she's lost the nerve. All I need is a witness. Someone who will believe me. Believe Alice.

When you see, call for Elias. Send him for the constable. It's all you will need to do.

"Do you want to read the narration, Lionel, or shall I?"

"I want to eat the cake." He has the face of a man satisfied that all has settled to peace in his abode.

"No, I think it should be you. You read so well." I pluck the cards from the box and hold them out.

He doesn't argue. Just balances his plate to his knee and takes the cards.

The hinge on the lantern squeals as I open it. I hold the slide up to make certain I set it right, then push it in place.

Lionel straightens the cards and clears his throat. *"ONE."*

The sheet before us fills with color. A barn door. A man in a tall hat and a woman pleading from just outside the screen.

"*ONE: I saw her with him and he said no not you I do not want you anymore you've ruined everything. And she said she wouldn't leave and then he pushed her and said he's chosen. Don't come here anymore! he said. But she did come.*" He pushes his glasses up the bridge of his nose and blinks. He peers at the image. I watch him in the mirror, the way his brow wrinkles and he looks puzzled. "I don't . . ."

Cathy holds her fork in midair. "What's this?"

The hinge squeals. I replace one slide with the next. "Go ahead, Lionel. Card two. It's perfectly marked. Alice was fastidious about things like that."

"*TWO: We're going for a row, Let's go in the boat, Liddie. And Lydia said—I'm not feeling well. But the fresh air is good, Cathy said, and, Alice mind the babe, you can do that, can't you, Alice?*"

The air is still and so brittle I feel it will crack.

I yank the cards away. "You don't need a slide for the next bits. You already know the scenes." I press my thumb to the cards, then snap them up in my grip. I don't need to read them. They have burnt themselves to my brain. "In fact, I'll just read the last card. In case you've forgotten specifics. *SEVEN: He tied the rope around her chest and said don't let go of that end, Alice, it's dark. We both pulled and pulled with the rope around a tree trunk to hoist her because of the grasses. Her skirts were terrible heavy with water—*"

Cathy cries out. Her plate tumbles to the floor, leaving a streak of red jam and bits of cake. She balls her hands into fists and pushes herself off the seat. "What are you doing?"

"*And he laid her down. Liddie! he said & he stared at me. & then pulled at the hood but the knots were terrible tight. I caught it in my teeth and ripped it. Her head bounced and swiveled I thought she would say something but she was dead. Liddie! he cried. CATHY, I yelled. IT WAS CATHY.*"

Lionel crouches over, his hands scraping his skull. "Liddie . . ." His chest heaves as he slurps in air.

"Did you know, Lionel? Did you know what she'd done?" I squeeze the cards in my fist.

"My God . . ."

"You can get Elias now, Saoirse."

Her head wags back and forth, and her hands grip the edge of the sideboard.

"Tell him to send for the constable."

"No. No constable." Cathy's voice stutters. She lurches up, grasping the slide box. "Didn't I tell you, Saoirse? Didn't I say? Do you listen to yourself? Just like Alice, just like her."

Lionel bolts from the chair, grabbing my arm and dragging me out of the room down the hall. My shoes catch and slip on the floor, pulling the rug like an accordion. My elbow hits the railing, and I cry out as the splint ricochets into my ribs.

"Let me go."

His grip digs into the soft of my skin. I yank and pull.

"Let me go."

"Put her in her room." Cathy follows behind, pushing at his back.

A high screech careens off the walls. I catch Toby from the corner of my eye, standing behind us on the landing, his hands covering his ears. My God, did he see?

But still Lionel drags me. He is rage red, the muscles on his jaw like sinew. He kicks the door wide open. It smacks the wall and snaps back hard against my cheek and shoulder. He jerks me fully into the room and throws me to the floor.

I hear the grind of bone before I feel it. Before my vision bleeds red and white. The splint is cockeyed, the cotton padding peeking out. I pull my arm to my stomach and curl tight, shuffling away from him until I am tucked between my bed and desk.

Cathy pushes past him and drops next to me. "Give me the cards." Her hands tremble at her chin. When she tries to reach for me, I kick her away. She grapples and digs into my hand, pulling my fingers back until the cards I've kept hold of are free.

The desk leg screeches against the wood, sliding, then pummels my shoulder. There's a flutter of papers as the desk totters. The ink stand slides to the floor, upending the bottle and spraying black ink everywhere.

My stomach wrenches then. The velvet pouch and brooch are upended too. I push myself to my knees, scramble to grab it. But Cathy's faster. It's in her grip. Her expression twists, her mouth ugly and tight. She shakes her head, a snap of judgment in her eyes.

It comes to me, absurdly then. The clasp on the rose gold resoldered in silver. "It's Lydia's. Why do you have—"

"It's mine."

My eyes cut to the wall between this room and Lionel's office. As if I can see through the plaster and lath to the one picture of Lydia hidden on Lionel's shelf. There. It's there on her left breast.

The braided cord that holds my keys is stretched from my wrist, the fabric cutting into my skin before it breaks and the whole of it drops away.

"You go out when I say you will." Lionel's entire body shakes. He bends over me, pointing his finger at my face, then tensing his hand to a fist. "No more."

I shrink back against the wall and raise my arm to my head, squeeze my eyes shut for the punch that's coming.

My wrist throbs and lies dead in my lap. A drop of blood spreads in the folds of a white cotton tie. Then another. It is from my lip, which I've bit or split, the skin pulled from the stitch. Not from him.

"No, Lionel. No no no . . ."

The toe of his shoe pushes against my hip. I curl tighter.

But the blow doesn't come.

Cathy pulls in a breath, one gulp of air, then another. "You can go home now, Saoirse." Her voice trembles. "We'll take care of her tonight."

A slam of the door. The turn of the key.

I scramble across to grab the knob.

But it is to no avail. I can twist and pull as much as I wish, and pound my hand even longer. Peer through the keyhole at the empty hallway. Push my ear to it and hear the choked sobs of a little boy somewhere above and the shush of the woman who is not his mother.

The bones in my arm rasp and grind. I drag in breath that judders out. My vision curls and shoots spikes of black. I can't pass out now. I can't.

There's a thump behind me, next to the window. A ladder. Then the shutters slammed shut.

"What are you doing?" I scrabble across the bed, knocking against the glass. "Lionel. What are you doing?"

I grab the window frame and tug. The frame sticks, and with one good hand it is impossible to dislodge. The sharp thump of a board to the shutters, then the strike and riposte of the hammer sends me reeling back to the bed. He's nailing me in the room.

"No."

I twist from the bed, the coverlet sliding off and tangling around my feet, dragging across the floor to the window over the kitchen garden. I press my hand to the glass to peer out. The yard is empty, though the back door is completely ajar. I open my mouth to yell down, but then the ladder knocks against that wall and swings the next shutter closed. The nail is sent home. Darkness swallows the room.

I am jailed.

I've stopped yelling. It only makes Toby cry out. His voice—hoarse and edged with exhaustion—comes muffled from his room and has muted and thinned as the time crawls by. He starts pounding his door, little furious fists. They have locked him in too.

I lie on my back. Stare at the ceiling and the shards of light that manage to slip through the shutters. The sun will set the pond aglow with gold and then drop like a stone behind Barrow Rock. Night will approach and the slits of light will be snuffed.

Lionel knew.

My wrist and fingers are swollen, the skin hard and cold. The bone is at a horrible angle. I run my thumb along it, feel the poke of it, wonder if I have the stomach to push it in place. But the lightest of touches makes me dizzy and faint, as if the floor has been lifted along one side. I've held the hands of enough men who had proper doctors to fix this. Even a dose of chloroform would not stop my scream. How I regret throwing away the tonic. How I regret trusting Saoirse.

A scraping noise jerks me awake. A tray slides across the floor and bumps the rag rug. Saoirse's crouched down, one hand to the key in the lock, the other snaking back from the tray. She peers up to the bed, expecting me there and not in the corner behind the desk.

"Saoirse." My whisper is rough and too loud.

Her head swivels toward me, her gray-blond strands loose, her eyes rheumy and weak in the feeble light. She ticks her tongue to her teeth, then picks up something behind her and slides it across the floor. A white tin chamber pot.

The tray holds four slices of toast, a scrambled egg, and a sliced apple. No silverware. A pewter water jug. Not glass.

"Saoirse." I dig a heel into the floor to scoot forward, all the while coddling my arm. My hand is numb, but not the wrist. Not the break. I clamp my jaw, swallowing back a keen of pain. Scoot forward again. "Why?"

She shakes her head. "'Tis a cursed family, this one." Stands and hobbles back, pulling the door shut with a click and clunk of the lock.

The water jug is full and sloshes over the top as I slide it close. I bend to it. Lick the drops, then lift it high and drink. It is laced with brandy or another liquor; Saoirse's showing her guilt for betraying me. Apologizing with a sop of alcohol to ease my distress. That she caused.

A laugh balloons in my throat, distends it, and then pummels its way out. I should have known. It was careless.

The chamber pot clatters and wobbles like a top when I kick it. When I kick it again it careens off the wall and lands facedown and at the tip of a pair of shoes.

They are odd shoes. Women's shoes in blue leather and buttons saffron orange. The tops along the shin curve out like wings. Skirts obscenely short, bare legs pale and showy. A tattoo creeps the left shin, from under the shoe's tongue to the bone of the kneecap. Black-ink roses, petals picked and chewed by aphids. The right shin is flayed of skin and muscle, just bone and sinew and flecks of soil.

My breath rasps.

There's a chattering noise, the click of teeth when a body's too cold. *Click click click.* I won't look up. If I do, I know it will be Alice's face.

Chapter Twenty-Nine

All day I listen to Cathy's and Lionel's footsteps tracking paths through the house: parlor to study, study to dining room, dining room to front door. In again and up the stairs to stop at Toby's door, their own, down to the kitchen, whispers rough and low as they pass my door. Once there was Saoirse. Her shadow flickered under the doorframe, the bell of her skirt swaying. Then the shadow petered out as she walked away.

I shift my hip; some loose paper crumples underneath as I move. And I've wet myself. No matter how I tore and yanked at all the under-layers I couldn't get them off. Now I lie with piss drying along my thighs and soaked in my skirts.

My mouth is bone dry, my tongue sandpaper rough against the roof. My water jug is empty; I finished it in the night. Now it sits on the side table by a candle stub and a spot that once held a matchbox.

I push myself up with my elbow. Pain flares through my arm and across my shoulder. I grab at a bedpost and clamber upright. I blink to stave off the dizziness, and shudder with cold. My fingers throb as if on fire, though they are losing circulation, blue and white at the tips.

Think.

My brother has locked me in this room. Tomorrow he'll realize his anger is out of bounds with whatever punishment this is, and he'll let me out. No. Not anger. Rage. So much rage.

There's a thud against the wall, just behind the wardrobe. One, or both of them, in Lionel's office. I cross the room and bend to the keyhole. The hall is empty, the office door shut.

"Listen to me." But my voice is parched and no more than a breath. I rest my forehead against the wood.

A squeak of a door. I squint again. Calico skirts, blue and peach. Cathy bounces the palm of her hand against her leg. When she approaches, the skirt's swirls and flowers grow ever large and block my view completely. Then it's her eye, obsidian and not blinking, staring through the keyhole at me. "Not now," she says. Her gaze glides to the side then rolls back. With no other words, she stands and returns to Lionel's study.

I crumple to the floor and jar my arm enough the pain knifes up the bones, and I gasp a breath.

The ties on the splint are too tight. I press my nailbeds, one by one, hoping for the blush of color that signifies blood is circulating. But the beds are white now. The tips numb.

My teeth are useless against the knots, not as easy to loosen as the velvet pouch with Lydia's brooch. It's an odd thing for Cathy to have in her possession, like a trophy. I can't think Lionel would have proffered his dead wife's jewelry as a wedding gift to the second wife. But there it was in her drawer. Perhaps she has Alice's locket somewhere too.

I need the scissors. I crawl to the sewing basket, scrabble my hand through the mending—Toby's short trousers with the rip on the pocket, Alice's chemises too intricate for the rag bin—and clamp my hand on the scissor case.

The splint clatters to the floor as I cut the muslin straps, the wads of cotton rolling over my skirt to the floor. With my arm clasped to my stomach, I drop my head to my knees in relief.

Then I grip a chemise in my mouth, cut new strips, and wrangle new ties with my teeth. I stuff the cotton under my palm and watch the skin regain its color. A simple accomplishment. The white is speckled brown from old blood and red from new. I pull the stitch from my lip and fling it away. It lands on the rug stained black from ink.

"No. I won't." Lionel's voice is loud in the hall. "It's too much."

"Then I will." The office door shuts with a thud that makes the wall quiver, and Cathy's words muffle. The sconce candles snuff out one by one. Her tread, then his up the stairs.

It's pitch black now. I swallow and then lick salty sweat from my upper lip. A low moan claws from my gut up my throat. My body trembles as the panic stirs and hisses.

Shh. Shh.

I flash on the tintype of Lydia, the almost smile that crinkles her cheek. Lydia drowned in the pond. Out past the turn, where the shores pinch tight and the Sentinels stand guard.

My lids snap wide, though the room is dark. There's something, prowling at the edge of my vision. Something rustling. A starched apron. Harriet Clough's. A smell of lemon cake and chlorine bleach. Oily smoke and the fizzle of burning pages in the diaries Lionel took from Kitty Swain. The only way Alice spoke now burnt to char and ash.

Alice knew something she shouldn't. And died for it.

But not before giving the gift of the slides. She must have finished them just before Lionel took her away. Not on the inventory list packed so neat with her belongings. Trusting me to find them. To trust her. To listen. To see.

I open the wardrobe, pull out a drawer, and rest my hand on a stocking. The glass slides slip across each other. Five slides. I smile, cupping my hand over them.

I had gambled: Two slides to catch Cathy out. The five others were *Old Mother Hubbard.*

Old Mother Hubbard
Went to the Cupboard,
To give the poor Dog a bone;

When she came there,
The Cupboard was bare,
And so the poor Dog had none.

But she'll soon know I switched them. She'll come for the real slides. She'll come for me.

I watch. My view is the keyhole, and the world of the house flits across it, like the glass slides in Toby's magic lantern. I see directly to the front door. On my right is Lionel's office. He enters in the morning, sits and stews, then leaves through the kitchen door, also on my right. On my left is the staircase, the curio cabinet with glass ornaments and the hidden closet with the spring door that holds a broom, a bucket, dust rags, and a mop. Saoirse pops it open and takes out one or the other during the day, and when she sweeps, her skirts sway just like the broom bristles.

Very little light comes from the parlor on the left. The opening is muddy brown, as if the curtains are always drawn. At night Saoirse lights the sconces in the hall and the lamps in the parlor, then lugs herself up the stairs to light the rooms above. When she's done, she takes the three short steps to the kitchen to start the evening meal.

Meals.

I am brought my food separately, though it is the same as Cathy and Lionel eat. Even a slice of ginger cake cut and set to its own plate. Not glass. Never glass.

Farther along, on the right, the dining room. There is lovely light in the dining room, and most of the day it brightens the hall and the thick wood door. Cathy wanders in and out, sometimes with an armful of flowers and sometimes poring over papers and tapping a pencil to her lip.

I press my lips to the metal lock plate on her third trek from the parlor to the dining room. "Where's Toby?"

She lifts the corner to the page she's reading and doesn't stop on her path from parlor to dining room. "He's in his room."

"Let me out."

Her step stutters. She looks into the dining room and then back to my door. "I can't." Her fingers bite into the sheaf of papers. She pulls them tight to her chest. "I really truly can't, Marion."

"You can't keep me here." I raise my voice. "Is this what you did to my sister?"

"Your sister knew how to get out." But she stops, gives an angry jerk of her head, and returns to the parlor.

I dig my thumbnail along the doorframe. The columns of roses waver; the pattern is mismatched. A small square patch peels along the frame. I've seen it before, thought nothing of the penciled marks. I run my finger along the edge abutting the arch until my nail catches on a loose bit of it. Below is yellowed glue and plaster. The paper tears in a strip, straight up to the top of the frame and the turn in the arch.

There's a ripple under the plaster. I dig and tear, but here the glue is thicker, and the plaster pulls away in a clump. The strip swings and thuds the door.

I freeze. But no one comes or calls out for me to be quiet. With a single rip, the paper is free. I stare down to the water jug. If I wet the paper it will come loose.

The chair wobbles as I clamber down, the seat corner knocking the wall.

Still no one.

I crouch, lay the stretch of paper to the rug, and dribble the rest of the water to the clump of plaster. I dig my finger to paper, curling it back. Bit by bit it emerges.

The plaster crumbles. A swath of fabric. Lemon yellow. A pattern of ferns. Each leaf like a saw's edge.

Evidence: One hood. The knots still intact.

"Are you there?"

I jerk up, scuttling back from the voice that floats through the keyhole. My teeth chatter and my breath comes out as a moan. "Toby?"

The knob turns one way, then the other. I scramble for the candle, holding it out. He stares at me, then puts his lips to the lock plate. "I'm going to rescue you," he whispers. He turns his head. Now it's his pale cheek I see. Then his eye again and lashes so long they brush the plate. "Don't be scared."

My body crumples then, because I am scared, and I can't stop the sob escaping through my fingers. I press my palm hard over my mouth and teeth, swallowing it back. "I'm not scared," I say. "You don't need to rescue me."

Light pierces the keyhole. He's left. Just the moon cutting through the front window. "Toby. Oh, please don't go."

A movement then, near my knees. Toby's pushed his fingers just under the door and wriggles them. Slides them right and then left until I catch them in mine. He tugs at them, a motion that sends me to my stomach, cheek to floor. Then he pets the top of my hand.

"How did you get out of your room?" My voice slips across the doorjamb.

He doesn't answer. I hear him breathing, open mouthed. Then he slides a long pin over the jamb. A songbird in blue, tipped with pearls. Alice's hat pin.

"She taught you."

"Now you can escape. I'll be right here."

We stare at each other. "I don't know how to pick a lock."

A floorboard creaks above us. Toby twists to peer in the hall, then scrabbles along the wall, springing open the understairs closet and sidling inside.

Lionel's feet plod the stairs. He stops at the bottom, taking a step to the dining room, hands curled in the pockets of his dressing gown. The blue silk glimmers in the light. His feet are bare and he curls a toe against the parquet before turning into the parlor and rummaging around for a drink. The hinges of the cabinet protest, then give way. A twist of cork and a glug of liquid to a glass. He must bolt it down, because the glass is refilled once more.

He paces. A minute or ten, I don't know, but long enough I wonder if he'll ever leave. But then the glass thuds to the felt on the game table, and he is back again in the entryway. He faces the hall and me and, please God, hasn't heard a thing.

He rubs his hands over his face, and sighs. "Oh, God," he mutters. "Oh, Jesus."

And then he takes the stairs again and shuts the bedroom door.

I wait. Toby waits. The moonlight shifts in the hall until it is a single arc of gray light through the window.

There is a click of a latch. The small door opening. Toby slips out and steals back to me. He kneels to the floor and I follow suit. I slide the hat pin back to him. "Try."

He scoops it up. I can hear the scratch of the pin against the lock tumblers. Silence when he removes it, and then the scratch as he works the lock again. I run my fingers over the brass plate, with its molded whorls of dandelion stalks and feathery pampas bristles. A Snow & Son original design.

"It's not the same." Toby clicks the tip of the pin to the matching plate on his side.

I sit back, push the heels of my palms to my forehead.
Think.

"Toby." I push myself forward to speak through the keyhole. "Can you hide something for me? In your room."

"Yes."

"I'm going to give you something."

"All right."

I move to the wardrobe, grab out the stocking with the lantern slides, then kneel again to the floor. I press the stocking flat, the tinkling of the glass muted. He can hide them in his room, somewhere behind the books on his shelf.

I roll on my back and stare at the ceiling, pulling the stocking to my stomach and twisting the top. He's only a child. If she did look—

"Auntie." His fingers trill the floor, expectant. I touch them with mine, to still them, to feel the warmth. He's torn the nail on his ring finger.

"Put this to the very back of your toy shelf." Before I can change my mind, I push the slides to him.

"Why are you in trouble?"

I pause. "I think it's because the constable came. That made your father angry." My foot catches on the length of wallpaper coiled to the floor. Above me the plaster gapes and the lath looks like ribs.

"How will I get you out?" he whispers.

I drag in a breath. "Oh, I'll be out soon, when I'm not in trouble anymore. You'll be out, too, if you're a good boy."

There's no answer.

"Toby?" I dig into my thigh and peer through the opening. He's still there. "Toby."

"They're going to take you, too, aren't they?"

"No."

He sniffs. "I'm scared." His head disappears from view. The hat pin is pushed back to me, bent at a right angle from his endeavor with the lock. I kneel to look through the lock. He lifts his hand to the balustrade, just able to reach the newel, and I see the weight of this horrible house in the hunch of his shoulders.

"I'm scared too."

Chapter Thirty

The clink of a teacup wakes me. Then another. A patter of voices and one titter that is certainly not Cathy's. I roll on my side and stare and listen.

They are in the dining room.

Women.

I sit up in bed. Wait through a bout of dizziness. I appraise the paper I reset to the wall with toothpowder and spit. There is a ragged hole where the hood once was, and nothing I can do to fix it. The chunk that is missing is now stuffed between my arm and the splint. It is a witness. It is a talisman.

The murmurs run in notes high and low and come from the dining room.

"Well, of course we would list all the names." The voice, watery bright, is followed by a crunch of a biscuit or meringue.

"Of the donors?" Cathy says. She sits at the head of the table. Her voice comes clear through the doorway and is tight with anxiety at this group of visitors she no doubt wished had come last week rather than this.

"Of the dead." A wiser voice ends with a disapproving *hmph* and cough.

"Yes. Of course. Of course, the dead." A clink of a cup to saucer, just a hair too sharp.

"We're thinking bronze."

I frown and try to recall the voice. One of the women from the park. Seeking the right spot for the future *Statue of the Fallen Soldier*. A statue and fountain.

"But not a fountain," she continues. "Everyone's finances are so pinched now . . ." Her voice trails away.

"Are you sure Mrs. Abbott can't join us?" Essa Runyon asks. "Or mayhap I could have a short sit with her?"

"You know how dreadful catarrh is," Cathy says. "I wouldn't want it to pass to you or yours."

Shoving the sheets off, I clamber to kneel at the keyhole. The hall is empty. I raise my hand to hammer the door, to call out to Essa, to any of the women.

"Just catarrh?" an older woman asks. Mrs. Flowers, who passed us by in church. "What a terrible, terrible thing. And in summer."

The tone of her voice stops my hand. I can see them all as if I were seated just behind them. The quick glances from one to the other and then averting their eyes from Cathy. Stirring milk to tea. Taking a tong to the sugar bowl and so careful to find the smallest lump. Scraping butter to a biscuit. The silence in the room. The curiosity in the pointed indifference to whatever Cathy might choose to say.

"Lionel has sent for a specialist. From Concord."

The gasp is on cue.

"Consumption?" one woman conjectures.

"One hopes only that." Cathy's answer leaves what is unspoken clear. "First Alice, now—"

I kick the door.

A chair rakes the floor. "Pardon me." Cathy's voice is louder. She moves into the hall, her hands to the dining room door, her eyes to the ceiling as if she were asking sympathy from God for all she must bear.

"Psst."

She hesitates, then cuts a quick look toward me.

I drop to the floor. Stick my hand under and crook my finger for her to come.

Her knuckles go white as she grips the knob tighter and tighter. "Pardon me a moment. Have another cake." She gives a quick smile to the women, shuts the door, and comes toward me.

I tap the floor for her to bend down.

Her green silk skirts billow out as she lowers herself.

I snake the hem in my fingers and twist. "I will break every window in this room if you don't open the door."

"If you break every window, you'll confirm what those biddies are thinking."

"There's nothing wrong with me."

"Let go of my skirt."

Instead, I pull it, reeling it under the door. "I know what you've done."

Her knee smacks the frame. "You're just like her," she hisses. "They know it. No matter what you do, whether you scream or break things, not one of them will listen." She yanks her skirt and stumbles back. "Not one."

Her shoes are sharp, heels harpooning the wood as she returns to the room, lifting her head high as she enters. "I will be happy to provide funds."

The room constricts around me.

No one will listen.

In the evening, Saoirse slides the tray to me but doesn't shut the door. She gives a furtive glance behind her, then reaches in to run her palm on the top of my head. "You must regain yourself."

I wince. "Why do you help them?"

"Child." Her eyes are weary. She lowers her lids and rattles in a breath. "Leave the milk."

Then she is gone.

I pull the tray toward me, until the corners meet my crossed legs. A single matchstick. Peas. Bacon. A roll. Green apple slices. The milk, with a whirl of cream floating on top.

I bite a slice of apple. It is tart. Not yet ripe.

The peas are salted and steamed, as I like them, as Saoirse knows I do, so there is that. She does think of me though she is complicit in all of this.

The bacon is thick and crunchy. Three slices.

The milk is poisoned with the opiate Cathy spooned in my mouth when I first returned after the accident to the house. How attentive she'd been then. Each spoon an alleviation of pain and an onset of dreams twisted and chaotic. She's put it in the water here. To keep me quiet. To keep me pliant.

My mouth dries with all the salt to the meal. I swallow, pressing my tongue to the roof of my mouth. I stare at the milk. Imagine the cool of it down my throat and the way it will cause me to drowse. Imagine then the hellish visions that follow. As they have done every night until I have come unraveled.

I kneel and then stand, and push the tray with my foot to the wall.

I light the nub of candle and pace the room. Count the steps—ten from the mantel and rocker to the bedside table, three at an angle to the wardrobe, five across to the writing desk.

Lionel has sent for a specialist. No doubt Dr. Mayhew has rid himself of the Snow family, so he seeks help further afield. I am certain it is not a doctor with knowledge or interest in catarrh. More likely it is one with an unnatural interest in female unease. In all the various complexities of hysteria and the maladies of our wombs. Why wouldn't he do so? I have behaved just as Alice, flailing around, deranged, and filled with a self-righteous sense of being unheard. He would see nothing else. All those times he looked at me, the same look we gave each other growing up. Pleading in church to God that it be only her accursed. Only her.

Or so he will say to the specialist.

A paper crumples under my foot. I turn a circle, picking my way around the overflow of the chamber pot, the food I've left to stale and rot, the sheets spilling from the bed, the metal springs and bits of the clock I worked free in an effort to find anything that would open the door. There is the hole in the wall and the pasted paper so easily spotted. A room for a madwoman.

Cathy killed Lydia.

But if I say a word—

I must be calm. Regain my right self.

I tap my thumb to the wood of the splint, then pull the sling off, letting my arm free and working my fingers, trying to touch my thumb to the others. Over and over through the stiffness until I am able to pinch it to the middle finger without the room thinning into white and my stomach revolting.

One button at a time. Each piece of clothing removed and folded to the mending basket. There is enough water in the jug for a quick wipe with a rag. I shrug on a chemise, then Alice's stays and Alice's plaid skirt because my own mourning dress is too large. Her bodice sports tight sleeves, for she never was one for pufferies and fancies. Not when the forest called.

Brush the hair and pin it.

Shuffle up the papers and set them to the desk.

Make the bed.

Cover the piss pot with a pillow casing.

Push the windows full up to gain fresh air. I press my nose to the wood shutters and breathe in. Horses, hay. Ash. Tobacco smoke. Not Lionel's. Outside, the cicadas saw, their song a rough throb. It weaves with other voices. I turn my ear to the words. Cathy. Amos.

Nothing intelligible, just one voice hooked over another, coming from down near the weeping willow. Words traveling on smoke. Words that snare and stop, jab and raise.

Then, "What about the boy?" Amos is directly below my window.
"What about him?"

"You don't lay a finger on him. He's an innocent boy."

"What do you take me for?"

"What you are."

"You'll get what you want." Cathy's voice like a knife. "Burn the factory. That's the only thing you'll get paid for."

"I'll get more than that," he says. "You didn't pay me enough for the other."

Everything slows. My heart. My movements. *The other.* Alice. I peek through the gap in the shutters, try to find the figures in the small slice of yard that is visible. It is just dusk, the shadows long, the air murky. Nothing in view but the gravel path. Then Cathy, striding to the house, mouth in a thin line. Amos stepping to follow, then distracted, smacking the air and then his forearm. Quashing a mosquito. He lifts his hand. Stares at his palm. Then wipes it to his trouser leg.

My breath is shallow. An image flips into place. Another man, smacking a mosquito to his arm and staring at his palm. Straddling the peak of the asylum roof, eating his lunch in the sun as we carted Alice's body away.

The kitchen door bangs. I jump away from the window.

"Cathy." I clear my throat, afraid she hasn't heard me as she passes. "Cathy."

"What?"

"Where's Toby?"

"I—he's in the yard. Target practice. He's—shut up."

Ice slides under my skin. "You can't keep me in here. I know what you did."

"Who do you think will save you? Kitty Swain?" She kicks the door and tramps down the hall. Then she stops. "I have news for you." Her voice echoes in the hall. "Your Kitty Swain is dead. She hung herself from a clothesline pole. Poor dim girl."

Saoirse's brought me a candle and a match. It is only a nub of candle, and I'm hopeful it means this is all temporary, that I'll only need the few hours of wax and wick proffered. It has been three full days and now tips to the fourth. Lionel has walked to the door each night, but said nothing. Tonight he stumbles, throwing his hand to the wall to stop from falling over. He breathes through his mouth, quick gasps, and knocks his forehead to the wallpaper.

"Marion," he whispers.

He freezes, then slants his head to look back down the hall. He straightens, losing his balance, then teetering back and swinging out a leg to catch himself.

"Lionel?"

"Shh." He wobbles forward, blocking the view from the keyhole. But then there is the scrape of a key, and he slips around the door. He is overcareful as he shuts it, his hand on the knob, his eyes boring into the door before he clicks it shut and falls back against the wall. He picks at the cuff of his suit, and now there's a hole and four errant threads. One more and the entire thing will unravel. "It stinks in here."

"You knew what she did," I say to him, my voice quiet, not wanting to give Cathy cause to come down the hall.

He puts his hand over my mouth and squeezes his arm tight around me so I cannot move away. His breath is sour, hot against my cheek. "Be quiet."

I wrench and twist, but his grasp tightens, pinning my arms. He digs his fingers into the hollow of my cheeks. "You shouldn't have come back, Marion."

I bite into his palm, clamping down until he loosens his grip.

"God damn it." He closes his eyes and wags his head, then sucks on his palm. In the candlelight, his eye sockets are dark black.

"You knew."

"No. I didn't . . . Lydia knew about Cathy. 'It's all right,' she said. 'Men are like that.'" He gulps a breath and slides down the wall. "I didn't want—there was another child coming. I had to tell Cathy no. No. It was too much. She wanted too much. I promise you, I didn't know she meant it. She laughed when she said, 'I'll kill her, then. You'll be free.' Then one day she came to the factory and said, 'It's done.'" His mouth pulls into a strange grimace. "She doesn't like to lose. She won't lose. And it's all out of control; I don't know where to stop it."

"And Alice?"

"She made one too many complaints."

I roll my hand in a fist. "Amos pushed her. Didn't he?"

"I put her at Brawders to save her," he says. "God, she was so—"

"But you didn't save her. Amos pushed her off that roof. And you let it happen." I roll my hand into a fist and try to yank away.

"I didn't know. Not about that, not about Lydia. I promise you."

"You're a liar."

"No. I thought Alice was safe."

"Wasn't it enough to *commit* her? Why? *Why?*"

"You were coming home. You would have listened. You *did* listen." He gulps a breath and his hand drops from my arm. With shaking shoulders, he cries, hand tight to his mouth to hold in the sound, skin glistening with tears. He reaches out to me—for what? Forgiveness? Solace?

"The Asylum for the Insane is sending two men. Tomorrow morning."

"You're committing me?"

"For your own good. For your own *life*, Marion."

"And what happens when she sends Amos for me? What then?"

"She won't. Once we burn the factory, he'll get his money. That's what he wants. It's all planned. New life."

"You can't get away with this Lionel. You're just as complicit."

"But we can. It's all planned. We burn the factory. Get the insurance. New life."

I can barely breathe. "Did you ever love Lydia?"

"I'll live with my mistake." He pushes up from the floor, bumps against the wardrobe. "Where are the slides?"

"You helped kill her."

The knob on the wardrobe snaps in his grasp. "No."

"You're a liar. You knew exactly where to find her. You knew to bring rope. You knew because you waited—"

He lunges toward me, shoving me to the bed, his hands pressed on my shoulders. "Shut up. I'm trying to save you."

"Have you even thought about your son? Cathy hates him."

"Shut up."

My blows slide from his shoulders and land on his back, then against his waist. "Let us go. Both of us. I won't say a word. Look at me, Lionel." I ratchet a breath. "I know you love her. Let it just be you and her. Just you and her. Like you've always wanted. Isn't that what you've always wanted?"

He swallows and lifts his chin.

"She'll kill him too," I whisper.

"No." He pushes me into the mattress as he stands, staggering to the door. "It's all planned. The hospital will keep you safe. I'll keep him safe."

"Leave the door open and let us go."

"I never meant—"

The swing of the door snuffs the candle.

"Auntie . . ."

"No, Toby."

Lionel spins around. "It's all right," he says, bending down to the boy. "Shush and go back to bed."

"Toby . . ." My voice cracks. The floor shifts and sways as I stand; I set my feet wide for balance. Grab the bedpost to maintain myself. Then I thrust myself past Lionel, knocking him against the rocking chair. I grab the pitcher and swing it hard at his head. He lets out a groan, pats the back of his head, and stares at the blood. Then he grabs the mantel, stumbling and collapsing with a thud. Benjamin's picture smacks on the floor with a loud snap of glass.

My ears ring with the next sudden silence.

"Toby?" Cathy's voice glides down from the top of the stairs.

He turns toward her.

"No, Toby. No no no. You need to run."

"Toby." Cathy's voice is sharp.

"Auntie—"

I can see his toes, the white soft of his bare feet, the sharp juts of ankle. "Go through the kitchen. Go to the fort."

"Auntie—"

"Run."

Chapter Thirty-One

Cathy steps to the entryway. Her skirts peel round the last post. She doesn't rush. Just stands in place. Listening.

But Toby's gone. I sit up, gulping air into my lungs. He's out the door. I can see him in my mind's eye. He's fast, like a deer, eluding the moonlight.

"Lionel?" A singsong. One step on the hardwood, the next muffled on the runner.

"He's in here." I squeeze my eyes shut, then open them and slink to the mending basket, watching the doorway. I pull the cord to the skirts—*clever Alice*—and the bands lift the hem just above the ankle, enough so I won't trip on the fabric.

The etui rests on the pile of clothes. I stick my thumbnail to the clasp, listen for the click, then turn the box upside down. The scissors tumble out. Such small shears. I squeeze the handles and hold it against my skirts.

Cathy is just outside the door. The key rattles in the lock, the tumblers grinding, metal on metal. She pushes the door open, silhouetted in the sconce's light. She holds her bow near her thigh, the arrow nocked in the catgut string, tip pointing to the floor. Her head swivels to me. "Where is he?"

I set my feet, hoping against hope she won't lift the bow in time. Then I lunge.

We careen into the wall and tumble to the floor, the wood splint slamming to her ribs. My vision goes white. I feel her twist under me, pushing against my shoulder as she gets to all fours and shoves me back to the wall. I gasp for air.

She clambers to her feet, clasping the bow again, bending down for the arrow that's just outside her reach. But it's inside my reach; I kick it away. When she turns for it, I scramble to my knees and ram my shoulder to her legs so she buckles. The scissors stab through the rug, but I don't let them go. They're all I have.

Her arms flail, and she kicks out, crawling backward and grabbing up the arrow. And it's nocked again in the bow, the string pulled back. "I don't lose," she says, closing one eye and pulling the string tauter.

She cries out. The arrow corkscrews straight into the ceiling plaster. The bow clatters against the wall as her hands scrabble forward, clawing for the scissors I've buried in her thigh.

Run.

The moon slices bright through the woods, painting shadows that hide roots and stones, nettle and chokeberry. Something cuts my foot—a broken limb, a shard left over from the glass house and the bonfire. I don't care. I wind through the trees, each limb silver in the light, the leaves copper and iron. Up a narrow path that twists and gives way to the graves. Mounds and shallows.

"Marion?"

I circle once to the sound, then peer in the forest for the path to the Sentinels. To Toby.

There. Just beyond Alice's grave. I bolt across, crashing into the brush. The sling catches on a gnarled branch, snapping me around again. I give a tug to release it, then pull my arm free and let it hang loose. The fabric flutters against my chest when I spring forward again.

To my left, I catch glints of light from the pond, like a cat's eyes winking. Soon I'll be at the Sentinels. My breath slices in and out like a razor. I can't feel my legs.

But I feel her. She's coming.

Pine needles soften the thump of my feet as I grapple up a rise, digging my fingers into the rough of the rounded rocks. I slide down, scraping my face and shins.

"Marion." Cathy's voice bounces off the trees and stone; I can't determine where she's at. "I just want to talk. You're safe, now."

I clamp my hand to a sapling growing between two boulders and push my toes to the stone.

But I can't pull myself up. Not with one arm. I dig my feet and knees to the rock to climb. All I need is enough purchase to hook my elbow.

"It wasn't me, Marion."

My hand can't hold any longer. I slip down the stone and topple back to the ground.

"It was him. Lionel did it. Not me." Dry leaves and empty cicada husks crackle under her feet. Slow steps. Stopping to listen.

I hold my breath. The katydid's song ebbs and saws. Above, the topmost leaves rustle.

A snap of a branch. Right next to my head. I scramble back and hunch against the rock.

"Where's the boy?" Amos hoists me up by my shoulders, then hangs on because I'm trembling too hard to stand.

"I won't have anything happen to him." He shakes me like a sack.

"What are you doing here?" Cathy steps from behind a tree.

He lets me go, turning to her. "I changed my—" His words are cut off, as if sliced by a scythe. His body doubles into itself. He grunts and staggers back before collapsing to his knees. He rolls forward, face to the dirt, his hair tumbled forward, arms slack, the shaft of Cathy's arrow pierced so deep through his gut I can make out the fletch feathers along his spine. His ribs heave. Blood pulses and bubbles. One more heave. One more heartbeat. Then the hollow rattle of a final breath.

"Well." Cathy moves her weight to one hip.

"Why, Cathy?"

She stares at Amos and flinches, then shakes her head and laughs. "Sniveling, sweet Lydia." Her mouth curves down. "Do you know what it's like to kill your best friend?" She sniffs. "It's harder than you think." She looks at something to her left. I follow her gaze and my heart drops.

Toby.

He holds the little derringer with both hands. The barrel wobbles as he cocks the trigger.

"Toby, you shouldn't play with that." Cathy smiles and taps her index finger to the grip of her bow. She lowers it. Takes a step forward.

"Don't." He clenches his teeth, then chatters them. "I'll shoot you."

"No, you won't."

In one quick move, she grabs his wrist and twists away the gun. She straightens her arm and aims.

"No." I bowl into her, knocking her off her feet. The gun falls to the ground and discharges with a muffled bang.

She grabs onto the loose sling, twisting it around my neck, yanking me along. I clutch at the fabric, kicking my heels into the dirt to find purchase. She slows, loosening the fabric enough that I take in one huge breath and twist my torso so I am facedown. Then she pulls again, dragging me until the ground stops, dropping to the ink-black water below.

My ears thrum. Toby screams in the distance, as if he's in a far tunnel. Cathy's busy with the sling. It's the pretty one she bought me. Peacocks and fairies printed on silk. The fairies' wings quaver as she pulls the fabric taut, then tugs it over my face.

She'll drown me, same as Lydia. Leave me blinded and suffocating, paddling in circles until my lungs burst.

I arch my back, clench my teeth, and slam the wood splint to her nose. There is a loud crack, and a gush of blood spatters on the cloth. I claw and rip it away and swing the splint again and again.

The forest dims around me. I see the swing of my arm. Cathy's eyes glaze and stare into mine, the tiny red veins traversing the sclera bursting with each hit until the white in one eye is pink.

She lays her head to my chest. It is heavy as lead.

I swing in the air, and my arm drops to the ground. I'm too weak to lift it once more.

I open my eyes. The moon is low, just a thin crescent over the tree line. The water is indigo, streaked with wavering lines of pale sun. The water sliders skate on the pond's skin. Toby has curled next to me, his hands tucked under my arm, his knees to his chest.

Cathy is not here.

I scan the clearing. Amos's body is folded in on itself by the rocks. Just beyond are the snarls and twines of bushes, with one small opening in the buckthorn. The fort. There is a bright glint from a tree. Alice's locket. It catches the sun and spins, though the air is still. On the next a lilac ribbon. A stand of birch, young saplings. A silver maple. A bit of pearl lodged in the wood. A round red bead. The teeth of a key. The Sentinels.

Cathy sways between them, then puts her hands to her knees and stumbles forward.

I slowly pull my arm from under Toby's head.

His body stiffens when he sees her. His voice wheezes, as if he will scream. Then he digs his heels to the dirt, struggling against my grip, wanting to escape.

But Amos is dead behind us, and I won't have the boy see that. I kiss his temple. With my lips next to his ears I whisper, "You are safe."

There's someone coming toward us. Loud feet that stomp and don't mind if anyone hears them. "Mrs. Abbott! Someone answer!"

A man. He whistles, then calls again. "Anyone?"

"Here," I call. My voice is rough, and the sound dies out at my feet. Cathy trots toward him, waving. "Help me. Oh, please help me."

A man pummels through the laurel and into the clearing. He carries a bundle of cotton batting folded and cinched with leather straps.

"Mrs. Abbott? What in the . . ."

Cathy stumbles toward him and grabs at his arm. He shakes her off, then stares from her, to Toby, to me. His gaze lands then on Amos's slumped body. "My God."

"You've come from the asylum. You're going to commit me. You're going to keep me safe." My laugh becomes a sob. I'm too tired to stop.

Chapter Thirty-Two

The room is impossibly bright. A white linen tablecloth that sears my eyes. Porcelain cups and plates with bright berries. I push a spoon under a saucer to hide the reflection and shift my chair so I no longer face the sheen of sun scratching at the window.

"Are you comfortable now?" The man across from me perches on the edge of his chair. He holds his hands palm to palm, shoved between his knees. He twists his left boot tip against the floor. I think his feet are the size of a child's. His hands and all his features—the grand hair and mutton chops, the saucer eyes, his Adam's apple that struggles up and down his skinny neck—seem outsize to them, as if they were added on from the wrong pile or God had run out of the large. He's been squinting and peering all morning. Attentive to a fault.

"Would you like more coffee?" He gestures to the pot. "Myself, a cup a day. It is a rule. *Mmph.*" His voice is a thin rasp. He shuffles back in his chair. "Do you know who I am?"

"Yes. You are Mr. Finch. You were introduced in the hallway."

"Enoch Finch. *Doctor* Enoch Finch."

My head aches from the light. From his rasping, grating, horrible voice. I want to press my fingers to the bridge of my nose to stop the ache. But there are bandages there. And all across my head. I want the orderly to take me back to my room, so I can crawl under the bedding and let the pain dissipate in the dark. But instead, I rest my hands in my lap and shrug. "My sister-in-law sent me here. For you to examine me. To determine if I suffer from mania. Or not."

"*Mmph*. Yes. That is indeed right."

He frowns and looks over the railing to the whitewashed window. "I am one of the doctors here. I will be *your* doctor."

"Did you see my room, *Doctor* Finch?"

"Indeed, I did."

"This is the first day I've been let out in nearly a week."

"Is that so?"

"Yes, it is so."

"What do you think would cause—"

"You have this all turned around. I'm not the one with mania. Marion is. Her whole family is. I don't know what she told you on the ride here to . . . Where are we?"

"You are at the New Hampshire Asylum for the Insane. In Concord."

"Concord. She would have told you that I am awash in delusions and promulgate my own reality. That I killed my very best friend. But that was only due to the necessity that Lionel take some responsibility. And her sister, who did indeed die of an accident, a *fall* not a *push* off the roof. You should ask *her* who has the delusions. But before that—"

"Mrs. Snow—"

"Let me finish."

He tilts his head and gestures for me to carry on.

"Before that . . ." But there's saliva at the corner of my mouth. I dab the handkerchief Marion so kindly gave me to my lips, then tuck it into the pocket of the gown this horrid hospital provided. "Before that, her sister, Alice, lived with me and my husband, who, I am also certain you were told, had to then provide for her. She was just left at our door. And she was perfectly controlled. I made sure her life was in order. I did. I did everything for Alice. And if I wanted to shoot Marion with a bow and arrow, I would have. She would have been dead. I'm an excellent shot. I always win."

Dr. Finch leans forward, elbows to his knees, and his smile is so wide I see the missing molars in the top left.

"You're staring."

"I would very much like to take some measurements. Of your head. May I be so bold?"

"You may not."

"But we can determine quite quickly the nature of your condition."

"I don't have a condition."

"Rule out conditions, then. I won't force you. But I am a noted phrenologist."

"You may not touch my head. There is nothing wrong with me."

"As you say." He taps the table.

"I'll have some coffee, now, if you will."

He nods once. Lifts the pot to pour. The coffee is thick and brown. He blows on it, as if the liquid will burn his lips, then gives a grimace of surprise when he sips. He sets the cup down and pushes it my way. It sways in my grip; I can't stop the tremble of my hand. This man's opinion is all that stands between me and the state asylum for the insane. Which, if rumor has any credence, makes Brawders House the Queen's palace. I've been blubbering like an idiot.

"Do you suffer?" he asks.

"Like Alice?"

"Like someone who has murdered two innocent people and nearly two more." He curls his lips and swats a fly away from his sideburn. He doesn't change his focus. That remains upon me. "Never mind the monies paid to have Miss Alice Snow pushed from the roof."

I open my mouth, about to answer.

He pushes the sugar across, then the tongs. "I must know, Mrs. Snow. If I am to assess you. I am not a man of snap judgments."

"Where is my husband?"

"Directly across. Recuperating in the men's wing."

"I did nothing, Dr. Finch. He did nothing." But the red heat on my cheeks belies me. And his patience wears. "It would be more abnormal if I thought nothing of it. Marion tried to kill me. And she killed that man, that laborer. They plotted against us."

He swings his foot. It is so uncommonly thin. "And now you make up stories to alleviate your guilt. Blame others for that original sin. It is common to do so. Guilt is a corrosive beast. The mind is not made for it. Nor the heart. Our brains make up new stories to mop up the mess, hide all the rust stains and remorse."

"I didn't do anything."

"Indeed."

"Are you committing me?"

He makes a click of his tongue. "Yes. I am. To the wing for the criminally insane. The third floor. You'll have your very own room."

Chapter Thirty-Three

The coachman hefts my trunk to the livery boy, who straps it to the roof. "Heavy one," he says.

I shade my eyes and gaze up at him. "Books and toys. The next one's lighter."

Toby hops down the steps of the general store and slows to peer in the shadows of the porch. He pushes aside a tin tub and crouches, snapping his fingers to tempt a cat. Then he unrolls a bag and pours the contents to a pan. One more snap before he rises and dusts his short trousers and bare knees.

I watch him lope along the wood walkway and then jump to the road. He runs the tips of his fingers along the white wood of the post office and the brass plate of the bank.

"Bank of Turee," he says to no one in particular. He will be tall as his father. He'll need a new set of clothes before the school year begins. "Horse." He rubs the muzzle of the chestnut, and then strokes the nose of the bay. Then he steps next to me, fumbling in his vest pocket for his watch, making a show of springing it open and contemplating the time. He rubs his thumb across the glass. It was Lionel's.

It is the last of his father, as the locket around my neck is the last I have of Alice.

I haven't told him the truth of Lionel's commitment. I have only said his father knew nothing of Cathy's evil. I could not hide anything else. Toby had been too curious. He watched the slides. He knew they told the truth. He believed Alice. And she had kept him safe.

"Thirteen more minutes," he says and snaps the watch closed.

"What did you give the cat?"

"Jerky. Mrs. Flowers says it's his favorite."

The bay paws a hoof to the road. The driver climbs to his seat. "Milford, Nashua, Boston," he calls.

"We're off, then," I say. "An adventure."

He looks up at me, his expression somber. It will be long before he can sleep through a night. He takes my hand, fingers sticky from candy. "An adventure."

We won't be back. And I won't look back down the road. Saoirse and Elias have gone to her sister's in Newburyport. The house has been sold to the Runyons, who will tear it down and turn the whole of it over to sheep. They are glad for the pond.

Alice's stone came. White granite that sparkles in the light.

Beloved sister.

ACKNOWLEDGMENTS

Alicia Clancy, you are an editor extraordinaire. I am so appreciative not only for your keen sense of story, but for your support and encouragement. I am so lucky and honored to work with you.

Mark Gottlieb, can I say again how much I appreciate you? You are so generous with your time and ideas and advice and knowledge. Thank you.

Danielle Marshall, your vision for Lake Union is amazing. I am so honored to be part of this group.

Gabe Dumpit, you rock. Enough said.

Faceout Studio, what a cover! I am in awe.

Much thanks to Production Editor Laura Barrett, Copyeditor Laura Whittemore, and Proofreader Patty Ann Economos for such detailed attention and reminding me that the devil's in the details.

Rebecca Stockbridge and the New Hampshire State Library, thank you for all the amazing details and primary sources you dig up for me. You are a true rock star.

Many thanks to these amazing historians and archivists whose input was invaluable to this story: Terry Reimer and the Museum of Civil War Medicine; New Hampshire Historical Society; Michelle Stahl and the Monadnock Center for History and Culture; Deb Salisbury and the Mantua-Maker series; Robbin Bailey and Ashley Miller, Concord Public Library.

KC Taylor for giving wise advice right when it was needed. Jennifer Springsteen for early story guidance. Kate Genet, I apparently can't start or finish a book without you. Thanks for the descriptions and book club questions and writing-in-general emails. Cathy Yardley and *Rock Your Plot* for giving story first aid when I thought I'd have to tear up every page and start over. Alan Hlad for our ongoing plot accountability and weekly check-ins—we both finished!

Thea Constantine and Alida Thacher for volunteering as first readers who waded through a remarkable mess, gave me a life raft, and helped Alice find her voice.

BOOK CLUB QUESTIONS

1. *After Alice Fell* has a great deal to do with the guilt that underlies a lot of our family bonds. In chapter three, Lionel accuses Marion of abandoning Alice, and Marion agrees with him. Do you think she may be justified in this? Does, however, the emotion of guilt have any use to any of us in the end? What would be a healthy way of dealing with the emotion of guilt?

2. The responsibility for those who need our constant care can be a hard burden to bear. Who do you think should have looked after Alice? Was she Marion's responsibility? How differently (if at all) do we deal with family members with mental illnesses now?

3. In the novel, much weight is given to appearances—what would people think? Do you think that this consideration of appearances is still prevalent today? And if so, is it beneficial to a community, or not?

4. The novel opens with Alice's body being brought home. Marion washes her and holds vigil. We rarely any longer wash and care for our own dead. When dealing with death in our modern times, do you think we've become alienated from it?

5. Lionel and Cathy took Marion into their home to live after her husband was killed. This sort of obligation toward extended family members was usual then, but now isn't so

much an obligation at all. Do you think this is a change for the better or worse?

6. Marion has questions about Alice's death, and everyone else wants her to put them aside. By the end of the book, we know there is a greater reason for this, but before that, did you wonder whether she was right to keep asking her questions and looking for answers? What motivated her to do so? Was it guilt? And do you think she may have been personally better off leaving it all alone?

7. We all have motivations for our actions—some healthy and some not so healthy. What do you think motivated Lionel to go along with everything Cathy wanted? What sort of hold over him did she have?

8. In the novel, everyone acts because of some sort of emotion. Which defines each character, and how healthy do these emotions seem to you?

9. "Guilt is a corrosive beast. The mind is not made for it. Nor the heart." Do you agree with this quote from chapter thirty-two? If so, what is the remedy for guilt?

10. Everyone has secrets in *After Alice Fell*. What do you think are Marion's own, particularly in regards to her marriage and her relationship with Alice? And how far do you think they influence her actions?

ABOUT THE AUTHOR

Photo © 2020 Upswept Creative

Kim Taylor Blakemore is the author of *The Companion* and the YA historical novels *Bowery Girl* and *Cissy Funk*, winner of the WILLA Literary Award. She is also the recipient of a Tucson Festival of Books Literary Award and three Regional Arts and Culture Council (RACC) grants. Outside of writing historical fiction featuring fierce and dangerous women, Kim is a novel coach with her company, Novelitics; a history nerd; and a gothic novel lover. She lives with her family in Portland, Oregon, and loves the rain. Truly. For more information visit www.kimtaylorblakemore.com.